The Extremities!

The Extremities!

A Novel

SAMANTHA KIMMEY

The University of Iowa Press · Iowa City

University of Iowa Press, Iowa City 52242
Copyright © 2025 by Samantha Kimmey
uipress.uiowa.edu
Printed in the United States of America

Cover design by Kimberly Glyder
Text design and typesetting by Jessica Shatan Heslin/Studio Shatan, Inc.

No part of this book may be reproduced or used in any form or by any means without permission in writing from the publisher. All reasonable steps have been taken to contact copyright holders of material used in this book. The publisher would be pleased to make suitable arrangements with any whom it has not been possible to reach.

Printed on acid-free paper

Library of Congress Cataloging-in-Publication Data
Names: Kimmey, Samantha, 1987–, author
Title: The Extremities! / Samantha Kimmey
Description: Iowa City: University of Iowa Press, 2025
Identifiers: LCCN 2024053349 (print) | LCCN 2024053350 (ebook)
| ISBN 9781685970246 paperback | ISBN 9781685970253 ebook
Subjects: LCGFT: Novels
Classification: LCC PS3611.I479 E98 2025 (print) | LCC PS3611.I479 (ebook)
| DDC 813/.6—dc23/eng/20250416
LC record available at https://lccn.loc.gov/2024053349
LC ebook record available at https://lccn.loc.gov/2024053350

The Extremities!

Health Effects of Wildfire Smoke Wide-Ranging and Possibly Fatal, New Study Finds

Recent wildfires that have brought weeks of smoke to local skies have people wondering: What are the health effects of exposure to such smoke? One new meta study found that exposure to wildfire smoke—which contains a mixture of gases, soot, fine particulate matter, and dangerous volatile organic compounds—is correlated with a slew of health problems. The skyrocketing number and geographic extent of wildfires in recent years have repeatedly broken records of annual acreage burned. Experts predict the trend will continue. This year's wildfire season alone has burned an unprecedented one million acres. Most locals are familiar with some of the immediate effects: cough, stinging eyes, and shortness of breath.

According to the Centers for Disease Control, inhaling wildfire smoke has long been known to also cause chest pain, headaches, fatigue, and irregular heartbeat. Vulnerable people such as children and the elderly, along with those with preexisting conditions such as asthma, are especially susceptible to harm; exposure in such populations is linked to increased rates of hospitalization. The latest research suggests more long-term consequences for all populations.

A recent meta study that examined dozens of papers from the past decade found that despite the mixed quality of past research, exposure to wildfire smoke was correlated with increased rates of cancer and increased mortality, as well as other respiratory issues.

June Grayton, a professor and researcher at Stanford University who has published extensively on health and wildfire smoke exposure and was not involved in the meta study, says that "as little as one week" of sustained exposure has the potential to cause stroke in certain populations, especially seniors, and is also linked to premature birth and fetal mortality in pregnant people. "It's not just about coughing for a few days and assuming it'll clear up on its own. Once you breathe in enough smoke, there's no telling what could happen to you in two, five, or even ten years from now. It might be the death of you."

Further research is ongoing.

The Day It Was Born

The disorder was born on deadline day, while I was on my computer, my very favorite place. I was typing typing typing, fingers striking, fingers blitzing across the keyboard to record what was happening, following each word of that very interesting and yet very boring meeting. Until that moment when I couldn't. It was like someone had pressed the smoldering end of a cigarette into each fingertip. Or maybe more like my fingertips had themselves become the burning tips of cigarettes, and if I didn't put a stop to it, my fingers would burn up into smoke and ash. Then I'd be left with just palms, sad pathetic palms, the most passive part of the hand!

Anyway.

The birth of the disorder feels so far away, even though it was only nine or so months ago, like a baby stubbornly refusing to leave the womb . . .

But was it really born, or was it just awoken?

Or did it enter me like poison from some mysterious sting?

Or maybe like one of those spiders that crawl into sleeping people's mouths, though obviously it's a myth, it's human hubris to think spiders want to make a home in the hot sauna of our mouths, the creepy hallways of our tracheas.

Or maybe the disorder came from nothing, like the Big Bang!

But all these words are based on the idea that it didn't come from nothing. This document is seeking cause and effect, it came from something, it came from somewhere, since maybe only the Big Bang itself can truly come from nothing.

Focus focus focus!

The disorder happened on deadline day, as I live-streamed a meeting about fire management, and I only looked through the window a few times, as the sky outside was glowering red, like a pit of dying embers, and I only wondered for a second if the sky had looked like that up north last year when that village burned up because of course it had and of course I looked at pictures of that village many times.

I'm not yet certain which details might be important clues, or signs, or if signs and clues are the same. I don't know if it's important that I was typing on my computer, or that the whole sky was red. But I hope what is important will eventually become clear, or maybe the opposite of clear; I hope the important bits find each other and become opaque and solid, a meaning so stable I can stop wondering what else in my life might be suspect—and more and more things seem suspicious now but I don't want to mix up the present with the past, I want to write about things in order. An answer will appear and it will be like that moment when you jump high enough in some game and are thrust into the next world, and you can't go back to root around to make sure you didn't miss some revelatory portal, since it's possible to reach the end but never truly finish.

I should have started taking notes right when the disorder was born but I was busy, I was working, I was stressed, and to tell the truth I didn't want to write about it. I didn't want to make it more real than it was. Now I don't know if things are more real when they're only in your body or when you make a document out of them.

I need to be as detailed as possible, and yet I can't remember exactly what I or anyone said. So this is a reenactment of sorts, like in shows about true crime, and although reenactments in true-crime shows are always very bad and embarrassing, I need to fill in the gaps so I can finish or at least get to the end.

The Day It Was Born (Redux)

Like I said: when I lost the ability to type it was deadline day at the newspaper and I was watching a meeting about fire management. At that moment, wildfires were affecting us enough to cover fire management but not enough to travel to the meeting.

The town stood at the edge of a large forest, and smoke had traveled hundreds of miles from one of the biggest wildfires in the state's history to smother our skies, and they said the air quality was the worst in the world and on this day in particular we awoke to a sky again densely red, as if the whole town had become a darkroom for developing photographs, and people were told to wear special masks to filter the dangerous particulates in the air, to keep the microns of faraway houses and trees out of our lungs, where they can do quite a lot of damage.

A government commission was debating how much of the forest should be set aflame on purpose, to reduce the thickened brush and accretion of fuels, which was a big part of the problem. But they were also debating existing policies to just let some wildfires rip, which had resulted in a few hamlets accidentally burning to a crisp, which was blamed on unexpected winds and thinly stretched resources and poorly maintained power equipment that had started the blaze and on the horrible heat and just how disturbingly dry it was. Burning more forest on purpose would result in fewer wildfires spiraling out of control in the future, if we ever reached the future, but the scale of the problem was monumental, and it was also tricky because the government had long been blamed for putting out too many fires and was now being blamed for putting out too few.

"Do you think they're going to decide anything?" my editor said, suddenly beside me. Because of my headphones she could only watch the mute mouths of professionals offering expert testimony in the streaming video, but she seemed to find this engaging. She kept looking at them and not me. That wasn't surprising because she rarely looked straight at me anymore. Instead she would look at a document, an email, a story draft as we hashed out final questions on the one day we were in the office together. We were usually standing because I had my standing desk, since my body was already having problems, which may or may not be important. My editor was taller than me, but when I got the standing desk I started wearing sad-sack platform orthopedic clogs to work, bringing me to her height, and this slightly softened the loss of her gaze, as if it made sense not to look directly at someone at the exact same latitude as you.

"Probably not. They love putting things off," the other reporter said, from his desk right behind mine, and he said it as if he knew things I didn't and I didn't like that. Maybe he was upset. He was interested in disasters too but hadn't been assigned the fire-related stories. Not yet. He had written important stories, exciting stories, but the closest he had come to writing about disasters was a short report on an extremely mild earthquake, when a famous fault line just across the road from our office, buried in the bay, slipped the tiniest bit in the middle of the night. He scrambled to find someone who witnessed the jittering of their precious objects, someone who might say something about a moment, a fragment, of fear. Even so, I had been jealous and made sure I was the one who got to write about this meeting, which made sense since I'd previously written about smoke, though that article had barely scratched the surface of its potential hazards.

"They'll recommend something—or if not, I can make a delay interesting," I said, and I was annoyed because their voices interfered with my immersion in the world of the meeting.

My editor nodded and left to do all the things she needed to do to finish the forthcoming edition of the paper, and the other reporter started typing again, so I could again concentrate on the proceedings. The experts laid out all the ways they knew to address the dangers of wildfire, but still it wasn't clear to me that anything would make enough of a difference, that disaster could truly be avoided.

Finally the public spoke, a public full of people either very emotional or temporarily asthmatic or stir-crazy from being inside for days and days to protect their lungs, and I got excited because the public comment period was my favorite part of meetings. Some people criticized the government for letting the situation become so perilous. They pleaded for fires at the perfect times and in the perfect places. But others worried; could they keep every fire, prescribed or wild, under control? And what about the smoke, a hazard to our health? But there was going to be smoke one way or another, someone else said. A few said wildfires should be left to burn so people would be more thoughtful about where they chose to live. Some people whose homes had burned offered up for the public record the heart-crushing fear of running for their lives and returning weeks later to the charred rubble of their possessions. At one point a commissioner said that if people were upset now they should wait until whole towns on the edges of wilderness might be stopped from building new homes or rebuilding in the aftermath of destruction, and then some people started yelling, and the commissioners threatened to make people leave. Everyone quieted down and I was glad, because although chaos could be interesting, ultimately people should respect the rules of meetings.

Near the end of the public comment period a few people from our very small town stepped up to the lectern, and in my word processing document I clicked the bold button and paid even more careful attention and prepared to capture their every word.

This wasn't difficult because I could type quite fast.

It was a skill I took pride in.

I took almost verbatim notes even though I could use only a few direct quotes from this meeting, since we had reserved only a few hundred words of space for the story in the paper. But I couldn't help my method of note-taking. I wanted to capture on the page all of the words that were spoken, even if some comments weren't really germane. The weakness of my memory didn't seem so tragic as long as what transpired was safely logged somewhere, and the computer was the safest place, much safer than my notepad and my mind. So I took detailed notes, especially on what people from our town said.

One person said the area was becoming so expensive, and what about that? Another person worried that even though our coastal town was a fire danger zone, it was often cool, which brought inland tourists escaping the heat and overcrowding the town, and what about that? That started a whole parade of complaints about tourism generally, not about fire at all, but it was common for people to travel far to make comments that probably belonged in the public comment period of a different meeting entirely.

⁂

The disorder arrived at about five p.m., right at the conclusion of the public comment period and about four hours into the meeting.

⁂

Was the timing important, that it started after listening to hours of unavoidable facts of fires and climate and people offering up opinions as if it mattered, or was it more important that my fingers had been moving nonstop, or was I thinking actually of something else entirely as I took notes?

⁂

The first thing most people do to rid themselves of pain is to shake the affected body part, as if to fling a rock out of a shoe, and this seemed to make sense in my case, because the pain in these first moments appeared in my fingertips, and fingertips are a person's very outermost points, the most extreme extremities, as if something—something—had only just gotten in and might just as easily fall out. So I shook and shook my hands, my wrists limp like dead flowers. But the pain in my fingertips amplified like something getting louder or brighter, like something becoming certain of itself. I flexed my fingers out like sea stars and retracted them and did that again and again, and I rolled my wrists around and around. These acts were meant to interrupt the signal of the pain, if pain is a signal, a sign, and I am no longer sure it is. It probably looked like I was trying to free myself of my hands, or my hands were trying to free themselves of me.

It took about ten minutes for the pain to reach its full potential as I kept typing and my emotional state moved from irritation to frustration to confusion to anger to fear and then not even fear because the pain in that moment left room for nothing but itself.

The pain was like:

The pain was like:

In the months after it was born I would try very hard—and still, still I try very hard—to find just the right description for what it was and is like, but there is no more ridiculous act than to try to describe pain, which is the most complete way of experiencing the present, and I think the best way to describe pain would be to come up with a million defective metaphors and layer the text of them on top of each other on a page until only the barest specks of blank document were visible.

My editor was tweaking the layout of the paper on the office computer, ensuring that each block of text and photograph was perfectly aligned and harmoniously arranged. The other reporter was engrossed in a precarious school budget. I saved my document and grabbed a notepad and, still listening to the meeting through my headphones, started taking handwritten notes. Handwriting isn't as pleasurable as typing but the pain softened into something that could be borne. Later I thought about how—after others pointed it out—the predilections of my pain were suspicious.

But in this moment I was just grateful the others were occupied. This was especially true of the other reporter. His desk was behind mine and when someone is behind you and facing you and you can't see them, it creates the constant low-level hum of suspicion that they might be taking note of everything you do. He probably wasn't. I wanted to switch desks but I didn't have a good reason and he would have thought I wanted to watch him. I did, but not him specifically; I wanted to watch anyone in that way, like a one-way mirror.

Or maybe I did want to watch him in particular, because he was the better reporter and maybe something in the manner of his body or something he searched for on his screen might offer some kind of revelation of how to be more like him.

The meeting was still going after everyone had left the office and it was finally time for the commission to issue its opinion. I tried to write by hand as fast as I could, but my handwriting was small and looked like it had been shredded by a garbage disposal, almost indecipherable when I wrote too fast, even to me, and during the meeting I realized I couldn't capture what people said verbatim. I grew angry. Most of the public left before the decision was made because they had to go to work or take care of families or because the rest of the meeting would be so long and boring. Management issues are very boring, and this was why, I told myself, I was important, because I kept listening. I made a record, a reference, a kind of proof.

I wondered why some people had such bad handwriting, whether it was genetic or related to a disorganization of the mind. That is why I loved the typed words on my computer. They were uniform and precise and organized and professional.

If only my entire life could be a typed document.

I worried the meeting would end tepidly, that the commission would defer its opinion to some future meeting. But in fact the commission recommended that the state burn hundreds of thousands of acres of forest on purpose every year, though they would prioritize municipalities and communities that pitched in financially. They also agreed to put out more wildfires, even though putting out fires in the past was part of the problem. Regardless, a few grumbled that there shouldn't be so many people living in the woods.

Once the meeting was over, I had to write the three hundred words and email them to my editor by midnight. I typed them using the hunt-and-peck method like an elderly person. I thought making my fingers straight and immobile would help, but it didn't make any difference.

Here are some things the pain was like:

It was like my fingers were piano keys and someone inside me who was not me was trying to figure out how to play a melody with a harpoon.

It was like something had speared my fingers as if to be roasted over a spit.

It was like my hands and fingers had been disassembled from the inside and something was attempting and failing to put me back together again, and merely touching my keyboard was proof that the wiring inside me was still all mixed up.

I paused after every word to shake my hands or just to hold one hand in the other because that is another thing a person does when a particular body part is in pain: the person holds it, although sometimes the person might also squeeze it, as if pain were a thing that could be extruded.

Sometimes there isn't anything to do but useless things.

I should be careful when I say I lost the ability to type. My fingers were not physically frozen. My fingers were not removed from my body.

I looked at my hands.

They looked normal, not discolored or swollen. They gave nothing away.

Which made me admire them.

I looked back to the screen, to the glow of the page and the precision of the typed words. I had written an inelegant sentence so I deleted it and this act was excruciating but the crisp clean disappearance pleased me, the kind of disappearance impossible on paper, since on paper when something is crossed out, there is always some trace of the rejected words. Finally, at midnight, I sent the short article to my editor and went home to bed.

The Next Day

The next day I woke up and I was alone.

Usually I wasn't alone, but my boyfriend was out of town at a two-week wilderness retreat, which would be over in a few days, which is yet another circumstance that could be important, but whether it could be important because his absence triggered something or his looming return triggered something or whether it actually wasn't important at all is difficult to know, especially so early in this document.

Maybe if he hadn't been gone, he would have made a poultice or applied some infused oil or administered a special tincture before the disorder had time to settle in.

Though maybe he's glad he was away, maybe he's glad after all that the disorder settled in, because it helped convince me to—

No, I don't want to mix up what's happening now with what happened then!

Anyway.

I woke up and before I moved a muscle I knew whatever had

happened was still happening. My hands felt strange, something inside them was ready, like the anticipatory hum of a speaker. I was surprised and then fearful, because I'd thought it would go away in my sleep, the way certain things just disappear into the night. I lay in bed longer than usual, trying to think of how to make it go away, if there was anyone who could help me.

When I finally got up I went straight to my desk in the living room, which was also the kitchen and the dining room. I had a makeshift standing desk, a splintery wooden table my boyfriend found on the side of the road, which we topped with stacks of books, mostly old dictionaries from the thrift store with thick, weakened spines, along with tomes on plant and bird and mushroom identification that my boyfriend switched out depending on the season. Each stack was a particular height for my laptop and special keyboard and mouse so I could be ergonomically correct.

I laid my hands on the keyboard.

But I didn't know what to type.

I looked around my living room but nothing inspired me, and then I looked out the window, and the smoke seemed even more ominous than the day before, which meant another day of remaining mostly indoors, and the light coming into the cabin had a deep amber hue to it as if trying weakly to preserve everything just as it was so at least it didn't get worse. But I didn't want to write about the smoke or the light, because those were things to be written about properly and knowledgeably for work.

Whenever I have nothing to write but want to experience the corporal pleasure of it, I start with *Hello*, a proper greeting to my computer, or maybe to the void—sometimes you don't know quite who or what you're addressing when you begin something!

Then I move on to the bland biographical facts about myself: *Hello, my name is Kim Smith, I was born in Huntington, West Virginia, I'm twenty-eight years old . . .*

The pain appeared in pulsing bursts, and on this day, the second day, it didn't stay in my fingertips. In fact it started at some point farther in me, maybe my palm or my wrist, and shot up through my fingers and into a few of my fingertips like fireworks, and then it lingered there, as if all the energy and effort to reach those places in me necessitated rest. But then it started popping up randomly in different fingertips, and it threaded my fingers and it dotted my palms, like my body had created a sophisticated algorithm to make pain appear in a pointillist pattern I would never understand. My hands were beginning a life distinct from the rest of my body.

I dropped my hands and stood still and eventually the pain calmed down a bit.

But then I didn't know what to do. I needed to go to work.

Luckily that morning I had interviews in person, situations in which I took handwritten notes and used my voice recorder, but soon I would need my computer.

I couldn't suddenly take time off work. Of course, if I'd died or fallen into a coma they would have still gone to press each week. Still the idea of not working wasn't an option I really considered, but more a theoretical possibility I felt obligated to conjure in order to dismiss. Without the paper I wasn't sure what the point of myself was, and of course the other reporter would take even more of my stories!

I could have called my editor on the phone to explain what was happening.

Given the problem that would have been logical.

But for the past few months almost all of our communication had been over email, except for Wednesdays, but Wednesday was a whole week away, and anyway: I always preferred to communicate complex or confusing things in writing.

Often when I talk, I trail off or speak tritely or ineloquently or confuse myself or say I believe in things that maybe I don't believe in. People often take speech as so viscerally true, but sometimes you need to say things to figure out if they are true or not. If you say you didn't mean what you said, it's always the edit that is deemed a lie, not the original statement, even though editing can make things more accurate.

My computer had built-in dictation capabilities so I opened a new email, clicked the microphone icon, and spoke. But my laptop was old, and when I originally bought the computer—or to be truthful, when my father bought the computer—I skimped on RAM, and the message on the screen didn't much resemble what I said. I fixed everything with my fingers. I could only touch a few letters before my hands had to rest to let the pain fade enough to start again. Maybe it was possible to think my way out of it, like people who walk on coals. I imagined each key as a coal and my stupid hands as coal walkers, and this made sense in a way because the keys were black and the letters on the keys were glowing lights, but that didn't help, and the pain was like:

The pain was like:

The pain in my hands appeared and disappeared and appeared and disappeared like the signal of a submarine on a radar screen.

In my message I tried to sound upbeat. I told my editor I was beginning to have a little pain in my hands but probably it wasn't serious, probably it wouldn't last that long, it was probably akin to aching legs after a runner's grueling race.

Since I knew she would ask for specifics, I said my hands felt numb and tingly, even though they barely tingled, and I don't think they ever really felt numb.

Really it was just painful. Really it just hurt.

But tingling was how a problem from typing was supposed to manifest and I wanted the pain to be how it was supposed to be. I wanted to be believable.

I said it might be a good idea to stop typing for a bit, as if it were a choice, because a choice made it seem less serious, but I'd come up with a simple solution: I would write all my interview notes and each story by hand and I would say every word of every story to my computer, and how difficult could it be, because at this point wasn't technology almost perfectly attuned to us, maybe it would be better and faster, maybe this was how it was supposed to be.

Then a name popped into my head: *Lee*.

Lee was a woman who had volunteered in the national park watching seals, trying to count them or help them, or maybe counting and helping were the same. I'd met her through my boyfriend, who also briefly volunteered in the national park, though his job had been to answer questions beside the guardrailed cliff as tourists watched elephant seals copulate on the beach below, huge sand-crusted males slightly bloodied from battle rippling across the sand and, with their arched bodies, pressing the females into the soft and salty shore.

At a volunteer party once, I talked to Lee briefly; she stood out, around my age amid a sea of retirees who found new meaning in their lives in talking to people about birds and sea mammals. In our stilted conversation she mentioned a problem with her hands, with typing, which had spurred her to leave some trajectoried career in the city for a job here waiting tables in town. Having pain in one's hands from typing happened all the time!

We exchanged emails as if we might become friends, but neither of us ever reached out. I tried a few times to formulate an email. Even recently, before he went on his retreat, my boyfriend suggested I reach out to Lee; he worried about my lack of close friends, which was understandable since there weren't many people my age around. But I never knew what to say. Now though, there was something concrete to ask: advice. Maybe, I thought, we could bond over it.

I found her email address and started dictating another message.

The First Doctor

The next day, still waiting to hear from Lee, I went to a doctor. My dad was a doctor and I believed in them, at first. (Or did I?) The doctor would have a diagnosis. The doctor would have a course of action or at least he would give me options, and options are nice. I knew vaguely that worker's comp existed, that I should already have requested it from my editor. But maybe I could quietly resolve it on my own, I thought, maybe I should draw as little attention to it as possible. I was fearful of disturbing it, like the disorder was some animal that would go berserk if it realized it was confined in the cage of my body.

So I went to the local health clinic and sat at the edge of an examination table, although no one ever closely examined me. I waited, looking at all the posters, like the one titled UNDERSTANDING HIGH BLOOD PRESSURE, with pictures of individual organs at strange angles and the clocklike face of the blood pressure reader, and the menacing picture of a saltshaker, and pills raining down from some mysterious above, and there was so much tiny text that it was hard to imagine anyone would leave understanding high blood pressure. The poster that said THANK YOU FOR WAITING frustrated me, because I didn't want to be waiting for a doctor, I wanted to be working. I had things to work on. A story about a preschool struggling because of low enrollment, and a story about how much money tourism generated annually in our town, and a story about a disease newly striking pine trees in nearby forests, and then there was a little tidbit I wanted to look into that was maybe a story, something Mona—I'll get to her later, since maybe Mona and what she gave me is important—mentioned a little over a month ago: that someone had offered, out of the blue, to buy the house she owns but doesn't live in, all cash, and she claimed, eyebrows raised, it was happening to other people too. I brushed her off at the time, or actually I didn't brush her off but sometimes I wasn't listening to Mona so much as waiting for her to run out of the steam that powered her long and sometimes nonsensical ramblings. But if there was something juicy to it, if home sales were escalating, perhaps even some hedge-fund real estate speculation, it might impress my editor, and my editor wouldn't get any ideas that I was too weak for this work.

Finally an amiable physician came in and asked what was wrong with me, and I told him, and I asked if it was that syndrome often considered the culprit in such cases.

He nodded. "Definitely, likely, yes," he said, and maybe he asked if I felt some numbness and maybe I said yes though I really didn't. He pulled himself up to me on one of those rolling stools that doctors use to maneuver around their patients and explained to me the syndrome. "Do you know about the three nerves that extend from the forearm into the hand?" he asked, and cradled the back of my right wrist in his clammy palm. I thought maybe he would examine my hands then, see some subtle sign I'd missed, but instead he used my arm for a demonstration. First he named the nerves: ulnar, median, radial. He traced the line of the median nerve along my forearm with the tip of his thick forefinger. "It travels through the carpal tunnel, a passageway in the wrist bound by bones and fibers, to certain fingers," and here he circled with his pointer finger the place on my wrist where the special tunnel was located. Sometimes the carpal tunnel became inflamed, he said, possibly if the hands are bent funny during sleep or because of bad posture while typing or maybe bad luck or genetics, or who knows why. "Sometimes we don't take good care of ourselves, right?" he said.

I nodded. He returned my wrist to me. He had only pointed at my body parts, but he was confident in his appraisal of the situation, and I thanked him for labeling my problem. He said people worried but the symptoms might go away in a few weeks. He said to take ibuprofen every day. A nurse fetched a pair of black padded wrist guards for me to wear at night, and the doctor slid them on my forearms. He pulled the Velcro tight, and I shivered slightly at the pleasure of the constraint as he instructed me to pay attention to the correct and neutral position the brace forced my wrist and hand into.

"You want to be in neutral as much as possible," he said, and I nodded again and repeated the word in my head: neutral! neutral! neutral! Why is it hard to keep bodies in neutral positions? Why are bodies always ready and willing to curve and bend, to twist and contort so fantastically?

If the pain didn't go away, an injection of steroids might fix it for at least a few months, he added.

I left and told myself I should feel good because one way or another I would be able to type again in a few weeks, a month or two at most, I would return to my previous state and write in a normal way, if I didn't decide dictating was even better.

I Downloaded Mirror

Lee responded to my email, which she claimed to check sparingly, a couple days later. She said her symptoms were different than mine; she suffered numbness that morphed into a terrible wrenching pressure. Yet the same cause could have different effects, she mused, our bodies might be trying in different ways to tell us the same thing. She herself didn't have a firm diagnosis but said that she was working on interpreting something she firmly believed would provide her with answers.

But she did have one concrete suggestion: a voice dictation program she used called Mirror. She said the program took time to get to know her voice but that it was of the highest caliber. "I think it improves my writing," she wrote, "that it clarifies me . . ."

Thinking of Lee speaking this message to her computer, I was unsettled by the ellipsis, since it meant she had literally spoken the word *ellipsis* to convey some level of uncertainty, feelings she couldn't quite put into words, a spirit of uneasiness about what she had just said. Of all things, no one should ever speak an ellipsis out loud . . .

Attached to the email was a zip file of Mirror. "It's expensive, but you can have a copy of mine," she wrote. "Of course, if I were you, I'd try to take some time off work. Maybe travel, get away from this smoke! But if you're determined to keep at it . . ."

Of course I was!

I was desperate to make it easier in the office. Already there were moments when I couldn't bear to speak to my computer, or someone else in the office was speaking, or the urge to preserve the transmission from body to computer took hold. Then I'd hold a pen and jab the letters on the keyboard. Sometimes I very slowly pressed each key with two outstretched pointer fingers like it was some kind of ceremony, hoping that by moving slowly enough I might elude it. But always within seconds, the pressure of fingertips on the keyboard, each keystroke, even using a jabbing pen (though how that could have hurt I still don't understand) felt like—like what? Perhaps screws swirling into my fingertips, or the equivalent in touch of the sound of nails on a chalkboard.

Then carefully I would lay my hand on my mouse and turn on my computer's sad dictation program, and do something like declaim an email to a person I needed to interview. I always sounded timid; the information I needed quickly always felt like an imposition. I had to remind myself that this was my job and my job was important and my editor expected certain things of me, she expected me to press people, to wheedle myself into all the crevices of what they knew, to the point that they would wonder why I needed such granular information, and although I took pleasure in the collection of details about other people's lives and jobs and projects and knowledge, I didn't like to make people uncomfortable, and I was apologetic. When I had to speak these emails aloud, I had to listen to that version of myself multiple times until my computer got it right, except it never got it right, and I would again make manual changes, and this took a long time because I would type a letter and recoil in pain and wait and then do it again like I was trying to enter a body of water that was simply too hot for human beings.

The other reporter said he tuned me out when I spoke to my computer, but sometimes as he brewed himself coffee in the kitchenette, he turned and gave me a sad pitying look, or said he needed to speak on the phone and this meant I couldn't do any dictating because it would catch his words and jumble things together on my screen.

And so without a second thought I downloaded Lee's zip file. Of course I could have paid for it, but it was expensive and I didn't make much, or maybe the newspaper could have paid for it, but every time I imagined asking, I saw my editor's face in the glow of the email, her lips drawn inward in a mixture of concern and suspicion at the prospect of investing in yet another accommodation, especially when I'd just suggested it would probably go away soon, and I didn't want to give oxygen to any glowering embers of doubt she might already harbor about the cause of my disorder.

Mirror wouldn't fix all of my frustrations; I would still have to speak to it. But although Mirror would struggle at first, Lee said, it would get better and better, eventually it would work even in a loud room with multiple people talking, it would be able to pick out my voice, and perhaps for me, I thought, it would work perfectly from the start. Perhaps Lee didn't speak clearly enough, perhaps she didn't care for her computer the way I did, and perhaps Mirror would understand me so perfectly that it would forge me into a better version of my voiced self, and I wouldn't long to type, because my voice would be able to exert such control that I could get rid of the whole clunky standing setup and bring my computer back into my lap the way I used to always write, and my computer and I would be closer than ever.

So one day at lunch, when the office was empty, I started the tutorial for Mirror. A dime-sized circle stamped with the icon of a microphone appeared in the bottom-right corner of the screen. I was instructed to click the microphone and say *Mirror is a program designed to understand the cadence and inflections of my voice. Using Mirror in place of typing will become as natural as taking a breath of fresh air! The more I use Mirror, the better Mirror will understand me. Mirror is me!* Then the program taught me to make the microphone sleep and wake up, how to capitalize and make numbered lists and parentheses and how to make a new paragraph and fix a word and spell things when I needed a word Mirror didn't know. It taught me to command it. The goal of Mirror was to evade the physical act of writing completely, to create text purely with voice, and I had no choice, and wasn't this the future anyway, text manifested without hands? And yet using my voice in this way made me squirm, and I wished there were a way to go back to the beginning, when I arrived at the paper, when I was excited and eager yet blank, when all the interviews and notes and documents and figures and storylines hadn't clogged and frayed my mind, hadn't turned my mind into a pile of knots that even if untangled would only be a mess of weakened useless string.

Soon My Boyfriend Came Back

I didn't contact my boyfriend when my disorder was born.

I didn't want to bother him on his wilderness retreat, and he had little phone service, and I thought maybe by the time he returned my pain would have faded away.

He posted a couple of times on a photo-sharing app when, at higher altitudes, he had reception. First it was pictures of lush valleys sliced out of their dramatic granite surroundings, and rock-ridden streams where water was always rushing somewhere, and close-ups of insects and plants hashtagged with their genus and species. Then toward the end it was pictures of yellow and then orange and then red skies, with captions that assured no fires were near enough to be threatening, that he was safe. His pictures were sharp and affecting. I was impressed because most phones automatically altered and softened the new eerie colors in the sky, but clearly my boyfriend had taken the time to manually change the settings to correctly capture the strange light. I myself had struggled to take pictures to text my dad that reflected what the sky really looked like.

I considered texting my boyfriend then that he should come home, his lungs must be burning, that smoke wasn't healthy, which I knew because I'd written a brief piece about the effects of wildfire smoke for the paper, and the piece had been interesting or at least there were interesting and even dangerous details. The smoke could contain metal and plastic, and the smoke could make lung diseases worse, and its presence increased the chances of premature birth. I guess when there was smoke in the air pregnant bodies didn't want to be pregnant anymore. And research was still being done on the long-term effects of smoke, so who knew what other horrible things it might do to human beings?

But my boyfriend and I rarely suggested things like that to each other, as if it would infringe too much on the other's autonomy. So instead I blandly texted: *hope you're okay, i miss you.* He never responded. In fact in his final week he didn't post anything, and I texted again the day before he returned, asking *are you okay?* Instead of issuing his own response he appended two reactions to my text: a thumbs-up and a heart.

As I scrolled through my boyfriend's pictures, I thought briefly of posting something about what had happened to me, but I didn't want most people to know, people being my few followers, mostly people from high school and college who lived in cities and posted pictures of themselves in beautiful or quirky places or pictures of food of such high resolution that you could see the finest fibers of a neatly sliced chicken breast or microscopic-level detail of charred cauliflower. My account on the other hand featured a few uninspired pictures of pretty views and the one time I saw three snakes writhing in a hedonistic mess, one of the few pictures I found myself looking at from time to time. But I preferred words to pictures, and usually when I saw a beautiful vista, I was with my boyfriend, and he posted it. And anyway there wasn't an interesting picture to accompany what had happened to me, not like people who post an *I'm okay!* selfie in the hospital after a dramatic brush with danger. I'd taken a few pictures of my hands and texted them to my father, thinking that although he wasn't a doctor of such things he might detect something. But he didn't see anything either.

⁂

My boyfriend came home soon after my disorder appeared.

When he arrived and collapsed onto the couch, I was standing at my makeshift desk. I'd been trying to google whether there was anything to what Mona had told me about the cash offers homeowners had been receiving for their homes, but I was behind on other assignments, so I switched to something I knew was a story: the disease newly infecting trees in the nearby national park. I moved the cursor with the mouse and turned on Mirror. I kept saying "pine sap canker pine sap canker" but it kept transcribing *times are candor*. I looked at the keyboard and longed to touch it, to press my fingertips into that neat grid of letters.

But instead I left my computer and sat next to my boyfriend but not yet touching him. The smell of sagebrush and clean dirt and the concentrate of his body odor hung over him, and the air around him felt difficult as if he had brought back the thin atmosphere of high altitudes. This was the fourth time he'd gone on a retreat, and each time there were those strange initial minutes of acclimation in which the brief question arose of whether our respective atmospheres could come together again.

He had been gone for two weeks, the longest he had ever been away.

The other retreats focused mostly on generalized nature connection and animal tracking and plant identification and sometimes there was a challenge, like each person being left alone to build their own shelter, but this one was a little different. He had to bring tools he made himself and he had to be ready to forage rare herbs that had required extra study, and he practiced in advance for the onsite concoction of herbal remedies.

He looked around at the walls of our little cottage as if he had forgotten entirely what it looked like or how it felt to be within a solid structure. He rubbed his eyes. As if that were some cue that he was ready to readjust, I placed my hand on his arm and slid it up to his shoulder and squeezed, and he put his hand on my hand and then pulled me into a half embrace there on the couch, still not quite looking at me, each of our bodies awkwardly trying to soften toward the other.

"How was it?" I finally said. "Your pictures looked so beautiful—at least until . . ."

"Right. Yeah. It was . . . good. It was mostly good."

"So you were outside the whole time?" I said, trying to prompt him into speech.

"Yeah. Sorry, I'm a little out of it. It was incredible, mostly," he said, finally getting going, and he discussed at length how within a few days his mind had felt refreshed. He thought of nothing for hours at a time and had never felt so at ease, mostly. He referenced forest bathing, though it was a term he usually derided. He used words like *quiet* and *simple* and *vivid*. He even felt camaraderie with the other participants, which for him was rare. They traded tips on perfecting forest tea blends. They debated the source of pellets of matted fur along the trails. Still, my boyfriend found ways to criticize them, either for knowledge they lacked or for friction in the values they espoused under a pine tree compared to the way they described their day-to-day lives.

"It was peaceful. Hard but peaceful. But then . . ."

"The smoke," I appended.

"Right," he said. "I don't know—we talked about skipping the last week. It looked ominous. But far away. We knew it wasn't the apocalypse," and he wanted it to be a joke but his laugh wasn't convincing. Still the laughter further dislodged the weird atmosphere he had brought into our cottage, and I laid my hand on his leg and gently squeezed his thigh, and this act, of my hand, didn't hurt, and I comforted myself that affection was an important thing my hands could still provide. "I don't know. It was bearable. And it felt like we shouldn't leave just because of the weather."

I told him then about the meeting I'd watched about fire management, and prescribed burns, and wondered whether someday they would ban people from living so near the forest. He remarked that something had to change, the forests needed to burn more, and yes, all of us—or most people, but perhaps not ourselves—should move farther away from the forests, or maybe some national or worldwide catastrophe would occur and disable computers and the internet and return us to some more elemental relationship with the environment.

"That'd be horrible," he said, but I wasn't sure if he meant it. Then he added, "And I know how sad you'd be, not being able to look up every little thing."

"Right," I said. "But I don't think there'd really be news . . . Well, there would be news, but not *the* news."

"Well, would that be . . . anyway. Anyway. I missed you," he said, perhaps a little reluctantly, not because it wasn't true, but because like me it always seemed that the minute a feeling left your mind or heart and entered the world it started to feel false, that somehow it became compromised the moment it left you. As if to make up for it he smiled and his head fell into my lap and I stroked his hair and he sighed. "How's the smoke been here, anyway?" he said. "How's the news?"

"Oh, you know. The sky was orange, then red. Now it's just a little smoky. It's been fine inside—I guess this place is insulated," I said, although I always wondered how the air inside was so much better than the outside and where the inside air came from if not ultimately from the outside.

"Well, we pay enough for it," he said, and I thought he would begin grumbling about how we should go live cheaply in some converted shed with a composting toilet and a solar-powered shower, although even around here cheap was somewhat expensive.

But he didn't, and finally I took a deep breath and recounted what had happened to my hands, although I didn't even know what had happened. I meant to watch him carefully as he listened, because his reaction was important to me, and maybe his forest clarity would allow him to intuit things, but by my third or fourth sentence each word I said shook just a little more than the last, each word its own little earthquake, which surprised me because I'd been thinking about it nonstop but hadn't actually talked about it aloud till now, and somehow talking about it aloud caused me to start shaking and then to start crying, so instead I stared down into my own lap because that's where you look to keep yourself together. So I'm not sure what his face looked like, but he hugged me and said something like, "Oh no," and gathered up my hands and held them in my lap, but then he held them up and examined their backs and palms and considered the various fingers, his gaze steady and focused the way it was when he was identifying a plant.

"But you can use your phone?" he said skeptically, still looking at my hands.

"Well, yeah. I mean, my fingers—the fingertips—they do feel uncomfortable a lot of the time, they feel . . . funny. But it's bearable except when I type. It makes sense, if you think about it—when you scroll on a phone you're not pressing down so hard, you're not striking striking striking with every finger . . . Do my hands look different?"

He said no, but kept looking at them. "Hold on," I said, and I got the black braces the doctor had given me and explained I would wear them at night. I strapped one onto my left wrist to show him. He was skeptical; did it really have to do with how I slept? It must be all the typing I did while I was awake, right? "Maybe I could make something for you," he said.

"I guess you could look into it," I responded. "But it'll probably go away in a few weeks. Maybe a few days. Something's probably just flaring up. Something got irritated. Overworked."

I told him then that I'd emailed Lee about it, since she'd said she also had some hand pain. It was an unfortunate occasion, but maybe, I said, we could build some kind of bond over our shared adversity. She'd even emailed me a copy of some expensive dictation program, I said, and he'd been nodding along and saying he was glad I'd reached out to her but at this his smile—it tightened . . .

When I asked what it was, he brushed it off. He just worried about me, that the first thing I would think about was how to keep working instead of how to heal.

Or maybe he started on that point a little later in our conversation, and here he said the mention of Lee had made him briefly relive his doomed time as a park docent.

My boyfriend had thought being a docent might lead to something, since the thing he liked most was to be outside, and the volunteer training had emphasized the joy in connecting with visitors, and maybe he could train in outdoor education and leave his job at the bar behind. But he quit after a few months. He was tired of offering up the same facts to tourists over and over, and he didn't like the pressure to be entertaining, as if he were competing with the fornicating seals.

"Well, I'm going over to her place next week, to talk about—hand stuff or whatever. If I need to talk about it. Like I said. Maybe it will be gone tomorrow."

His attention returned to my hands, gently massaging them. "Maybe," he said, some new idea arising in his mind, "your body is, like, doing what all our bodies should be doing. I mean, we're all insane, spending all this time on our computers, eyes burning out and bodies getting all hunched and—maybe your body is telling you something."

"No!" I said.

"Maybe you should take time off work. You could go on a retreat or something."

"I don't want to do that." I took my hands back. "My job's important. I have all my assignments. And—remember that tip I got? From Mona? Maybe more homes have sold this year. It could be a big story."

"Hmm. Doesn't seem like news to me."

He didn't really take my job seriously. Some weeks he didn't even finish reading the paper, even when I left multiple copies around our tiny cottage.

"It just doesn't seem urgent," he went on. "I mean, what if you got paid time off? Couldn't you ask? It hasn't been so great there recently—" But he stopped short at the look on my face. "That's what I'd do. God, I wish I didn't have to go work tonight."

My boyfriend worked at the local bar. He didn't like alcohol much but it meant he was free to hike during the day, and his days off were during the week, so when he went to the woods it was mostly unpeopled.

His job wasn't part of his identity the way it had become part of mine.

He thought my way was unhealthy, though I thought it was unhealthy for a person to have a job they didn't even like, to inhabit a role they hated.

I think he would have understood me more if he read the paper. He read my articles, usually, but I didn't want him to read my articles just because I wrote them. I wanted him to read the whole paper because it was important to know what was going on around you, even the boring things.

"Well, you're not exactly fond of your job . . ." I said.

"I don't hate it. And you didn't answer the question."

I sighed and got up to open a bottle of wine and I poured myself a glass, which took up some time while I considered how to respond.

"I—No," I told my boyfriend. "I'm not doing that. I just want to go to work."

"Okay, okay," he said. "I just—you know, you get so stressed. Sometimes it's good to take a break. I'm worried about you," he said, and even though we were kind of arguing, the arguing had opened up something that allowed us to close the weird gap caused by his absence, and then he was kissing my neck, one hand cradling the back of my head and the other slipping under my shirt and upward, and I fell back on the couch and he came along with me, and I moaned because it had been weeks and his hands were urgent and knowing. Even after all his clothes came off he still smelled like smoke and juniper and I wondered what I smelled like to him although whatever it was he liked it. Or who knows. Maybe he didn't like it. Maybe he was urgently touching every part of me so I smelled more like him. I begged him to fuck me hard even though I couldn't come like that. I could only ever come from sex that was excruciatingly slow, and yet I wanted to be fucked very hard. Desire is stupid like that. Afterward we were quiet and happy in bed and I wondered if his return would fix me. It would be a relief to wake up back to normal. Yet it would have been disconcerting, for his appearance to be the cure, and ultimately I was relieved when I woke up the next day and the disorder was still there.

Mona Visited Me at Work

Mona came by the office about once a week, on Mondays, a practice I inadvertently encouraged by helping her some Monday long ago, even though Mondays were busy, days I was finishing interviews and ensuring I understood what I needed to understand. Hopefully I'd already started organizing information into orderly narratives, and then of course I'd start to worry about whether I'd angled an article unfairly or if someone might believe their perspective was misrepresented. I'd check to see who hadn't responded to requests for comment, though I sometimes guiltily hoped they wouldn't call; they might say something so important I'd have to reshape my story, instead of just noting that they didn't respond.

On this Monday I was working on an article about a state project to replace a very old bridge. It was simple enough or should have been; the bridge was extremely short and it took about five seconds to cross it by car. But even short crossings can be complex, and there would be reams of environmental analysis, and people had a lot of opinions. During the bridge meetings, people alternated between asking the state agency why the bridge needed to be replaced, as if old things were entitled to exist forever, and debating each other about a whole decision tree of issues that the fate of the bridge had triggered. I wondered about the great weight everyone was putting on the replacement of a tiny bridge when the world was—well, we all know the state of the world! But the debate made my job interesting, forced me to push past my natural inclination to believe in authority.

A few people, the prominent environmentalists who showed up at every meeting, worried about the fate of the fish in the creek beneath the bridge, although at least one older woman, who never missed a public meeting and always came with a long list of fauna and flora to fret over, never showed up. Other people were upset because the replacement of the bridge would require a years-long closure of one of the two entrances into the tiny village center, where most everyone got their groceries and ran their errands and into each other and either had nice little interactions that helped you through the day or uncomfortable interactions you endured while your mouth coagulated into something benign but stiff through which no more conversation would flow. The prospect of the closure, which would mean only one way in and out of town, triggered fears over what would happen in an emergency? And what if a fire blazed when tourists were clogging the roads in their cars going to look at some stupid shipwreck from the '90s or a long-defunct lighthouse?

Tourists—they love love love to see nature foregrounded by human decay!

This was about when people stopped directing their comments at the state agency and started debating among themselves.

Someone said we needed those tourists, because the tourists were keeping the town and keeping people—at least some people, the ones who worked in town—afloat by buying cheese and oysters and kayak expeditions. But other people complained there would soon be too many tourists (if there weren't too many already!); as it got hotter inland more and more tourists would start visiting our cool climate. Then somehow the conversation turned from tourists to ourselves.

Someone brought up the sewer system that had been proposed to deal with our shit, which had been getting into the local waterways, but there were rumors the sewer system might allow for more homes, but if more and more people who loved this place actually lived here the character of the town would be destroyed, destroyed! someone proclaimed, and then there would also be even more people to deal with during an emergency, more and more people breathing in this wretched smoke that had still not completely dissipated. A couple people—people I now realize are part of the practice group, which I'll get to soon enough—argued we in fact needed more housing, it was so expensive here and you could only buy a house if you were rich, not just rich but very rich, and the population of the town had fallen according to the most recent census, and how could a town function if it kept losing people? Here it came to light that the stalwart environmentalist missing from the meeting had recently and suddenly sold her home for an astronomical sum. Even that woman, so devoted to protecting those stupid little birds that nest in the open sand, idiotically vulnerable to predators, sold out on us! someone lamented. But others worried about more people in a place at risk of fire, more people living near a bucolic forest that should be protected from people and all their impacts. Then the meandering comments turned back to the bridge and what could happen if the bridge were closed in a real emergency! I imagined that Bruegel painting of all the people dying and the world in flames. I didn't tell anyone about that though because it would give the impression that I didn't take the situation seriously.

I did take it seriously.

Although part of me had always wanted to be part of a catastrophe.

I never admitted that to anyone, especially my boyfriend because I was usually the one who needed to convince him a catastrophe would be bad. I just wanted a temporary catastrophe that would last a few days, a few weeks at most. That sounded like a nice amount of time to be trapped. Of course I didn't have many skills that would be useful, because the ability to compose easily digestible but engaging news articles would not be an important skill during a minor, temporary catastrophe. I could identify a few mushrooms and maybe two species of edible berries but a lot of people here could do that. My boyfriend made sure to keep dried goods around, ostensibly for his backpacking trips but also just in case, so I could be helpful through him. Maybe a limited catastrophe that affected everyone simultaneously would bring me closer to the town, although maybe that's not what I wanted, since one of the reasons I became a reporter was because it was a useful way to be an outsider. If I were useful at all it would only be after the catastrophe was over, when I could write something important about it.

Anyway.

At the office I started writing the bridge story in a notebook. The notebook was actually for drawing, and I may have bought it by accident but the pure blank pages mimicked the screen of my computer's word processing program. I wrote slowly so it would look professional, like it deserved to be in print. But still my handwriting seemed less objective. It showed not just that a person was stringing the words together but that a person had inscribed the words, letter by letter, stroke by stroke, that everything had come through the messy conduit of a person and that person was me. Although I dreamed of being objective like a window someone could look right through, not even a window is objective and I would never rid myself of the smudge of my private thoughts and judgments. That had been bearable before, because on the computer I could pretend my words were only from the mind but these words on paper were clearly from the body, and I didn't like it.

In the background of my pencil's scratchings, I listened to the other reporter's typing, which was fast but not too fast, and I thought maybe I should record the sound of his typing and play it whenever I wrote. Maybe it would soothe me or guide me like a metronome.

Eventually and begrudgingly I took my rough draft to my computer. If I filed it that night I would be on top of my workload. I moved the mouse to wake up my computer and saw a word I'd typed earlier, even though I wasn't supposed to do that, and of course the pain had appeared immediately in my fingertips like a fresh wound somehow fully festered. I sighed and turned Mirror on and started dictating, but when I tried to dictate a quote I liked, in which a man used the word *eternal*—these projects never end, they're eternal!—the program kept transcribing *terminal terminal terminal*, and maybe I would have gotten stuck there forever if Mona hadn't come to the office.

"Hello?" she said hesitantly, and then she saw the other reporter, and her eyes narrowed suspiciously because she'd never seen him before. She didn't get along with most people. She then looked at me, her eyes slightly unfocused and wide. She had long whitish hair like cumulonimbus clouds and wore a muumuu, the kind most people would call shapeless although everything has a shape. She was holding a piece of paper in her hand.

"Who are you talking to? Who's that?" she asked.

"Oh, that's my colleague. And I was just getting off the phone," I said, because I didn't want to explain Mirror to her.

I looked at the screen and suddenly her words appeared in the search bar: *hello hello who are you talking whose that that's my volley i was just giving off a foam.*

The first time Mona came to the office, I thought she might be one of those unhinged people who told long rambling stories they thought should be reported on, sometimes sinister conspiracies and sometimes mundane events, or someone in town was walking their dog in a place where dogs weren't allowed, or a neighbor's loud music made it difficult to hear the morning chorus of the birds, or perhaps they self-published a book five years ago but forgot to tell anyone and now they wanted an article about themselves.

But Mona just wanted to buy kale and rice at the food cooperative next door, where she'd been banned. When I asked her name, she refused to reveal it, telling me names were a form of power over others. But later I found out her name was Mona and she lived in her car although she owned a decrepit house that she thought was bugged by the government. She was banned from the normal grocery store and the library and the thrift store, because she stole things, although in her telling this was cruel because she was planning to pay eventually, once she figured out how to avoid money, which led her one time to reveal she'd once been a bank teller. "All that dirty money!" she'd cried. I thought she meant dirty in a metaphorical sense, but no. "The germs! People sneezing on wads of cash they handed to me!" And there was to me a big blankness between being a bank teller and who she was now, and how exactly had that shift happened?

When she encountered people who had wronged her, she bared her teeth at them. She had a pretty good memory. Maybe that's why I kept buying her groceries: I feared her wrath as if she were some lone Greek fury somehow separated from the other deities.

She asked me to buy her macadamia nuts, brown rice, and carrots, and handed me a bag of quarters.

I went into the cooperative and as I weighed her nuts and rice, I thought at some point I should stop buying things for her; I should not support someone who was banned. I strove to obey rules. But I also had a difficult time saying no to people. When other people were upset with me, I felt something shrinking inside me, my body collapsing in on itself, even though this job was supposed to fix that part of me.

The other reporter was gone when I returned, and she was more at ease as she thanked me for the groceries. She remained in the doorway, seemingly waiting for me to ask her something. "How are you today?" I finally said.

"I . . . ahh . . . You know, you know. The vibrations of the earth today are really off," she said, her voice full of her own breath. For at least twenty minutes she talked about her various ailments. The tone of her voice suggested she was confused, even though she was saying how certain she was about these problems. People said she was a few cards short of a full deck or a few bricks short of a house and her pupils sometimes bobbed up and down like buoys in a pool. But there were recurring themes, like her scoliosis and lupus and leaky gut and multiple chemical sensitivity and vertigo and something about her chakras and osteoporosis and sensitivity to smartphones and Wi-Fi and gluten. She was always mixing up reasonable, believable ailments with ones that seemed implausible, although those were also ailments many people here claimed with relative frequency. Most people who claimed them, though, were not like Mona. I tried to follow the thread of her speech, whether to figure out some way to help her or to find my own way out of her endless monologue, the length of which always terrified me, as if I might be trapped by it forever. When she pressed me about whether I believed her, which was often, I said I did, although I didn't.

"I'm sorry about your—troubles, that they don't seem to be getting better . . ."

I wanted to ask her then about her claim, about her house, about the pressure to sell it for heaps of cold hard cash, but in that moment I couldn't bear to invite another half-hour monologue.

I looked at my computer and saw again in the search bar bits of words she said. It transcribed them better than my own speech, which felt like a betrayal. But maybe, I thought, it was my own fault, maybe I was mumbling as I was wont to do or somehow holding something back from it.

"Are you all right these days?" she asked earnestly. She always asked me this and I wasn't sure if she was being caring or waiting for everyone to befall her own fate. I said I was fine but added gently that I needed to get back to work, and she left, she usually left when I asked, I think because she did respect my job, sometimes she even praised my articles. But this time she returned.

She asked us to consider at least using recycled paper or soy. I said yes, of course we'd look into it, and was about to truly move her along when I noticed again the piece of paper in her hand. "What's that?" I asked.

She seemed confused at first but then shook her head mournfully and began ranting about all the wasted paper. She was notorious for removing posters from community message boards because she felt using trees to make paper for all the little messages people posted was a travesty. I was always fearful of pointing out that taking announcements down might only encourage people to replace them, so I instead offered to recycle it, and although she always said *reduce before reuse!* she handed it to me. It was a flyer that said, succinctly: MEETING TO DISCUSS PRACTICE TOWN EMERGENCY EVACUATION, to be held at the defunct church.

Once she left, I put the flyer down to look at later more closely while I finished the article about the bridge. I highlighted the jumbled text we had said and deleted it, then started to speak again. I said "yellow bridge" and the name of our town, since the bridge was only known by its horrid caution-tape color. *Yell orb ridge*, Mirror wrote. I took a breath and said "yellow bridge" and again it wrote *yell orb ridge*. So I said it again but slower, with less inflection, and it finally wrote *yellow bridge*, and I told myself this different voice I was using was still myself, it was still myself but just a different version.

I sighed. I took my hand off the mouse. I hadn't taken a break in a while. I tilted my head back to look at the skylight. The sky was orange and quickly dimming. I turned back to my computer, to the words and the glow. I was tired of standing. I wanted to sit like everyone else. There had to be some right way to arrange my body.

"Why are you talking to your computer?" Mona said, having suddenly returned, and I jumped, though her eyes were steady with genuine concern.

Hesitantly, almost against my will, the way a surprise will sometimes let something loose out of you, I said I couldn't type anymore, my hands were in agony.

Without a pause, as if she expected me to say such a thing, she said, "Oh, that's no problem. I know what you should do."

She pulled from her backpack a thick workbook. Its flimsy plastic cover featured a clip-art brain hovering in an abstract orange-red glow, a brain unbound by a skull or a head and its body nowhere to be found. The brain was liberated, or maybe just purposeless. Maybe the body was on some other workbook for other people with different problems. The workbook said *Painful Emotions: How to Think Your Way out of Chronic Pain* in large shadow font, and I wondered why people used those kinds of fonts. Who exactly wanted words to have greater physical dimension and who wanted words to cast shadows, who dreamed of words frozen in their attempt to lift off from the page?

She explained excitedly that it was a workbook. She hadn't finished it and her pain hadn't yet gone away completely but she had decided in advance that she fully believed in it, it would cure all, or at least some, of her problems. Some aspects of her health, she'd learned, could be traced to trauma from her youth. She carried spare workbooks with her for exactly this situation, since so many people were in agony, and her only sorrow was that she couldn't help nonhuman beings, not that human interference ever helped the natural world much, she said.

"So you—what, journal about your woes . . ." I said.

"You should take this seriously," she reprimanded me. "He's a respected doctor. It's a guided workbook. You'll see. Do it today. *Today*, Kim. Maybe we'll both be better soon," she said, finally leaving with her macadamia nuts.

The workbook, I saw as I read its opening pages, claimed that chronic pain was, for many people, a manifestation of incorrectly processed trauma, like some improperly canned jelly. And of course most trauma wasn't correctly processed, because the world is messed up and most people don't know the right way to process it. So some doctor created worksheets to guide a person in dealing with this un-dealt-with trauma, and by the end you were totally and completely free of pain!

I imagined writing about sad-sack memories and the pain suddenly disappearing, which would make me feel like a complete idiot. Then I imagined writing about my sad emotions and nothing happening at all. It was hard to know which one was worse.

Worksheet 1

You *are here because you are in pain. Traditional medicine and perhaps even alternative medicine have failed you.*

As you read in the first chapter, your pain may be the result of emotions and memories you have failed to process. Your body has reconfigured those emotions into physical distress, perhaps at the site of a previous injury. This is not "psychosomatic." Your pain is real. *You must reconfigure the disordered neural pathways that are creating the experience of pain, by processing your unresolved emotional pain and anger.*

So consider: What memory is most painful to you? What is the worst thing someone has done to you—or that you have done to someone else? Think deeply, especially about your youth. Who was this person? What was their relationship to you? What happened?

※

In a way what happened between my mother and me happened because she didn't work and I judged her harshly for it.

My mother worked but only before my sister and I were born. The first job she had was in high school at a fried chicken restaurant in the Midwest. She was fired after six months, when she refused to sell rotten coleslaw, a detail I always make sure to remember because it seemed a kind of taking charge. Somewhere in there her mother died, although I think that must have been before she was fired for not selling rotten coleslaw because she was barely a teenager when her mother died, and then she went to a liberal arts college and studied the classics. She claimed she liked the professor but it always seemed more likely that she was drawn to reading the words of the dead in a dead language.

After she graduated with a thorough education in the classics she panicked.

Maybe she realized that if she continued studying the classics she would end up teaching the classics, and maybe she didn't want her life to be about the past or the dead. Or maybe she did, but she resisted her own inclinations. Of course she could have studied the classics and become an adventurous archaeologist, or something, but she wanted a family, even though she wasn't a people person, and maybe she thought that kind of life was incompatible with a family, especially back then for a woman.

I don't exactly know why because she never quite articulated it and I never asked, even though *why* would be an obvious question for whenever it was she relayed this juncture of her life.

Anyway.

She turned to the living: she applied to medical school only minutes from the shore. Coasts are supposed to be healing places, or at least that's what people said when I moved to the coast, although I moved to the opposite one. Maybe looking at the ocean for so long puts you at a point of decision. Either you go crazy from that dizzying enormity or you gather the strength to live with it.

My mother survived medical school while looking at that huge enormous ocean, and a residency and an internship, which is impressive, because for some reason she specialized in internal medicine, and internal medicine requires interacting with many people, often the same ones for years and years as their ailments shift and morph and get better and get worse. My mother should have chosen a specialty that did not require so much empathy, since she believed that some people—really most people—were bad and could never be good. She should have chosen a specialty involving brief devastating illnesses that could have confirmed some of her beliefs about the world.

But maybe she had her reasons for choosing what she chose. Maybe she wanted to alter her very nature and maybe she was looking for a catalyst. The fact that it didn't suit her was the point, but it didn't matter because she never practiced after her residency.

There were a lot of reasons. She wanted badly to be a mother, a desire related to the quick and early death of her own mother, some aunts once told me, many years ago, as if it was necessary to fill the void of her mother with her own self. The world was a dangerous place, and she needed to protect my sister and me from whatever bad things were out there, so she gave up working. She had little money of her own and she was pretty miserable in the end, although her misery had many causes.

But anyway.

One day when I was a teenager I was eating a bowl of Cheerios for breakfast and my mother came downstairs from her bedroom and sat down beside me with her black coffee. She liked black coffee and cigarettes and red wine, she often told me, though I always already knew, and she never mentioned the other things she liked, the things she might have liked much more, but maybe *like* isn't the right word for those other things. We were alone in the house, since my dad was at work and my sister, who she was closer with, was older and gone to college. I was surprised she was awake because she usually stayed up late. After my sister left I started to stay up late with her, at least on the weekends, when we would watch raunchy late-night television together and she would laugh her absolutely insane duck-honking laugh. I was trying to get a little bit closer to her, in the absence of my sister, but then I'd stopped staying up late. I'd decided to be healthy, and being healthy meant not consuming sugar and waking up very early.

She sipped her coffee slowly and stared at me. Whenever she stared at me like that, she was trying to think of how to impart an important message.

"You shouldn't depend on other people," she finally said. "You need to be able to take care of yourself."

She didn't say financially but that is how I took it.

"I will," I said.

"Things don't just work out for the best," she said.

"I know," I said. I ate a spoonful of Cheerios and she didn't respond and we were quiet for a minute as I kept eating because I knew it would get soggy quickly and my head filled with the echoey crunching of cereal and slurping of milk, but she was patient.

"Well, what do you think I should do? With my life?" I asked.

"Oh, I don't know. Don't major in the classics. But don't become a doctor either. Major in whatever you want. But then make sure to sell your soul to make a lot of money afterward. Actually, no, I changed my mind. Go to law school. You're good at arguing."

Finally I said, "Why don't you get a job? You could get a job and have some of your own money."

She snorted. "I'm old. And I'm tired." But she wasn't old and didn't even look old. She had long hair, down to her elbows, straightened and dyed dirty blond and it always seemed a lot of effort considering she only left the house about once a month.

She was silent again for a while and then she said, "If I could live my life over again, I wouldn't have married your father."

I slurped a spoonful of grainy milk.

She reached over and took the utensil out of my hand and ate a spoonful of my cereal. "Listen—I don't regret you and your sister. You two are the best things in my life." She said it not with fervor or sarcasm but as objective fact, as if she had analyzed all other possibilities.

"Hmm," I said.

She patted my arm and took her coffee upstairs to her room. I don't know exactly what she did on this particular day but in my head it was one of three things: she read a mystery novel or watched the Home Shopping Network or searched on some online auction site for paraphernalia from a midcentury genocidal European government, the last of which was disturbing, but she was Jewish, which made it less disturbing or just disturbing in a different way. For some reason she had become fixated on this genocide—I didn't ask, maybe as a teenager it had made some intuitive sense that my mother would become fixated on this genocide, although now it drives me crazy that I never made her articulate it—and this led her to purchase things like Juden stars and old newspapers in a language she couldn't read. She asked me a few times if I would take the language as an elective at school to help her. In retrospect that was perhaps some twisted effort at bonding but I always said two things: *What's wrong with you?* and *No. No no no.*

I thought about following her to her room that day, which I never did because I didn't like to see her room, but I wanted to press her about the contradiction she had posed to me since she couldn't regret her life and yet not regret me. I was young and when a person is young they haven't always figured out how many statements and beliefs and assertions can really be true at once. At the time I believed that if I pressed her, I would ferret out which of the two statements was true and which was false. But then she did another thing she did sometimes: she confined herself in her room for two days with the lights out, only occasionally emerging to make a cup of coffee or pour some vodka into a mug, though eventually she just stored the vodka in her room. It was on this occasion of retreat, and in particular during a ten-minute interval when she was smoking a cigarette on the back porch, that I quietly went into her room and for the first time took something from her, a newspaper from 1942, and I don't know if I took it because I thought she would not notice or because I thought she would, and I threw it in the trash.

The Worker's Compensation Clinic

I wore the wrist guards and took the ibuprofen and did a worksheet and waited patiently for these interventions to do something. I wanted my hands to feel blank again. Writing by hand felt so unnatural, and Mirror struggled to understand me. I complained to Lee in an email, which itself took a long time to compose. She reassured me, said it took time for Mirror to understand her too, that she would try to help when I came to her place for advice and commiseration. I thanked her, yet couldn't help but end the email by saying again that the pain might go away soon. Lots of people have chronic conditions that come and go, that flare up and calm down, I lived by the shore after all, maybe it would be tidal in some way.

But the situation hadn't improved, not after a few days and not after a few weeks, although to be fair to the worksheets—not that I believed in them!—I'd only done one. It couldn't do any harm, I thought, and it hadn't, except certain thoughts and sadnesses started surfacing, which made it harder to focus on work, which was already a struggle. I'd wait a while before doing another. In the meantime, I went to a worker's compensation clinic an hour away, in the urban center of the county.

The examination room there had a poster with a man in a hard hat and orange vest, grimacing and holding his own back, with text listing rules for safe workplaces, like only doing what you've been trained to do and never wearing unstable shoes. Maybe I hadn't been trained properly to type. Maybe I wore shoes with too much support and some weakness of my arches was rippling through my body, or maybe it was too little support, my feet slowly collapsing and crying out for help in the opposite extremity.

While I waited to be examined, I read the news from elsewhere on my phone: articles in regional and national newspapers and in-depth features in respected magazines, which I did whenever I wanted to pass the time and imagine the important things I might in the future write about, although I remembered the content of these articles only vaguely; if anyone had asked me to explain what I'd been reading, I could not have done it very well, as if the words passed through my body undigested, like tomato skins or niblets of corn. Still, I liked reading the news on my phone, tapping from one article to the next. My phone was small and reading was like peering through a crack into an organized universe, and I liked knowing all I had to do was tap the back button to trace my own whereabouts, which made my forgetting a bit more bearable. Many people find it disturbing that every swipe and click is tracked. But I was comforted that everything I did was copied elsewhere, in case a series of moments needed to be reconstructed. It was unlikely that such a comprehensive log would ever be necessary, but it was comforting, the way it's comforting to take thousands of pictures on your phone that you may never look at again but that you could look at again, all in the palm of your hand.

I switched from checking the news to checking my email. There was nothing new, though one message stood out, one that I hadn't responded to; a week old now, it was an email from my editor about whether I might want to take some time off.

Time off.

After filing paperwork with the worker's compensation clinic, she'd realized worker's comp might pay some portion of my salary, perhaps two-thirds, for a couple months. She could probably find freelancers to fill in. She repeated that this wasn't my first ergonomic issue. She was concerned. I needed to figure out how to care for my body. I hadn't even lived most of my life yet, hopefully, and then she digressed about how, when she was my age, she worked the crime beat, subsisting on stale infrared-warmed sandwiches from gas stations, in some city much bigger and grittier and therefore more interesting than this mostly pleasant and mostly bucolic place where she'd ended up. It was the longest email she'd sent in some months, and she did seem genuinely concerned, especially toward the end when she circled back to this potential offer of time off.

All I could think was: no.

There were a number of practical reasons for saying no.

Two-thirds of a salary wasn't a full salary and I already spent half my income on rent. My father would have helped but after arriving here, I promised myself I'd stop asking for help, except if I was dying, and this wasn't anywhere near dying.

Then there were the savings bonds my father had found and given to me just before I came to this place.

But they hadn't fully matured yet. They were close but not quite done.

And even if my whole salary could magically be covered, I would say: no no no. Work gave me a role in the world, and I did not not not want the other reporter to pounce on my stories, because even if I soon returned fresh and healed I'd never get them back.

Yet I couldn't bring myself to respond to my boss's offer. I should tell my boyfriend about it, I thought, or maybe talk about it with Lee, I should get a second opinion before dismissing it, I thought, shouldn't I?

As I sat in the swirl of my thoughts I got a call from *Caller Unknown*. I thought maybe it was some tip, and the clinic was taking its time anyway, so I answered and said hello but only got a curious recording: *If you're ready, press one; if you're not ready, press two; if you'd like a callback later, press three.* "For what?" I asked, but it only played the recording repeatedly. A woman in scrubs appeared before I could make a decision and because I was the kind of person who felt obligated to respond, even to a recording that wouldn't respond to me, I pressed two and hung up. It was strange, but the woman in scrubs was quickly weighing me and so I didn't really think about it, and instead I answered questions about my pain and what was its severity on a scale from one to ten? I think I said seven, although whatever number I offered I later felt guilty about. Perhaps the number was an exaggeration, since as long as I let my hands hang motionless at my sides they didn't bother me much, although when I did type, even for a few seconds, the pain felt beyond ten, felt beyond the scale, although then again the pain felt beyond that scale only in this one part of my body, whereas every other part of my body was fine, and so maybe in the end it did average out to seven.

She went away and a man in a plaid shirt entered the examination room wearing glasses with lenses so thick they enlarged his eyes, as if to better inspect me. "Okay," he said, hands on hips, like we were really about to get something figured out, "so what's going on?"

I attempted to describe the pain in my hands, and I believe I said it was sudden and sharp, although perhaps I said it was quick and shooting. He took one hand in his and flipped it back and forth, considering each side, and asked if they felt numb or tingling.

I said something like: "Not really . . . I mean—yeah, maybe? Rarely . . ."

But it wasn't wise to articulate aloud my uncertainty, because people pick out what they want to hear, because what's said aloud can be easily distorted in the open air between your head and other people's heads.

Although maybe the problem wasn't what other people heard. Maybe the disorder tracked all my confusion and became more confident in itself.

I could have said: Sometimes it's like a pin. But not pins and needles, more like a single pin jabbing inside me as if looking for a good vein to draw blood, or pricking me over and over out of curiosity, as if I were an alien, or like an animal you poke to find out if it's dead or alive, even though it's always dead by the time you get to poking it.

Maybe there was an unmetaphorical, precise way to explain

it, but I can never say the precise sentences in my head aloud because they start to change once they exit me.

"Okay, and can you place your hands like this?" he said, more or less unfazed, perhaps used to people being inarticulate. He pressed his hands together with the wrists bent at a ninety-degree angle, as if to pray. I was happy because the other doctor hadn't evaluated me, hadn't asked me to do any special maneuvers, and so I did as this doctor asked and he waited quietly, studying my face with his magnified eyes for a sign of something, awaiting fresh agony.

"You don't feel any tingling?" Now he was skeptical.

I said no. I felt as if I'd let him down.

If a person has the famous syndrome this prayer pose will usually catalyze numbness or tingling. I never felt different in prayer pose, but the doctor didn't let the failure faze him. He tried a different tactic. He asked me to squeeze my hands into fists, then to squeeze his thumbs. I enjoyed following his simple instructions. Afterward he still thought I had the syndrome. He prescribed physical therapy and acupuncture. "Although sometimes, you know, this stuff just goes away on its own. You're young," he said.

Whenever anyone heard about my problem, my age was often the first thing they remarked on. The body is supposed to start falling apart eventually, but not at my age, and their comments suggested that my body might soon understand that it had acted prematurely and quiet down for a while longer. But I didn't want the pain to simply go away, because pain is supposed to have a cause, it's supposed to have context, and meaning: a leg breaks in a car accident or lungs inhale asbestos or a stomach protests rotten food. I wanted the pain to go away after a treatment had eradicated it; I wanted to establish cause and effect.

He said to come back every two weeks so the clinic could monitor my progress, and to limit my fine manipulation—anything that required precise movements of the fingers—to two hours a day.

"That seems like a lot of things, a lot of different kinds of movement," I said.

As I sat in the parking lot after my appointment, I pulled out my phone and searched online for activities that required fine manipulation. One website said fine manipulation included anything involving *a small movement and/or accurate force control of a tool interacting with objects.* It said fine manipulation was pervasive in daily life. It cited examples including using a fork and knife, or holding an egg. Typing of course involved fine manipulation. Handwriting seemed to fall into the definition of fine manipulation, but although I could feel the disorder when I wrote by hand it didn't reach that threshold when weirdness becomes pain and pain becomes unbearable, perhaps because there was so little movement, really, just the fingertips pressed against the thin object but the fingers themselves not really moving at all. Washing dishes didn't seem to involve too much fine manipulation—just holding the sponge, circling. But the handling of the dishes and the way you hold the sponge, how you might scrape dried-up avocado from the plate, those movements did seem to be varieties of fine manipulation. Hand jobs didn't really require fine movements, but a person has to be careful and delicate, applying enough pressure but not too much, and if holding an egg constituted fine manipulation, then a hand job definitely did. Flicking a light switch involved fine manipulation but just one second of it. I would need to flip hundreds of switches before reaching my limit. Two hours seemed a strange amount of time to prescribe as a limit, since only a few seconds of typing triggered my disorder, but if he ordered me to cease all fine manipulation, I would just have to sit in a chair or lie in bed and be still. I could have walked, I suppose, as long as I was careful. If I could have been completely motionless for the rest of my life, I could have told that lady in the examination room: zero! Zero zero zero!

Get off your phone, I thought, before you're reduced to sitting sadly still forever!

But I needed to do one more thing. I went into my email and responded briefly to my editor's offer, with an email that kindly but succinctly said: no no no!

Okay, I thought. Starting now: no more phone for the rest of the day!

Or at least a few hours . . .

Then of course it rang.

I wasn't completely surprised. I was a reporter.

But I wasn't expecting any calls, unless *Caller Unknown* had surmised that only an hour or so after their original call, I was now and finally ready, but this call was not from *Caller Unknown*, or perhaps it was, because the caller, according to my screen, was still not fully known.

The screen said: *MAYBE: Lee.*

Finally! She had put me off over the past few weeks, claiming she was busy, which had frustrated me, I wanted to commiserate with her. Although I also wondered if I truly wanted to talk to Lee about the pain in her hands and the pain in my hands. I sometimes wanted to talk to someone who might be going through something similar, but also my experience was something precious and private, something to protect from outside influence even as I tried to obliterate it.

Anyway.

I thought: Don't undo the easy vow you just made to not touch the phone for at least a few hours, be kind to your hands!

But then I thought or felt or felt the thought: it doesn't matter, and did I really believe that the man in the medical office park was going to be the one to recalibrate my body?

I tried to push back the negative thought. I needed to believe things were possible. I looked for hope but by this point a guardrail had appeared around my heart or brain or wherever hope lives in the body, and even though guardrails aren't even that tall I was not the kind of person to breach formal barriers.

I slid my finger across the glassy screen to accept the call.

"Hey, Kim," she said, her voice a little more gentle and grounded than I remembered. "I know we said we'd meet later this week, but my schedule shifted a bit, and—it's last minute, but I think I know something that might help. With your hands."

I took in a breath as if the extra air inside me could be a protective padding.

"Okay," I said evenly. "What—what's the deal? Like—medically, or . . ."

"It would be easier to explain in person," she said. "I could show you the setup."

"The setup?"

"You could come by my place. This evening if you want."

I paused. "So it's a thing?"

She repeated that it would be easier to explain in person.

Lee

Lee told me where she lived, an address that seemed vaguely familiar though I'd never visited her before. It was a small neighborhood nested in a hilly mess of tangled roads. The roads changed their names the farther they penetrated into the woods, as if to mark how far certain people had ventured, or maybe every so often even a road can change too much or confront new circumstances, necessitating a new identity. She offered detailed directions, noting turns and distances by the color and size of houses or especially sharp swerves or dips in the road. She cautioned that it was better to follow her instructions since some phone maps still sometimes got her location wrong.

In her voice was the quiet pride I'd heard before from other people when planning interviews at homes for which smartphone maps had the wrong location, like it must be profound that the app thought a person's house was a quarter mile farther up the road and as if it wouldn't probably soon be remedied, the little digital pin finally piercing the correct coordinates and affixing them securely in place.

I left the parking lot and repeated the directions to myself in my head so as not to forget and resort to my phone. Luckily her directions were clear, which was helpful because the deeper I drove into those hills the more dense the evening fog became until toward the end, when I turned off my headlights entirely. They seemed not to illuminate but to further cloud and obscure the road before me.

The familiarity of the address struck me only when I passed the main house, near the beginning of the initially well-paved driveway: I had reported on the property. In the waning light I recognized the main house from the drawings and computer-generated images, when it was just a plan submitted to the county government for approval. A couple from somewhere bought an old cabin and hired a high-profile architect to figure out how many appendages could be soldered onto it, additions all the more elaborate because they emerged from that renovated but still somehow decrepit heart that was the original cabin. It had to be that way because the neighbors protested the original plan to completely demolish it, even if the property was so isolated that the neighbors couldn't actually see the structure. It was very old, it might have been a monastery, and that—not the religious tinge but rather the old and vaguely spiritual tinge—was important to people.

The owners had claimed they originally believed the cabin too decayed to be saved but found a way to preserve it after all.

But as I passed the house it was clear the couple hated that original cabin.

The truth was in those appendages, including a wing at the

back of the house I now saw but didn't remember seeing in the approved plans.

The driveway got bumpier and bumpier until finally at the far back of the property was Lee's tiny cottage. I remembered this part of the plans too: the addition of an affordable rental. It was even smaller than my small place. But my cabin looked tired and dumpy and sad, as if the wood of it wished it could belong to something better. For this tiny home the owners had put more money into it than they would ever get back in rent. The owners had perhaps built exactly the place they really wanted in miniature, and so could look at it with a certain longing from afar. My boyfriend would have judged it as something the owners built to pretend they cared about providing local housing while flaunting their stupid taste and wealth.

The little home, made of reclaimed redwood, was long and rectangular with a front awning that reached out strangely far. The front was all windows, now glowing warmly, and the roof was not flat and not an A-frame but instead one steep stark angle. The whole thing reminded me in a way of coyotes I sometimes saw on hikes, lean and comfortable in their bodies but also acutely aware of their position in the landscape.

I parked my car. I felt the blooming of an internal struggle. I didn't know what she might show me, and I'd never wanted to be one of those sad sacks seeking answers in chakras or crystals or vibrations. I was about to start physical therapy. If I piled one treatment on top of another, how would I know what was working? On the other hand, Mirror wasn't working that well, was it? My voice wasn't quite right, was it? And I'd done that worksheet too, so why not pile treatment on treatment, why not keep trying and trying unlike a certain parent of mine who just gave up?

I was apprehensive but excited to meet with Lee. I liked seeing the insides of people's homes, an occasional but important part of my job, especially for profiles; never was my weak impulse for touch so awakened as it was in other people's homes, my fingers fascinated by tables made of rare wood and couches of luxurious upholstery. I always felt on the verge of something in other people's homes. I never quite reached it but still, even when a story didn't especially excite me or maybe especially when a story didn't excite me, if an interview was going to take place in a subject's home, I looked forward to it. And maybe, I thought, one day Lee could be a subject, maybe she had some new radical treatment for pain and someday I could write about it, not for the paper but for something bigger like a national magazine or at least a prestigious website.

I left my car and walked through the dark to the door and knocked before I realized she had a doorbell, so then I pressed that too and it made the sound of a temple bell. Lee's voice told me to come in and I entered quickly to keep out the cold air and it was as if I had walked into one of those coffee table books for tiny homes.

Standing there a little dumbfounded, I said, "Wow," before I even said hello.

Lee nodded. "Yeah," she said.

She hadn't gotten up from the cozy love seat built into the back wall. She looked so at ease and so part of the interior that it was a minute before I realized she looked very different from the only time I'd met her in person. Before she wore tight jeans with her hair frizzy and tied up in a loose bun on her head. Now her clothing was loose but architectural and her hair was cropped short with the part straight down the middle of her head as if each aspect of herself was efforting to be in a precise balance.

I sat down in a wingback chair that seemed designed to eject people. My body stiffened slightly. I kept looking around the interior of the cabin, trying to imprint all the functional and sedately beautiful details to take back with me. Almost everything was pale. A staircase built of the most beautiful drawers I'd ever seen led to a lofted bed. The kitchenette had cabinetry without doors, so everything to be consumed was visible. There were many mason jars of herbs. I saw no wine or liquor.

I took off my coat and even my cardigan, the cabin warm and pleasantly dry from the woodstove, though after looking at the little flames I realized the fire was fake. Real woodstoves weren't allowed in new buildings anymore, because of the smoke. To some a fake fire might seem absurd, but it gave a nice ambiance.

She saw me looking at it and said, "Pushing a button is a lot easier than building a fire every day in the winter. And the owners pay for the heat—they don't want this place getting moldy. The owners put a lot of money in this place. They're very particular about it. I had to agree to rent it furnished. Down to the mugs." She raised her eyebrows suggestively at this imposition on her agency. "At first it was a little nerve-racking, worrying about breaking or scratching anything. But I'm kind of glad, actually. Maybe it's good to be a little more careful with things."

She got up and poured us steaming cups of ginger tea and sat across from me. She went on about the owners, noting with a mixture of judgment and awe that their home had five bedrooms and remained empty except for the holidays. They were planning to move in soon, she said, which was a slight disappointment.

She knew it was a waste of space but admitted she preferred to be alone on the property, especially in the summer when she would use the main house's porch because her own cabin was so cowed by trees and hills that only little chips of sunlight managed to fall on it. I remembered then that there had been some public debate about the number of trees the owner would need to cut down for the project and so they left more standing around the affordable cabin. But she liked it here and she'd always wanted to live in a rural place but never had the courage to upend her life until her health issues arose, and then she asked me how I'd gotten here and I explained I applied for a job at the paper and somehow got it and took it, and somehow I was still here.

"I'm glad you came over," she said.

I took a sip of the tea. It burned the back of my throat.

"Me too," I said, but then I wasn't sure what to say and I looked around for some guidance since this place seemed full of intention. "I'm kind of in awe of how neat you keep this place. There's not a lot of storage. My place is so messy," I said.

"Oh, there's all sorts of nooks. Even parts of the floor come off and I store things there. But I like all this open cabinetry, too. Keeps me tidy, organized. Kind of forces me to maintain this—aesthetic or whatever."

"Right. It's—calming," I said, looking at the crocheted thingamajigs on the wall, two tightly woven and geometric and another with looser braids that petered out into many hanging cords, which matched her ceramics, which did have some remembrance of color but were somehow even paler than pastel, as if their makers were ashamed to keep making things and so subdued the colors more and more, either as penance for the accumulation of things or so it wouldn't be so noticeable.

The only thing that didn't belong in the palette of the room was a laptop connected to a garishly yellow box that did not seem made of natural materials. Or at least not its plastic exterior, since its insides were probably full of silicon and other elements mined from the earth.

The laptop was not sleek. It had a bulky, almost industrial look to it. The box was also bulky, the size of a thick dictionary, and on its front was a row of tiny red lights along the bottom. Above each light was a number, one through eight. There was also the outline of a human form, like the shape police make around a cadaver on the ground. There were also red lights on each hand and foot and the belly and the head of the outline. One cord connected the box to the laptop and another to a black strap.

"So—how have you been?" she said, I think seeing my attention unable on its own to look away from that almost primordial computer and wanting my focus not over there, at least not yet. "Have you managed work okay, or . . ."

I thought of my feelings in the days leading up to this evening, the hope that I might find some true understanding in Lee and yet also the hope that there would be no understanding at all, our situations would be different and my disorder could remain singular.

"It's—okay. Or—it's not really okay. It's been hard. You obviously know how frustrating it is—to not be able to type," I said. "I'm about to start physical therapy. Maybe it will help. But to be honest," I said, suddenly deciding to at least try to be honest even though she was a stranger, because maybe by being honest I could get somewhere or maybe she could become my friend in this place where I struggled to make friends, "I'm worried it's going to get worse. My hands, they just feel weird most of the time. Is—did yours feel that way? I just—and more and more I just—I dread going to work, or not even going to work but working wherever I am . . ."

Yes, yes, she said, nodding. She understood. We talked about the specifics of our respective pains, or at least as specific as we could manage, which for me wasn't very specific except for the locations, which were very specific. She was better. She didn't pause or hesitate like me. She had removed alleged inflammatory foods like dairy and gluten from her diet, which partially helped. Her mention of food sensitivities made me suspicious, and the specificity of her problems started to dissolve the hope for kinship and the possibility that I might ask her what I'd wanted to ask her in my email: *Do you think I might be conjuring this pain from nothing? Do you think it's possible there's no real cause? Do you ever think maybe you're totally crazy?*

But somehow it was like she saw the thought in my mind. "Are you worried this is . . . all in your head? Because," she said, not waiting for an answer, "it's not. You're not crazy because of this weird pain, or because you're trying all sorts of things to cure yourself, like those worksheets, and you're not crazy because you're having trouble with Mirror. You know, I think the issue with Mirror is—well, you do mumble a bit. I can imagine you're trying to be quiet, but you need to speak as clearly as possible. But maybe if you can just manage with Mirror a little longer, it won't matter. Maybe I could—well, maybe I could actually cure you. I don't want to promise too much, but . . ."

Our eyes turned in unison to the primordial computer.

"So that's the Axon," she said.

She began then to tell me about how someone's relative with chronic pain had heard about the Axon deep in some message board threads on the internet, which had led the relative, whom Lee described as both open-minded and somewhat desperate, to hunt for someone who owned and operated an Axon in order to receive the treatment. The Axon, Lee went on, was computer software and hardware allegedly invented by a scientist from an elite university, whose specific credentials Lee did not detail. You entered certain details about yourself and your problem into the program, and connected yourself to the hardware, wrapping the black strap around your head. She said it was about the connection between you and the world. The machine tapped into your energy and the energy of the universe, it used a process blending holistic medicine and quantum mechanics. She talked at length about how everything in a person's body vibrated at different frequencies, including viruses and blood cells, organs and toxins, allergens and bacteria and even emotions, but sometimes these frequencies were disturbed. She was getting excited, losing a bit of her pastel calm, as she went on talking about all the ways the body's quantum frequencies could be disturbed. Her own frequencies were becoming extremely active, and she radiated the fresh energy of a convert. She was a far cry from counting seals, I thought.

Sometimes, she went on, the various frequencies of the body's history and its maladies interfered with each other in unfortunate ways, in ways that intensified them, when it was important that certain frequencies be allowed to peter out, be absorbed by the world. The machine could detect the energetic state of one's body and determine whether levels of minerals and vitamins and sugars were in balance, both from the vibrations it read and also of course from my hair and spit, small portions of which she would insert into the machine. Sometimes the machine could detect illnesses from long ago, if their effects lingered in the body. She compared it to a virus scan for a computer.

After analyzing this information, the Axon used special energies and quantum vibrations and electromagnetic waves to calibrate the body's frequencies and levels to once again be in harmony, to equalize with the universe. It's both a treatment and a diagnosis, she said.

"I know it sounds a little bizarre," she added. "I was skeptical. But . . . what can I say. What works works. I'm a certified operator now."

I looked at her blankly. I wasn't sure how to arrange my face.

"I'm working with a few people now. We're really making progress."

I sipped my ginger tea. It was somehow still warm. "Ohhhh," I said.

This is crazy, I thought. This is a joke.

Yet I also thought: It would be nice to return to this warm cabin with all its intention.

I thought: Maybe sometimes healing has to be a big joke!

But can anything ever be only a joke?

"I know we don't know each other that well," she said, "and this might sound a little funny, but—well, I thought of you, of course."

"Now?" I said.

"Oh no," she said, and she let the *no* linger in the air for a few seconds. She held my gaze while also seeming to take in the outline of air around me, as if she could see some special emanations from my body. "No, no, you're not ready."

I paused or maybe I truly froze. "But—what—*that*? But . . ."

She held up her hand. "It'll ask again when it's time."

As I drove back down the driveway and navigated the tangle of streets back to the main road, the fog had evaporated but still I went slowly because my vision was a little blurry and my vision was blurry because I was slightly crying, not much but similar in effect to a thick fog.

I Went to Physical Therapy

I didn't hear from Lee for some time after that evening, and I told myself I was glad of it. What bullshit! If it called again I'd press two again, *I'll press two forever!* I thought but only to myself, since the only person to whom I would have ranted was my boyfriend, and for some reason, when he asked how my visit with Lee was, I only said we'd talked very generally about our issues, and every time he asked what exactly we'd talked about, which he asked many times as if hoping I'd suddenly reveal that she'd pushed me to take a break from work, I'd change to subject to my new focus: physical therapy, which I hoped would massage my problems out of me. And soon I was driving two days a week, an hour's drive each way, to a nice physical therapist named Nick who, at the beginning of each session, delicately wrapped my forearms in a heating pad, swaddling them like a baby, and I sat for five or ten minutes while he attended to others.

I didn't speak to other patients at the clinic. There seemed an unspoken agreement that we would remain silent unless we were speaking to a physical therapist, as if their ministrations were a spell that discussion might obstruct. But now I wonder if maybe I created the silence and when I wasn't there all the injured people spoke freely and expressed wistfulness or frustration or hope. It was an open office and there were multiple physical therapists tending to people a few minutes at a time. Some of the other patients had problems with their hands too, patients mostly wearing khakis and button-ups, office workers, and although I knew it wasn't really appropriate I strained to listen to their conversations and I heard terms like *carpal tunnel* or *tendinitis* or so-called *repetitive stress injury*. These were the patients more like me, I suppose, which was a disappointment, because they looked very boring. But Nick and the other therapists handled all kinds of ailments related to work: twisted ankles, aching necks, pulled knees, backs in all varieties of distress, ailments from sitting for hours and hours in front of a screen but also ailments from moving heavy things or doing dangerous work, or what is commonly considered dangerous work, and typing is not dangerous work, or if it is considered dangerous it is a sad and curiously tedious kind of danger. The patients who worked truly dangerous jobs wore sturdier pants and more casual shirts and in my recollection some of them are even wearing hard hats, though the hard hats must really have accidentally hopped from the posters I'd seen into this memory, and I was a little jealous because they seemed more interesting than the office workers and I wished I were more aligned with them. But there was a way in which all of them were more like each other than me, because they probably all lived in this city, where it might only take minutes to reach this clinic, where they didn't have to worry as much as we did about fire, because they didn't abut the forest. Though of course they, like everyone, would be subjected at times to the smoky air that seemed poised to return each fall.

As I waited for my arms to warm up, I thought about work. I had to go to the clinic when I was supposed to be at the office, so I worked in my mind, since much of my work took place in my mind anyway, or in the continuous loop between my mind and whatever material I inscribed my thoughts on, because my thoughts were wispy, threatening to evaporate at any moment. At least the important thoughts. The thoughts I wanted to forget or at least not linger on were the strongest of all, and instead of thinking usefully about work I started thinking about the other reporter. When I said I was leaving early that day for physical therapy, he used it as an opportunity, a springboard to ask the question he seemed hesitant to ask before, which was an unusual posture for him because in his work he was confident and dogged, the kind of person who waited politely outside homes or offices or bars if someone he needed to speak to wouldn't return his calls, whereas I was happier on my computer, combing the internet for tidbits of information. I liked emails. I liked scheduled conversations. I liked reports. But in order to cold-call people or approach them on the street or interact with them at all, I often told myself I was a different person. Not a specific person; just not quite me. I would say to myself, in my head: *I am not me, I am not me, I am not me* . . .

Anyway.

I remembered the other reporter asking me *So what's wrong, exactly?* and I said carpal tunnel, well, maybe carpal tunnel, and he asked for details and I gave him some of the details. Then he asked what bothered me besides typing, and I could tell he loved it, the accretion of details, and I said I don't know, sometimes other things, like peeling an orange, or . . . but I said then with forced finality that he shouldn't worry, it would resolve itself. Still, he offered to research anything for me, if I wanted, and I said thanks even though I didn't want his research. He asked if it was numb, and I said maybe, and I kept trying to describe it for a while, and finally he said, Well, that is an odd condition . . . and I said, Odd? and he said, I just mean, of course I believe you, but like you say, I'm sure it'll ease up.

Clearly he didn't believe me. But what did I care?

Or maybe he was just trying to get into my head.

Luckily Nick wheeled back over to me, having cycled through his other charges, and directed my stretches, and so I could just focus on this, the beginning of my healing. I held one arm out and pulled my hand into a high-five position with the opposite hand for about fifteen seconds and then pushed the hand the other way, down, as if I wanted someone to look at a ring on my finger, although I didn't wear any jewelry at all.

He asked how my hands felt, if my fingers hurt at all, and I gave him an answer that made him frown and say that I sounded a little uncertain.

I wished in this moment that each body part had its own brain and mouth and vocal cords and could just speak for itself. But none of them could and so I tried to remember exactly how my hands felt when I came in, and how they felt in this moment while one hand was stretching and the other had just been stretched, and whether either hand was a little worse, and if that little bit worse seemed a function of moving my wrists as he told me to or more like the typical fluctuations my pain cycled through, the ebb and flow, the way the pain gently came and went when I did nothing like the gentle breath of a sleeping monster waiting to be awoken.

"The stretching aggravates my fingers a little," I said, trying to sound certain.

He told me to be extra gentle with my hands, with myself, and then we did more exercises. He gave me a piece of clay to mold carefully in each hand. He told me to roll my wrists clockwise fifteen times and then the other way. I did as he said and he watched me. Every motion had to be balanced with the opposite motion. I wondered if for all the years I had been typing I should have been doing the opposite of typing for the same amount of time, whatever the opposite of typing was.

After that, I sat for a while in my car, which I'd been doing more often lately because it was the only inside place to truly be alone. Even at home when I was alone, and my boyfriend was at work or running errands or wandering in the woods, he could come back at any moment, unexpectedly returning early from some place, and in that way being at home was never quite being alone. But no one ever unexpectedly opened the door to my car. So I sat quietly in the driver's seat and vowed not to touch my phone for a while and maybe not even until the next day, so the treatment had its best chance at success. My blood would find its way back to my neck or hands or wherever it was he said my blood needed to go, without the fine manipulation of my fingers like some horrible wrench tightening certain inside parts of me and making them impenetrable. The vulnerable parts of my body could remain porous like healthy crumbly soil, the kind of soil that water can easily percolate through, which I had learned was important for rain to reach roots and for human wastewater to slowly cleanse itself before it reaches other waters.

My Boyfriend Found Mushrooms

When I got home from physical therapy that evening, my boyfriend was on the couch, paging through a mushroom identification book, his jeans brown and damp from kneeling in the woods. On the coffee table before him were a few specimens he'd picked that day, after waiting weeks for rain. The first rains of the season were supposed to start just after Halloween, or that's what longtime locals said, but in recent years the rains had started later, and during the recent drought there was of course barely any rain all.

But finally a rain did arrive, and it cleared the air of the last bits of smoke and brought up from the dirt the first flush of mushrooms, and for me that was a relief because my boyfriend had been antsy waiting for them. Or that's what he said when I'd asked recently why he seemed a little antsy, a little on edge, a bad combination: you don't want to be jittery on a precipice. This was an unusual mood for him. His natural state was one of calm critique, often of how this place where we lived was changing or becoming too expensive or being inundated by the wealthy or tourists or both. But he kept saying his new jittery mood was temporary; hiking was what calmed him and he'd been hiking less because of the smoke, and he'd worried the rains wouldn't come, and after his last wilderness retreat he didn't have any major excursion to look forward to. I wasn't sure he was telling the truth, or at least the complete truth; it wouldn't matter so much, would it, to be between seasons or far from another retreat if he was content in his life or his job?

So I was glad the mushrooms had come, because then I knew or thought I knew what was occupying his mind. If someone can't figure out how to be happy, at least they can be occupied.

"What do you have there? Any of them edible?" I asked after pouring myself a glass of wine and sitting on the other side of the couch with one of his fern identification booklets. I was behind on work but still I was trying to keep myself off the computer in the evening, and wouldn't it be nice to learn about ferns? They seemed emblematic of this place, thriving in the cool coastal fog, which I myself could only pretend to have affection for.

"No, I don't think so," he said, then turned his gaze from the mushrooms to me to my cup. He asked how my appointment was and before I could tell him he noted that alcohol was inflammatory. "Maybe it's not the best thing for whatever's going on with you," he said, and reached over the couch and gave my hand a tender squeeze.

I squeezed back, but took a sip. The wine was light and tart. I reveled for a second in the bracing pleasure of being completely immersed in it. "It's relaxing. Don't be overbearing. It's my own body," I said, though clearly I had no idea how to care for it.

His face took on an overly chastened aspect. "I'm not trying to tell you what to do. It was just a thought. Lee mentioned to me once that it helped her . . ." but he saw the look on my face and returned his attention to one of his fungal specimens. It was one I'd never seen before, with a broad orange cap covered in tiny hairlike filaments. He scratched and sniffed its stem, then looked at it intently, yet with some hesitancy, or actually it was more like unease, an unease I didn't typically see in his gaze, at least not his gaze upon the natural world. He said none were edible, or at least pleasant; they were medicinal or potentially medicinal. As he moved between his specimens and his identification tome, I lost interest in what he was doing, because I was only interested in what could be eaten, and also I didn't want to be a woman watching a man being absorbed in something, and anyway it was an unspoken element of our relationship that we would never too closely approach the other's passion.

It was actually our passions that had brought us together. I first met him by interviewing him for an article I was writing about a new mycological society in town. My editor told me to find one mushroom enthusiast who didn't want to belong to a society, to at least give some voice to those who didn't need to make their hobby so organized. I found my boyfriend in the town's online message board, where he answered people's occasional and usually foolish questions about mushrooms. When he agreed to let me come along to forage, he asked if I'd prefer a popular and therefore blown-out spot, which he would show me freely, or one of his personal spots, a journey that would require me to be blindfolded. I was taken aback, but at that point I'd talked to a number of people who were extremely cagey about their foraging spots. I agreed to the blindfold. We didn't end up finding much but trampled through the forest on a misty day and all the leaves were glistening and we eventually came across a firm pink mushroom that didn't have normal gills but rather an underside covered in what he called teeth, and the top of the mushroom was beaded with bright red droplets, and we crouched low to admire it. I asked him its name and of course it was called bleeding tooth fungus because people aren't very original. He rattled off a few facts about it, which I noted furiously in my notebook, its pages made fragile in the mist. I was a little enchanted. I ended up quoting something he said about identifying whatever he encountered, that he hated the idea of being so fixated and obsessed with edibility. He liked that. He liked the article. He didn't necessarily care what other people thought of him, he said later, but through the article it seemed I thought he had integrity. He made sure to tell me soon after the article came out that he'd read the whole paper and admired other articles too, particularly one about the bane of rising rents; my job was a different way of having a relationship with a place, he said. I got the feeling he didn't necessarily respect many people but he decided he respected me and my work. A few weeks later he gave me a framed spore print of a mushroom I'd picked from the ground.

"You know," my boyfriend said, snapping me back to the present, "Lee sometimes said her problems—they were a blessing in disguise. She really liked counting those seals." He broke the stem of a mushroom to examine the nature of its fibers. He again smelled deeply. He took some notes.

That phrase: *a blessing in disguise*. A cortisol rage shot throughout my body, cracking open in my chest and zipping into my extremities. I thought of it coursing through my veins, around and around like some trapped animal. I almost expected my fingers to start burning but of all things they were completely nonplussed. I took a long quiet breath as if my anger could escape that way.

"Are you saying this is a good thing?" I said, getting up and going over to my laptop. Ferns weren't going to help me! I thought. I didn't love ferns. I loved my laptop. It was open and ready at my makeshift standing desk, perched on the stack of dictionaries and also, now, the workbook, which my boyfriend derided when I brought it home, since he hated the idea of people undergoing deep psychotherapeutic investigation, finding that kind of search for meaning narcissistic, although later he apologized, begrudgingly encouraging me to keep at it.

"Kim, I'm not trying to upset you. I'm just saying, it's . . . not an unusual response to being all contorted and hunched over. It's not natural to be on the computer all day. Or maybe it's not an ergonomic problem. I mean, who knows? Maybe your hands are responding to something else in the computer. You can still write by hand, after all . . ."

"Come on, lots of people have carpal tunnel. And—natural? Tell me what contemporary job uses the human body's natural and ideal state, anyway? And I wasn't hunched over. I was standing. I had a whole ergonomic setup. Or—I don't know, I thought it was ergonomic . . ."

I opened up my email. My boyfriend asked what I was doing and I said I'd gotten a new lead on the potential spike in home sales. I didn't really have a new lead, but I could send a few emails to local real estate agents. I'd meant to earlier, before my physical therapy appointment, but got derailed by how long it took me to dictate some little article about who knows what. I opened a new email and tried to dictate quietly. I didn't want to be declaiming in our little cabin, it felt ridiculous, but Mirror was still struggling and even the initial explanation of who I was—*Hi, my name is Kim, I'm a reporter with the local paper* turned into *Hi, my aim is Kim, I'm going to report her to the local paper.*

My boyfriend said again that rich people buying homes didn't seem like news, wasn't new at all. It had been going on for years, people buying second homes to stay a few weekends a year or turning them into more short-term rentals. Why get so stressed, he said, over nothing? I breathed out performatively through my nose in frustration.

"Just let me worry about all that. It's fine."

"Have you talked to your editor about this story idea?"

"No, I haven't told anyone at work about it. What does it matter?"

"I just hope there's no more pressure on you than you're already under."

I nodded slowly. I said okay. I wasn't going to tell anyone anyway. I didn't want the story being taken from me. I changed the subject, asking my boyfriend jokingly if he'd found any mushrooms to cure me, but he got a look in his eye like he didn't find it funny, that his foragings weren't a joke.

He had in fact gone, with the manager of the bar, to a neighborhood where he sometimes prowled around the large fungi-rich properties of mostly vacant second homes because he wanted to search for medicinal mushrooms that could help me, he said pointedly. My boyfriend rolled his eyes while telling me that the manager, who asked to tag along, musing at the potential of some hip adaptogenic drink they might concoct, had almost gotten them caught at a house that wasn't as vacant as they thought. Then my boyfriend started grumbling about how he'd been reduced to creeping on private property—not that it was bad to use what wasn't being appreciated—because so much of the public forest was overgrazed with tourists wrenching from the earth any mushroom they saw, looking at it for ten seconds, then chucking it into the woods.

Anyway, he'd found a few mushrooms, he said, that were supposed to be good for nerves, though I didn't ask if he meant physically or psychologically.

Then my boyfriend said the manager had told him about the upcoming meeting about a potential practice emergency evacuation of town, that in fact the manager was helping to organize the meeting but they wanted a few more volunteers, and he'd asked my boyfriend if he was interested.

I snorted involuntarily.

"What?" he said.

"Community organizing isn't your thing," I said. "You're not a people person."

The look on his face shifted. He didn't like that I'd evaluated him. "Maybe it's possible to change," he said. If he was ever going to leave the bar like I always said he should, he went on, he needed to change something. It wasn't good, he went on, seeming to talk to the mushrooming tome in his lap instead of me, it wasn't good to go at certain things alone, he repeated a few times.

"Are you okay?" I asked.

"I—no, not exactly. I just . . ."

"What?"

"I got—something happened. On my retreat. I got lost. For a few days."

"A few days?" I said. "What—why didn't you say anything? What happened?" I didn't know what to do exactly, and I left my computer and sat beside him on the couch but still he felt far away, as if he were back wherever he'd gotten lost and was trying to find his way again. I rubbed his back but to be honest no one has ever found me the most comforting person, and my boyfriend gingerly moved my hand and laid it on my own thigh.

"I don't really want to talk about it, to be honest. Maybe later. But—I found a few edible mushrooms the day before I got lost. I ate them with my dinner the night before . . . I just—have been wondering, did I misidentify something, did I eat something a little bit . . . that made me slightly confused? I've never done that before. I'm very careful about what I forage. You know that, right?" he said, getting a little more upset, his voice starting to shake, which had never happened before, at least not in my presence. I again put my hand on his back and rubbed in circles like I was making some target or maybe some hole that only I could fill, and this time he let it stay.

Soon he said he just needed some quiet time and I said okay and went back to my computer and was about to start dictating but then he asked me not to, couldn't it just be quiet, and I said yes and I wasn't mad at him but the cortisol rage came back. I went back to reading about stupid ferns but nothing could push out the chorus in my mind of *why why why*. It was rare in my life that I longed to go backward in time, not that I was always overjoyed with the trajectory of my life, but I accepted it, usually, yet in this moment my body craved going back back back. Where, though, where could it go to fix things, where had I taken a wrong turn? Maybe not the very beginning, but maybe my mistake, where I would have gone back if I could, was the moment when my editor offered me a future at the paper.

Back When It Was Just Me and the Editor

My editor tentatively offered me a longer future at the paper near the beginning of my time there, back when it was just me and her, long before the disorder was born. I improved quickly, in part just by doing it over and over, writing thousands of words each week: about school budgets and local art shows, about businesses that were opening and businesses that were closing, about milk prices and cattle diseases and occasional retail thefts. I wrote and my editor rewrote and asked for more details. She always pushed me to go back and ensure I really and truly understood everything, and it was a little maddening, to spend hours trying to comprehend the tiniest thing that might just be a sentence, an ancillary detail that was somehow also important. She was kind and brutal as we sat together on Wednesdays, her looking at the screen of my laptop and me looking between the glow of the laptop and her, at her and her confidence and knowledge, at her intense gaze and her long and thick and manelike gray hair, sometimes distractedly wondering if my hair would look that graceful yet intimidating when it turned. Sometimes after the critiques were done and the paper sent to the printer, I cried, but I also improved. I learned to anticipate her questions, the particulars I should know before I turned in a draft.

After a few months she emailed me with the subject line *Your future at the paper*, which sent a sickly adrenaline through my body. Maybe, I thought, she was going to gently suggest I move along or outright fire me. But instead she praised me. Not that I was perfect or anywhere near it, but I seemed excited and enthused, and I hadn't mentioned any anticipation of returning or going somewhere else, and she'd for years wanted someone to hand the reins to, or at least delegate important duties, and maybe I would be that person. She'd like to retire someday, maybe, if she could save enough money and if she could let go of the news, which, with two sons in college, was like her baby, although she admitted that even when they had been at home the newspaper had always been her baby; her two sons grew older and older but the newspaper was always her baby.

I didn't have to sign a contract, but if I wanted, we could move forward with that intention, she went on, a few years down the line I might take on more duties, edit columns, perhaps even buy a small stake in the paper.

I remember sitting very still, reading the email again and again.

I hadn't imagined I'd be in this place very long.

But maybe I could stay for a while, I thought. I hadn't made friends but I was still enchanted by my own loneliness in a bucolic place. Even if I didn't make many friends, I could gain not just some experience but significant experience, deeper experience, be even more prepared for the next leg of my life, whatever it was.

And it's hard to resist being wanted.

I responded simply, something like: Yes, yes, yes!

And so I kept writing and writing and writing, with even more intensity because I had a real future in journalism. I wrote soft features, like the story about mushroom foraging. I wrote about county regulations and the sales of important properties, including the property owned by Lee's landlords, who only ever corresponded with me through email. I wrote about invasive grasses in coastal dunes and rare black bear sightings, about protections for shorebirds so eggs had a better chance of hatching, so in this one small stretch of beach they would be just a little bit safer. I wrote about public toilets overflowing from all the tourist excrement. I wrote or tried to write about solutions, though there didn't seem to be a solution for how desirable and hence how incredibly expensive it was to just be here, there didn't seem to be a way to depreciate the value of rolling hills and a coastline close but not too close to a city and coolly pleasant weather always compared to the Mediterranean.

And I wrote about water, especially since the drought was in its second year when I arrived. Conditions weren't quite as dire on the coast as they were inland. It was foggy and gray and cool just as it was supposed to be, but the mist in the air never collected into the downpour we needed. The local water company, a corporation that owned a number of other water systems in the state, warned of low creek flows that left the forest unsettlingly quiet when there should have been the comforting white noise of rushing currents. The big reservoir just outside town was shrinking, at first showing more and more of its muddy lip but eventually sinking so low it revealed a little bridge and two picnic tables, artifacts from its very creation, and at its lowest point a pair of motorcycles. The water agency first pleaded and then mandated restrictions on water use.

Then there was the controversy about the proposed sewer system, a story I covered from its beginning but not to its end—the first story my editor took from me!

Anyway.

I was happy when a water story arose. Water was potent. Water was elemental. In writing about water I felt connected to urgent worldly questions even as I reported on problems that centered on one bay or a single creek.

Although maybe it was just narcissism to hope that reporting on something important could make me important by proxy, make me more informed and therefore improved, better than people with only vague ideas of what was happening around them. Or maybe in my secret heart I hoped that writing about something clearly important would help me get a job somewhere else, somewhere bigger, since what was more important than having a bigger and therefore better job? That's what my mother would have wanted. She would have been so angry to find out I'd stayed so long at such a tiny paper. Sometimes it really was a relief that she was dead so I didn't have to argue with her anymore!

And yet it's becoming clear to me now that I never deserved anything greater, that I already missed things right under my nose.

Maybe if I hadn't been so drained by Mirror and the constant need to repeat and repeat and repeat myself, things would have been different. Or maybe it wasn't Mirror or it wasn't just Mirror, maybe if I'd been energized rather than drained by certain elemental parts of my job, like talking to people, I would have had more information about certain things.

Although it's not true that I hated talking to people for my job. I did actually like talking to people for my job.

Some people knew so much. Some people cared so deeply. People spent time patiently explaining their concerns about a particular invasive plant and the biology of how it spread, or an artist spoke hesitatingly about their art on display in a local café, and occasionally people answered my questions in the wake of personal tragedies, and I was humbled and moved and intrigued and excited.

Yet talking to people and pressing them for information induced sometimes a feeling of dread: what if my questions revealed my ignorance, what if I missed some key element of the story? Especially I dreaded the occasional necessity of making people uncomfortable, asking questions they wouldn't want to answer, although when I had documents to back me up, it was as if the documents were pressing them, not me. I have met people in life who thrive on making others squirm in the name of justice, but seeing people squirm only makes me want to squirm, as if inside me there is a strong sense of justice but my exterior only wants to mimic the world around me, to cause as little of a disturbance as possible, though I became a reporter to become a different kind of person!

Anyway.

The best part of any story was this: arriving at my computer with all the pieces of the story, at least the pieces I managed to find, and arranging things that had happened or were happening or would happen or might happen into as clear a narrative as possible, so people could understand little slivers of the little world of this place. And it wasn't exactly physical labor, it was in the computer, but there was something material about it:

rearrangement, sentences swapped, paragraphs freefalling below other paragraphs, kicked to the dark basement of the article, other paragraphs leapfrogging upward if in the span of a few hours or days something mildly important became absolutely critical, so important I wanted even the people who never read past the jump of the first page to see it.

But I don't know—maybe it was something about the adding and subtracting and editing and rearrangement that caused me to contort my body.

⁂

I reneged on my editor's offer of a longer future at the paper while I was working on a story about shit.

Before the other reporter and before my disorder and Mirror, my editor sat me down and told me what she knew about the proposed sewer system. She rolled up to my desk in her rolling chair. She was clearly excited. She sometimes complained that she missed the frenetic energy and grander scale of the city, but within minutes her manner would flip as she related some intriguing tidbit of potential news—the sale of a historic business, the replacement of a bridge—and we'd brainstorm questions that the turn of events entailed. On this day she must have talked me through a mix of assignments at first, issues that were definitely stories and things that were maybe stories, since many things happen that aren't really stories at all. Even when things were important, they weren't always stories. As we talked through assignments each week my editor moved fluidly between me and her laptop, its fan always whirring loudly, like something struggling for liftoff, as she skimmed through emails. The more she expounded, the more she got excited and the more she got me excited. Almost always her forehead was a little shiny from sweat, though the rest of her body seemed unaffected, like only her mind was getting hot.

She didn't know much about the proposed sewer project, but the county had announced a meeting about it in the wake of testing that found unfortunate levels of human waste in local creeks, which was apparently the result of the widespread failure of local septic systems, though no one was surprised given the occasional putrid scent in the air. By this time I knew the difference between a sewer and a septic system, the former piping human waste to a central facility for disposal and the latter allowing the wastewater to carefully seep out through the ground while the solid sludge of human excrement collected in some underground box, like buried treasure gone horribly awry, every few years siphoned and trucked off to some elsewhere place.

Then she said, "But now this part's *really* interesting," a common phrase of hers usually emphasized by hands gesticulating quickly. On this occasion the interesting parts were the suspicions arising among a few residents along the creek who had emailed her with theories that the county was being pressured by homeowners who wanted to enlarge their own homes, turn them into mansions or maybe even sell their land to developers for millions for large apartment complexes so the villages would no longer be villages but towns or even cities. "Take all this with a grain of salt. But it could be interesting," she said.

I was typing typing typing. "Yeah. But that kind of project—it would take at least a half a decade to get off the ground, don't you think?" I said, wanting to be knowing and familiar with the way things worked, and also perhaps trying to show I was just as intrigued and excited as she was. I wasn't the kind of person whose emotions easily expressed themselves. Even when I was curious and buzzing with energy, nothing naturally appeared on my face. But I did my best to seem lively, to extrude excitement from my pores like some decorative icing, because she said my writing became more sure of itself every week and I wanted to show her what that meant to me. She was excited to see me grow.

"Definitely somewhere around there, yeah," she said, her words slowing and her gaze moving to the skylight, the claw of her fingers sliding into her thick gray hair and scratching her head as if forgotten tidbits of information might fall out.

A few days later I was at home, preparing for the sewer system meeting. I was at my computer looking over documents and notes from talking to people beforehand, some with fears of development and others in favor of growth, not rampant but perhaps a few modest apartment complexes, and my brain felt fried, like all those voices were the oil I had to fry my mind in. As I worked, my back curled and my neck leaned even farther toward my laptop screen, leaning so far forward that my abdominal muscles clenched to hold my body in place like that, because in truth that's the shape I wanted to be in, that I put my body into week after week, and everyone says it isn't right, that computers force us into unnatural postures, but what is the posture of curiosity except to lean one's head forward as far as the rest of your body will let it go?

About an hour before the meeting a new email arrived from my editor: *A few more things* said the subject line. She offered up a few more questions I might ask of people at the meeting, but then the email changed registers.

She wanted to bring up again my future at the paper, since it seemed even more true that I wanted to stay for a long time.

She didn't mention it specifically, but I'd already moved into my boyfriend's one-room cabin, and I'd been there almost two years.

She said she'd decided to hire a second reporter—she'd managed to scrounge the money together—and wanted me to seriously consider whether I wanted to take on some editorial duties. Not right now, but soon, sometime in the next year or two, and maybe in five or ten years, I could buy into the paper, though that was contingent on—

What was it, exactly, contingent on?

Of course the email still exists but I'm relying only on my recollection.

And in my memory it was contingent on being more assertive, in my writing and how I pursued things. I needed to hedge less in my stories, to project more authority, to remove from my stories the occasional acrobatic attempts to avoid placing direct blame, and it might behoove me to be a bit more social about town, to be a person who would draw people toward me with their information and tips.

I wrote and deleted and wrote and deleted different versions of my response. One went into more detail about why exactly I'd moved in with my boyfriend, and one accepted her offer without reservation, and one said yes but with some reservations.

And why not? Why not say yes? I'd already said yes!

Why not stay forever even, or agree again to at least a couple decades?

But suddenly the antithesis came burbling up: no no no.

Yet maybe it wasn't sudden.

Maybe it only felt sudden because my simmering doubts now confronted a hard question. And what had been simmering was that I wasn't ready to give up on how my life might go, the mystery of where I could go next, of what greater thing awaited me—she told me so often how good I was!—or the thrilling moment I would flee when my boyfriend inevitably left me, because even though I loved him and he loved me, I didn't really believe that he would love me forever. I was sure that sooner or later he would run out of things to love about me, and that would be that. And I think too that in that moment, hunched over my computer, my mother, whom I thought of often but who was never a voice speaking to me, who had said nothing on that first offer, started screeching in some corner of my brain: *no Kim, no no no!* And I didn't like listening to my mother but finally I wrote back briefly that I was honored and flattered and heartened, but I no longer envisioned myself staying, no longer envisioned becoming her legacy, and maybe I wouldn't even be there another two years.

My Father Visited and It Was Mostly Nice

After the disorder arrived, my father visited for a long weekend. He liked to visit the beautiful place to which I'd moved, and also wanted, he said on the phone, to ensure I was all right. When I responded that of course I wasn't all right, I had a physical ailment, he edited himself; he wanted to understand. He was concerned. He wanted more information. Maybe if he understood it better he could do some research or seek out colleagues for advice.

I worried about his visit, about having to go over all the disorder's little details. And would I tell him about the Axon, that I'd potentially agreed to try—at least when Lee determined I was ready—some absurd diagnostic tool or treatment that harvested information from my brain and body and the universe? On the one hand I did want to tell him, to give a full and accurate picture of everything I was experiencing and considering. But obviously he would question my state of mind, that I would consider it. I didn't even think of telling him about the worksheets. I didn't want to talk about those things with him.

But I was grateful he was coming. I missed him. We had always been close or at least my family's version of close, which meant doing things together even if we didn't share our deep emotions. Even shallow emotions were shared sparingly. What were shallow emotions doing there anyway, so close to the surface? It was better for them to be deep deep deep, deep enough so that pressure encouraged them to fall ever downward.

Anyway.

We were close but then I moved far away. When I left, I said I wouldn't be here forever. I said that by living somewhere new and far away, I'd learn things but I'd return, eventually.

He was always in a good mood on trips to see me, and it was the same this time but with a new shadow of concern. His questions that weekend, at least questions about my disorder, always began with the word *so*, the kind of *so* followed by a pause like an ellipsis in the air, not the ellipsis of things that can't be said, but the ellipsis that gives the other person a moment to prepare. He tried to discuss the disorder on the first evening of the trip, when he and I and my boyfriend went to an upscale seafood restaurant near my house, the kind that made its tables from big slabs of scavenged wood thickly coated in clear epoxy to preserve their weathered state. My dad and I ordered wine. My boyfriend drank water. He was on the quiet side, maybe to let my dad and me catch up or maybe because he was uncomfortable or judgmental of the restaurant, although he'd sold his foragings there. I gave his hand a little squeeze as we ordered our mains, my dad the salmon and my boyfriend and I choosing fish considered off-catch that the restaurant sought out, either for some claim of environmental sustainability or to be interesting or because it was a challenge to turn the unfamiliar into something succulent. I asked my dad if he was sure of his choice. He rarely ate seafood. To tell the truth I didn't like the idea of him eating fish; my mother only cooked land animals, ones without the luxury of moving in any direction they pleased. But my father liked to go with the specialty of a restaurant. He must have been tired after traveling but he seemed happy in the restaurant's dim-dark illumination like some kind of halted twilight, or the vague ambiance of a campfire without the discomfort of breathing harsh smoke into your lungs.

Soon our wine came and we both took generous sips. He didn't use to drink but now he liked wine. The alcohol turned many things pleasantly fuzzy, like my insides and the chatter of the patrons. My boyfriend and I rarely went out to eat; we prided ourselves on simple meals at home. But it was nice to be there with my father and my boyfriend, especially after the first glass of wine, which eased the low-level stress I felt in combining these two people, who each admired the other in certain ways and yet reserved some uncertain, unadjudicated feelings about the other's life path. But for most of the dinner, we had a nice time, my dad praised the tender pink salmon and told stories about his most outrageous patients. I told stories about people I'd interviewed, eccentric people but also serious people and serious subjects so he would take me seriously. Between bites of off-catch that I found at first intriguing but that eventually overwhelmed my palate, I said I was looking into a spike in home sales. I'd tracked down some contact information for a couple of people who'd recently sold their homes, I said, drinking quickly my second glass of wine, but the numbers were disconnected and emails went unanswered. The buyers were obscured by opaque ownership structures, I continued.

"So . . . you're still able to work normally, more or less?" he asked.

"Well, I mean, the dictation software—it's been tricky . . ." And of course it was more than tricky, the software in moments seemed intent on true sabotage, but if I let myself say even a word about it I'd never stop ranting. I begged my boyfriend with my eyes to say something, and though he had been mostly quiet, he offered a few anecdotes from the bar. He had stories of absurd and combative customers, but also vulnerable emotional customers with whom he forged brief moments of connection. I think he found these fleeting but potent moments more mysterious and ineffable and somehow more meaningful than longer-term connections. Or at least the way he told those stories made me wonder. My dad hung on his every word.

The removal of our dinner plates spurred a switch of gears in my father, who started asking about my longer-term plans in life, if I ever thought about furthering my education, if I'd recently called my sister, who was at the tail end of a doctoral degree just a few hours away from our hometown in science or neuroscience or whatever about addiction, and had I ever thought about a PhD, he added, in like, anything? I said yes, I'd called her. (I told myself the past three months should be considered recent.) I was thinking about a master's in, well, something, a comment that drew a long, somewhat surprised stare from my boyfriend, which itself resulted in the slight questioning tilt of my father's head before he decided not to pursue it for the moment and instead he said, "So . . . how exactly did it start again?"

I went quiet, wondering if this was a good or bad place to talk about it, but in that moment I wanted to be immersed in the pleasant atmosphere, and though most of the diners were clearly tourists, I didn't want snippets of myself to catch in someone's ear. I didn't even want to talk about it in front of my boyfriend. I didn't want anyone to hear this stupid origin story over and over, as if it might become deformed, lose its structure or turn fuzzy at the edges.

So I said, "You just got here. Let's talk about it later. Let's talk about something more interesting," and I mentioned that my boyfriend recently went on a wilderness retreat, and I looked at my boyfriend pleadingly again. He didn't like being put in the position to turn his experience into entertainment, but he did it, though he left out the end, excised the part where he got disoriented and lost and terrified, a story that didn't belong in this kind of restaurant.

※

The next day we ended up in the forest, one of the two main places visitors want to see. It was either the forest or the beach, but on previous visits my dad never enjoyed walking along the broad banks of shoreline. All the sinuous washed-up bull kelp on the shore made him uncomfortable, he seemed to find them alien. Each one was long and thin and tapering as if a tail could be its own gloriously independent creature, and I'd googled pictures of kelp in its ocean habitat and showed him how beautiful their streamers were before they started rotting or curing in the sun. I hoped he might be more partial to other features of the sea, but try as we might we never spotted the distant spoutings of whale blowholes that were a major attraction, and our failure did not seem to disappoint him particularly.

So instead we took him to a trail I hiked many times back when I first arrived and thought this place could turn me into a nature person, someone who could identify plants even in the depths of winter, when some lost petals and colors. But then I met my boyfriend, who complained that the trail was too popular and took me to other trails, narrow ones, or off trail entirely, though I really didn't like going off trail. But the big wide trail would be good for a group, and my dad was happy at first; its slow curves gave you more time to appreciate everything you were approaching. Yet a rain had come recently, paltry but accompanied by a fog that refused to let anything dry out and was swaddling the coast, a fog that made it hard to remember how smoky and dry it had been, and my father struggled as the muddy trail slightly suctioned his every step.

My boyfriend led us to a side trail easier to navigate, and I talked about the weather and how grateful everyone was for the precipitation.

The smaller trail swept through a forest dense with the infected pines. I told my dad every last detail about the disease, trying to impress him with my knowledge of pine sap canker, to show that I was accomplishing things, that my moving so far away wasn't all pointless. When we saw an infected tree close to the trail, I became excited even as I felt disturbed at my excitement. I said, "There it is!" We approached slowly for some reason, as if that seeping gunk might collect itself into something animate and spring from that canker and drag one of us into that wound, though I wasn't sure who it would be. "Don't touch it."

My dad put on his reading glasses. We all leaned in for a closer look.

"That's interesting," he said nonchalantly, and his gaze turned from the canker to my hands. I put them in my jacket pockets and we all started walking again. Finally, after what felt like some necessary distance from the canker, he asked, "So . . . how did it start again?"

I tried to explain and to explain in a way that emphasized its probable physical origins, in a way that resisted any grander meaning at all.

"You've been really stressed too, though," my boyfriend added. "After that falling out with your boss."

"Well, I don't think that has anything—any bearing," I said quickly.

My father made a sound of acknowledgment like he was storing this bit of info in a special place reserved for info that was about me but that did not come from me. "Well, so I don't understand exactly—is it sharp or more like aches or . . . and what kinds of tests have these doctors done anyway?"

"Well, they just move different parts of my body to see what triggers my pain, and I do physical therapy, and . . ."

"And what?"

"And—and I'm about to start acupuncture," I said, which was true but I was also thinking about the Axon and the outline of the body with the lights. I should say no, I thought, if she decides I'm *ready*. I didn't want Lee tapping my mind, even scam-tapping into my mind, scam-analyzing my extremities. I didn't want to be her subject!

Did I really think that, though, exclaim it in my mind, especially given that I eventually gave in?

My boyfriend was quiet. He also didn't bring up the Axon, which I'd finally told him about. I'd asked if she'd ever mentioned it to him. He'd said yes, some months ago they'd run into each other and she talked about it enthusiastically, and who knew if it worked but why not? he'd said. He knew I was skeptical and he claimed to be skeptical but also intrigued, and wasn't it good to say yes to things, to experience something?

But anyway: my dad was there rolling his eyes at acupuncture.

"It helps a lot of people," I said defensively.

He shrugged. "I guess there's some positive literature on it," he said. "You know your mother tried that once," he said offhandedly.

"She did?"

"It didn't work. Then she tried other—well, one or two—oddball treatments . . ."

I was extremely curious but didn't push. He clearly didn't want to go there. He returned the conversation to my hands. On the way back to the trailhead, as I grasped for some metaphor to explain exactly what the pain was like, my boyfriend brought up to my dad that he thought I should take a sabbatical. My dad started to agree, and I interjected that I didn't need a break.

"—but you also have, you know, Mom's bonds," my dad went on. "You should cash them in soon. If you lose those pieces of paper, there's no way to get that money."

My boyfriend looked at me.

I'd never talked to him about my bonds.

"I also think Kim could consider—maybe leaving the paper," my boyfriend suddenly said. "It's stressful on you," he went on, looking at me.

My father made a hum of acknowledgment. "I was never sure it was a—long-term career path," he said. "Have you—two—

thought about moving elsewhere? What do you both want to *do*?" Since it was clear to him that what we were doing couldn't continue forever.

My boyfriend seemed emboldened by this questioning. He said we'd talked about moving north, or perhaps staying here if there was a way to live the way we wanted, more authentically on the land, in community, homesteading of sorts, or something, and I was somewhat shocked because although he'd vaguely mentioned this desire, it had never quite incorporated me before, especially since I had equally vaguely mentioned living in a city, since that was the way to take another step in my career, even though I still wasn't sure I was any good at the things my career required. But the triangulating presence of my father spurred something in my boyfriend. The previous night, after dinner, the mention of graduate school had caused an uncomfortable conversation about our communication difficulties and almost, just almost, spurred talk of the future, but somehow we hadn't, and it was only when asked by a third party that he could voice it to me, find the hole in the space-time of our habitual relations.

"Well," my dad said, dragging out the vowel, trying in the drone of the *E* to figure out how to respond. He didn't like conflict but clearly didn't like what my boyfriend had said. As we walked onward he finally asked, without looking at us but instead straight ahead, if that was something I was considering. Then he tried but failed to start another sentence. His brain was sputtering. Finally he said, "I can't imagine—what you would *do* up there, Kim. Or here, in the long term. As a—real career." And it wasn't clear if abandoning my current job was jeopardizing that career or if he was also implicating my current life. "Your mother would just—"

"It's just ideas in the air," I said awkwardly, also looking at no one, and there was a strange quality in the way we walked in a straight line, making parallel tracks across the trail. "I like my job. There's no imminent plan to leave. Or to cash in Mom's bonds," I said quietly and uncomfortably, because we so rarely mentioned her that I didn't know what to do with her when she came up. And part of me didn't even want the bonds, or I wanted the bonds but not the money, I just wanted the physical pieces of government paper she had left me. Maybe, though, if I had something more meaningful from her, I could let the pieces of paper go, and be at peace with cold hard cash. I asked offhandedly if her stuff was still in the attic. He sighed, and said yes.

※

At this point in his trip we were almost done with talking about the disorder. There was only one last reference, when I drove him to the airport and he told me about a patient whose thoughts were trapped inside his mind.

When I was a child, I often heard my dad on the phone in the evening, talking to nurses about patients, or to patients themselves. They discussed new symptoms or disappearing symptoms, or new medications because their old medications weren't working, and as the doctor he needed to keep providing new treatments, and it's like that old computer game with the snake, a game I sometimes played while listening to him talk on the phone, where the snake keeps eating more and more pixelated dots, and at first the snake is short and navigating the maze is easy, but as it eats it becomes longer and longer, always on the verge of running into the past of itself, and it meanders in strange ways to avoid its tail—though really its whole self is a tail—because when the head of the snake hits any part of itself it immediately dies.

My dad's patients often died, since that's what cancer does, but people with cancer can also live a long time. I once imagined he chose oncology because oncologists spend years treating patients, and perhaps those relationships were the most intimate and rewarding. But when, as a teenager, I asked him—maybe I asked him more questions than I asked my mother—he said an oncology rotation was available when he had to choose a specialty and that was that.

Perhaps my dad remembered the story about the man with thoughts trapped inside his mind because I had something terrible inside me, too, something that tangled all my efforts at expression. But my dad has a lot of disturbing stories and sometimes he just tells one out of pure silence, like some stories are just waiting for a pure silence they can spring themselves into.

During the drive to the airport, he began to talk about a patient from many years ago, a man with cancer in his brain, which is a very bad place for your cancer to be. When the man spoke, his words didn't make sense, at least in the order and context in which he spoke them. My dad might ask him how he felt that day, and the man would say something like, "Bunnies are throwing up on my rugs!" Weirdo sentences like that, though the man hadn't lost his sense of grammar. After the man spoke, his face would express frustration, his eyebrows furrowing, and he would sigh in exasperation. He would sometimes try to speak again, but the same nonsense would erupt. The same thing happened when the man wrote.

He clearly knew he hadn't expressed himself, though it seemed he could think rationally; his frustration indicated he knew he had spoken nonsense. But there was no way for the sensical thoughts to get out. His wife could only tell my father if her husband had obvious problems, like throwing up or fainting.

"At least you don't have something like that," my dad said.

※

When I got home from the airport, I didn't really want to start another worksheet. But with my father gone I felt suddenly my mother's absence, and I got out the worksheet to summon her up, even though the worksheets were a horrible way to do it.

Worksheet 2

Continue *writing, thinking of another significant episode. But now take agency over your emotional and physical responses. If someone wronged you, you may feel, deep down, you deserved it; if you wronged someone, you may feel intense guilt. When such thoughts arise, say aloud three times:* I Am a Good Person! I Deserve Love! I Love Myself! *to rewire the neurochemical basis of your physical pain. When you experience pain, do not become angry and fearful. Instead, say:* There is nothing wrong with me. *Then banish it with a phrase such as:* Go away! You are not welcome! *The paths the pain has established in the body will disappear. The pain will lose its way.*

⸎

The next things I took from my mother were mystery novels.

Boxes and boxes of mystery novels.

When my mother was alive she kept some Greek classics on a single bookshelf in the house. I never saw her read them. I never saw them move. But the other shelves became stuffed more and more with the two genres she confined herself to, books about the midcentury European genocide and mystery novels.

My mother loved mystery novels, or at least she read them constantly. For a while she read a series of mystery novels organized by the letters of the alphabet, and at one point she became engrossed in a series in which the detective had a Jewish girlfriend, as if even in the escapism of a mystery novel she couldn't be the protagonist, although perhaps she couldn't find a novel where the protagonist was someone like her. But most of the mystery novels she read were their own complete worlds and each had their own industrious investigators. The books were thick and squat and their covers were kitschy and menacing and the rough pages were tightly packed with text. Mystery novels are usually long and meant to be read rapidly. For a time when I was a teenager I read the mysteries she finished. But eventually I decided I didn't want to inherit this predilection, and anyway the crammed words that left barely any white space on the page tired my eyes, the words crunched so tightly as if even the spaces between them were a luxury, as if at any moment the letters themselves might start merging.

I never asked why she read so many mysteries. But mysteries offer struggle and darkness and often include retribution, with clear narratives and casts of characters. Usually at least one person dies. Usually there is a narrator who is good and somewhat flawed trying to solve the mystery. In mysteries there is a bad person somewhere but the reader usually doesn't know who the real bad person is for a while. The books tease at possibilities, but readers know they will be teased and in the end the bad person is almost always revealed, and my mother must have found satisfaction in the dark quality of the books and in the revelation of the most malevolent person.

Of course since I never asked why she read so many mystery novels, it's possible the reason was something entirely different. Maybe books were the one thing she could buy without drawing my father's concern, since books are supposed to be good, or at least not frivolous. The other things she bought—cigarettes, purses and shirts and sweaters and jewelry and makeup from the Home Shopping Network as well as the genocide paraphernalia from online auction sites—were more and more scrutinized by my father as items piled up and piled up in protective plastic sheaths around the perimeter of her bedroom, an accumulation that might have lessened a little if I'd ever accepted the few purses and shirts she offered to me. My sister, before she went to college, would take them as an act of mercy, if only to store them in her own room. But at this point my sister only took them rarely, when she came home on break, and so my mom turned to me even more but I always said no. I said they were ugly. I told myself this might convince her to stop buying so much stuff. But maybe it was just cruelty. Although cruelty, I think, is supposed to be a choice and it never felt like a choice.

When my mother finished a book, she never reread it but she wouldn't give it away, so there were mysteries everywhere.

When I was young she kept the mysteries on bookshelves in the living room and then bookshelves in the dining room. But as my sister and I grew older, she had more and more time to read, because the older we got the less we needed her constant attention. As we got older she also changed. We still expected her to do our laundry and clean the house and cook. But more things that needed to be done outside the house, like the grocery shopping, shifted to us and our father, especially once my older sister could drive. And it's not that we didn't need her, but the things we needed were less straightforward; we wanted fewer dinners and car rides but instead more difficult things she couldn't always provide, and instead she spent more and more time in her room, watching television or reading or looking at the genocide paraphernalia. And so as we got older the accumulation of mysteries intensified and the overflow from the bookshelves went to boxes in the basement and boxes in the garage and boxes in the attic. The one place she never kept them was her room, maybe because her room was full of all her other possessions.

One day she found all the mysteries in the garage gone.

I was at home working on a presentation for debate class, waiting for my debate partner to arrive. It was the second semester of senior year when most everyone stopped caring. But I cared, and although I was good at school when it involved being quiet at a desk, debate class gave me trouble. Every time I stepped up to the lectern it was as if I'd been suddenly struck with aphasia. The class wasn't mandatory but even back then I hoped to change myself, and also perhaps with enough work I could convince my mother through sheer logic that she needed to find a way to be happy, or at least less unhappy.

My mother came into my room as I was working on one of the many common topics in debate class—charter schools or the electoral college or universal health care or taxes on soda—and asked me to go to a nearby corner store and buy her cigarettes. I looked up at her from the pile of folders I was trying and failing to better organize. "They're not good for you," I said, wondering if anything on the soda tax proposition could be relevant. "And they'll only get more expensive. . . . Anyway, why don't you get them yourself if you want them so badly?"

In that moment I thought her desperation for cigarettes might overcome her problems, which I only vaguely understood but which made her reluctant to leave the house. Even if cigarettes were bad for her, it would be good for her to leave the house to get them, and she would probably be embarrassed to argue once my friend arrived.

But she remained in my room, and my friend arrived but she kept asking me to go and also to pay for them because she had no money at the moment. I thought to ask why, but even more packages than usual had come last week and she'd recently installed a clothing rack along one of her bedroom walls, walls now stuffed with clothes in plastic sheaths, including a calf-length tan leather coat with fox fur trim, which was totally insane and useless for someone who didn't go for even short walks in the cold.

She groaned and said, "Kim. Please. I'm about to make dinner."

It was Sunday, and every Sunday she made rare T-bone steaks, as if her distaste for cooking led her to cook things as briefly as possible, though she paid careful attention to thoroughly sear and char the outside while retaining the bloody redness within. "Can you cook one well done?" I asked. "I don't like it rare. I don't like it bloody like you."

She didn't respond directly. "Please, Kim," she said, almost moaning, and perhaps it was supposed to be a lesson, a performance to remind me more concretely to not become her, but also she was longing for cigarettes. I kept refusing. Eventually she went to her room and closed the door and soon I smelled the smoke of reserved tobacco.

I was not always nice to her.

But it was difficult to be nice to her because she was so miserable, and she was miserable because she had no money of her own and because she had so many ailments that seemed to be all tied up in each other.

I often wondered what order her ailments had arrived in, and if each had caused the next one or if they were unrelated. I think the migraines started relatively early in her life, or at least someone told me that afterward, and maybe the migraines, a sickness in the head but not necessarily psychological, were the first problem. The migraines could have made her depressed. The stress of her depression could have affected her blood pressure, or caused her to eat certain things to raise her blood pressure, and worrying about the pressure of her blood could have made her even more depressed, and the medication for her depression may have left her feeling dizzy or weak or anxious, and all of those problems made her stay at home and drink instead of going places, and to buy things on television and eventually the internet instead of going places, and she had purchased so many books and pieces of jewelry and items of clothing, she needed to monitor them to ensure that they weren't given away, which made her even more unlikely to leave the house, and this made her even more sad about the state of her life, and so forth. But the problems could have appeared in a different order. Perhaps the alcohol came first, and that made her tired and so she stayed inside, which made her depressed, and being depressed made her head hurt.

I'd probably understand it all better, or believe I understood it better, if I'd asked more questions. But like I said, I didn't, and when I did they were really pointed critiques posing as questions, or leading questions about what she should do to improve her life. Often I tried to convince her to get a job, but she said she couldn't work because she had too many headaches. She took medication for her headaches, but the medication changed all the time because nothing had much of an effect, or something would work but then stop working, as if the medication had given up, or it had too much of another effect and made her feel awful in a completely different way. I felt bad for her but also angry with her and judged her for being unhappy and defeated. I believed there must be some way to make her headaches go away, if she tried enough different medications, made healthy life choices, went for walks, or stopped smoking, the problem would go away, or at least shrink and become a smaller presence. If she only tried harder, I thought, if she kept trying, she would figure it out, and even if she never figured it out, she should keep trying, because why would you give up if you were miserable?

After my friend left, my mother came back to my room to continue discussing the cigarettes, but I didn't want to talk about cigarettes. Instead, amped up on the arguments my friend and I had worked through, I thought: *Maybe I can really change her life.*

I said there must be some way she could medicate herself so she could work, or do something to earn money and therefore get her own cigarettes, and couldn't she look up jobs on the internet instead of paraphernalia of the midcentury European genocide or cubic zirconia necklaces or well-reviewed mysteries, which were all in different ways disturbing to me. Then I said she would probably kill me with that secondhand smoke and what if I got lung cancer from the fumes? The lining of my lungs would fill with liquid as if to counter inhaling the remnants of a false fire, my body would have to be irradiated, I'd become weak and sick. "Sicker than you can imagine!" I kept on, and then my own father, whom she didn't even like, would have to try to cure me, and either the person she disliked most would be the one to save me, or he would fail and I'd die.

"So there must be something you haven't tried," I said to conclude my speech.

She looked at me and didn't say anything.

"There must be *something*," I kept on.

She closed her eyes and gently pinched the space of skin between her eyes as if to stanch the flow of something. "It's true," she finally said. "I probably haven't tried everything. You're right sometimes, even when you understand almost nothing."

I looked at her and didn't say anything.

"I'm so tired," she said, and sighed and closed her eyes as if to illustrate her point.

I looked at her and didn't say anything.

"Don't worry," she said. "You're too different from me to end up like this," and she seemed mostly but not completely certain and then she chuckled in a sad sputtering way. Still I didn't react and she sighed dramatically. "I guess I'm going to cook dinner now," she said, resigned to my silence.

She went into the garage to remove some steaks from the freezer, but then something was wrong because she began screaming my father's name, and it sounded as if his name were being ground up like a tough cut of meat, and I heard his footsteps above me travel from his room down the stairs to the door into the garage. He didn't open the door but instead said "What?" through the door. She asked loudly and aggressively what he had done with some boxes of mystery novels. He responded calmly but firmly that there were too many things in the garage and she had already read the books. But those were my things, she screamed. You threw away my things! He said he didn't throw them away. He donated them. Although it wasn't just my father who donated them. We had gone together to Goodwill on the way to the grocery store the previous day. He said it needed to be done because the garage was out of control, there were years of mystery novels along with the overflow of other things she couldn't find space for in her room.

My dad left the house briefly. My friend left and I came downstairs to keep working on my debate homework because I liked the smell and sizzle of steaks on Sunday. But I didn't say anything to my mother, who had started cooking dinner, and I couldn't concentrate. It was a bit dark in the room because it was near Halloween and my mother had recently put up black and gauzy curtains, and they let in a diffused vague light that kept the room dim. I got up to pull the curtains back and passed a battery-powered skull affixed to a wall in the living room that said *boo* every time a person walked by, one of the cheap, grim decorations that she purchased at Kmart, hollow plastic skeletons dangling from curtain rods and a candleholder in the shape of a vampire with blood dripping past its lips. When I sat back down I saw a text from my sister, which I didn't open for a while because I knew what it must say, that she knew I'd helped our father throw away my mother's things and I was cruel cruel cruel.

Soon my dad came back holding a new carton of cigarettes. He must have heard my mother and me arguing before. We could all always hear each other arguing in the house, sometimes the specific words and sometimes just the timbre of discord. He went to the kitchen, and she mumblingly thanked him. He usually would have said how terrible her habit was, but he just said, "No problem," and went to the back porch to look at the grass and the birds that came to his birdfeeder and to drink a single beer. He rarely drank, at least back then. A beer often meant a patient died. Back then I thought I'd be like that but even better, I wouldn't drink at all, not even if someone died.

My mother took a break from cooking and went out to the porch, and I saw her through the glass doors, standing and also facing the grass in the backyard, a cigarette pinched in the valley between two fingers, but I wasn't sure if they were talking because the back porch was the one place it was hard to overhear. I tried to look back over my debate notes and the plan my friend and I had put together for whatever resolution we might argue for or against, since our teacher never revealed who would argue which side until the day of the debate. But I kept looking instead to the glass and my mother standing there, the cigarette returning to her thin lips again and again, turning her head to the side away from my father when she inhaled and exhaled, at least some of the tension leaving her body with the smoke that blew out of her nostrils as if there were a house on fire inside her, and in profile she honestly looked as happy as I'd seen her in a long while, and that wasn't necessarily one of the last times I ever saw her happy but it is one of the last times I remember seeing her happy. Then I went upstairs and went into my mother's room. It was already difficult to navigate the room because of all the piles of things in it. But there on her bed was the pack of cigarettes she had opened after I refused to do anything for her. I took them into my own room, and I took one out of the pack and held it between my right pointer finger and middle finger just like her, and brought the sad cold cigarette to my mouth a few times because there isn't any way to actually know what's in another person's head, and perhaps the only way to understand them even a little bit is to reenact them, and I could have lit one and brought it to my lips and inhaled, in order to more closely approximate her, but instead I flushed all of the cigarettes down the toilet, including the one between my two fingers.

Later, after dinner, my mother cleaned the dishes, and then walked past the battery-powered skull that said *boo* and then went up the stairs to her room. I waited for her to scream my name like she screamed my father's, even though he'd gotten her a whole new carton, because every pack was precious. But she remained silent even after coming back downstairs to put the leftovers away. After that we didn't see her for a few days. Later my dad said one of the boxes in the garage had been filled not with mystery novels but older books from a long time ago, from before I was born. Neither of us had taken a close look. I wondered if the episode might convince her to get a job so she would have money and some kind of autonomy or even enough funds to rent a storage unit for her things. But when she emerged in a few days she just moved more of her things from the garage to her room, and she also, somehow, got a credit card, and eventually she racked up a large debt.

I Went to Acupuncture

I began going to acupuncture twice a week in addition to physical therapy, so I was driving two hours a day almost every day, not including the time spent on the actual treatments that were supposed to heal me. It was strange to me that a worker's compensation outfit would send me to acupuncture, which seemed a bit progressive. But it wasn't nearly as alternative as what Lee was proposing. I still hadn't heard from her. I vacillated between asking my boyfriend to intercede on my behalf to convince her to do it to me, whatever it was, and declaring I'd never do something so ludicrous. He also went back and forth between high-pitched encouragement and sudden hesitation. The subject had come up a few times, maybe as a way to focus on something other than the uncomfortable conversation with my father. My father, for his part, had stopped mentioning the disorder in our communications, and instead his outreach turned into emails containing links to doctoral programs in at least half a dozen disciplines he thought might interest me. I wrote back—I dictated back—only to say I'd look into it all when I was normal, although Mirror turned *normal* into *northern*, which didn't even sound the same. My boyfriend saw what Mirror did and consoled me in my frustration. I should have been grateful he was being caring, and I was. But maybe it was care in the service of making me suggestible to his future suggestions, and was that care or careful manipulation, or was there even a difference?

Anyway.

Maybe, I thought, acupuncture would be the answer until Lee decided I was ready for her scammy treatment, and then I'd start typing on that ancient computer myself!

※

I didn't research acupuncture before I started. I was trying to keep my mind open. In the town where I lived, I'd heard vague success stories. But if I combed the internet, attempting to understand the philosophy and mechanism, which I haphazardly understood as a redirecting of energy around the body, I'd turn too skeptical for it to work. I was losing control over my body, but I could shape the confidence of my mind. I had, before the disorder, read articles about placebos. If I believed in it enough, the treatment would work, the treatment would come true.

I could also have asked the other reporter, who'd repeatedly offered to look into treatments or ailments, as if our job couldn't slake his unquenchable thirst for investigation. He'd already taken stories that should have been mine, like the one about when the water in town, not just in the village to the north, started to taste salty, because as his dogged reporting revealed, the water company had sold ungodly amounts of water to a water trucking company that in turn sold it to indeterminate far-off businesses and communities that needed extra water in the summer, which must have depleted the aquifer and made the water taste like "something you'd use for an enema," as the other reporter put it.

He was good at his job. But still, I couldn't give him the one story I should be able to figure out.

And anyway, he didn't always succeed. He'd never found out who was buying all that water.

So I turned down his offer to help me with my disorder. I didn't want to give him anything of my disorder, my weakness. Maybe I felt protective, not of me but of it.

It's not entirely true that I never did my own research into acupuncture.

I did at least say the word *acupuncture* and maybe some other words to Mirror as I tried to search the internet. But as usual it bungled what I was trying to say. I said *treatment* and it wrote *tree mind* and I tried other words but they didn't work either, and my mind started to wonder if maybe I should have been searching *tree mind* instead of *treatment*. Maybe in some way the program was really trying to tell me something, and maybe there was a way in which it really did understand me the way it claimed it would, maybe it understood me and my needs better than I myself did.

Then I closed my eyes and closed my computer and took a breath and thought: Yikes. I didn't attempt any more research on acupuncture.

My acupuncturist was a woman in her late thirties, with the kind of voice that was even and soft yet well enunciated, with barely any syllabic emphasis, which maybe made people more likely to trust her with inserting needles all over and into their bodies. She had the kind of voice Mirror would easily understand. She said her name was Mary and motioned for me to sit on the medical bed. "Why don't you tell me about your troubles?" she asked, the last word said so gently she almost whispered it.

I told her about the pain in my hands and that I sometimes had pain behind my neck, near my shoulder, when I used the computer, and this may have been the first time I'd told any of the doctors about the other pain in the other parts of my body. "No one knows if they're related . . ."

"All pain is related," she said, and maybe with that she ruined it.

I lay down on the table as she played ambient music probably created by a computer, long synthy chords overlaid with the occasional piano key for a dash of humanity. The notes were so sparing that the whole composition had no rhythm at all, which maybe made sense in the context of the treatment. Rhythm can be calming, but rhythm means time and forward motion and people don't want to keep going forward until they are healed, and maybe some people prefer their healing to feel as if it's taking place in some synthetic, pulseless dimension. Of course she could have acupunctured people in silence, but in silence a person is always waiting for something to go wrong. Or maybe the music was just to cover the noise of other patients rustling against the paper sheets we all lay on. She always had three patients going at a time.

She pricked my forehead with a needle and then wanted to

put a couple between my knuckles. When I stared wide-eyed at my hand, she asked if I really wanted to watch, and I said yes. I needed to see the needles silently sink into me. She slipped the first one in, a quick pinching as it entered. Then she put a few more in my leg, a little below my knees, and these went a little deeper. The needles were so thin, their tops tightly coiled so she had friction and grip. I wished for a moment then that I were the acupuncturist, bodies lying quietly on tables for my inspection, sliding needles into body parts, watching needles disappear into people with virtually no blood, like a magic trick, knowing that the needles when first inserted could create a tingle of pain but soon the pain would disappear, and there would be a body activated and extended before me. But when I was young my father told me not to go into medicine, it was awful to be responsible for so many bodies. Maybe he was right, or maybe he saw I wouldn't be able to handle it. But why? Why couldn't I be like my father or Mary the acupuncturist or Nick the physical therapist—or like Lee, whom I was unsure how to define? Still I let the thought of me presiding over other bodies disappear, and instead I just lay there with pins all over me like I was a message board from which every tacked-up sign had been ripped away.

Mary left for twenty minutes to let the needles do whatever they were supposed to do. I looked at my hands. I looked at my legs. The needles seemed so shallow. It didn't seem like enough. The needles should go deeper or even all the way through. I imagined my hands impaled and pinned up like insect specimens. These weren't the right thoughts though so I tried to think of nothing like I knew I should during treatments. I imagined the needles were creating little exit points for all my negative thoughts and perhaps the pain too, maybe the pain was just looking for an exit.

She came back and removed the needles, and once they were out, it was quickly impossible to see where they had been. The skin closed neatly. Everything looked normal, but then again everything always looked normal.

She asked if I felt better, and if so, how much? By this time, I was accustomed to calculating my health in percentages. By twenty percent or so, I said. I didn't really feel different, but I couldn't bear to tell her that, or maybe I did feel a bit better, but I'd been lying motionless, and doing nothing can be helpful, and still there was an underlying strange feeling lurking, not pain but the foreshadowing of pain, an unnatural tight alertness, which never left, which was always ready to be present, to be conducted, especially once I was in motion again. Whatever percent I said was not so important because by then I couldn't really remember what hands were supposed to feel like.

The Worker's Compensation Clinic Again

At my next appointment at the worker's compensation clinic, not with the physical therapist but for one of my semiconstant check-ins, another three hours down the drain and not even for treatment, the doctor said she didn't think I had carpal tunnel syndrome.

She thought this because at the beginning of my appointment, I said with a new certainty that no, it wasn't numbness. "It's just pain," I said. She argued at first; the screen said numbness and tingling. But I persisted, it was just pain in my hands, and then I said, though I haven't mentioned it—or have I?—that before the disorder appeared, the pain in my neck had appeared, and a month or so before the pain in my neck appeared, my boyfriend and I had bought a wool bed and pillows, handmade by a friend of my boyfriend's from locally harvested wool, which over time compressed into a thin mat with bulging lumps like something was burbling nefariously under the surface.

She asked more questions, rewriting my case history. I spoke and she typed. I looked at her fingers with longing. She asked for dates, such as when my neck pain began. Then she said, "I'm actually not sure you have carpal tunnel."

"Oh," I said.

There were aspects about my problem—pain that was bilateral, pain in every finger, no numbness—that didn't add up. She said maybe I had repetitive stress, and I asked what that was and she said it was what it sounded like. Or maybe I had tendinitis. Or maybe some abnormal manifestation of carpal tunnel. "Possibly the problem is coming from the neck," she mused. "Maybe some ergonomic issue? We'll keep sending you to physical therapy and acupuncture. And get you a diagnostics test soon. Just be grateful you—well, probably don't—have carpal tunnel. This will probably all go away."

What the new doctor said made me uneasy. Carpal tunnel involved a tunnel and a tunnel narrowed and compressed had a logic to it. Repetitive stress was vague. I didn't want to be vague. Or what if it was coming from my neck? That idea was the worst, the least meaningful, the most boring.

※

When exactly did the pain in my neck arrive, anyway?

When precisely did I wake up one morning unable to turn my head?

It was most definitely after I'd turned down my editor's offer to inherit the paper, which shifted the tenor of our relationship, her curiosity cutting out whenever I offered up an idea and nothing I said and no question I posed was able to restore her enthusiasm. It startled me, like electricity that seems so unquestionable until some tree branch leans gently on a power line, and when it happens, it seems strange not to have worried, since it was clearly so vulnerable. I couldn't blame her for losing faith in me because I was after all someone who summoned my innermost *not-me, not-me, not-me* each time I interviewed another human being.

It was most definitely sometime after the other reporter arrived, fresh from some fellowship for a regional newspaper, on his way to significance. I was surprised he took the job. It didn't seem to match the trajectory of his ambitions. But maybe he saw a year or so in a small but quirky place as part of the grand arc of his journalistic career, or maybe he was sure that in such a small place there were things to uncover that no one had yet discovered.

Of course I could probably find a more precise date if I searched my emails or my texts. I must have told someone in writing about my neck.

But right now I'm trying to rely on my memory.

Perhaps the stress of those events at work contorted and tightened my muscles as if to freeze myself into some particular position. Or what about the fact that I started leaving work early to finish up at home to avoid them both, and my posture there was even worse than in the office.

Yet it's also true that the pain appeared after moving in with my boyfriend, after sleeping on the horrible mattress, perhaps causing my neck to quietly suffer.

The problem is that the pain appeared after a quarter century and more of my life.

The problem is that pain always appears after so many things have happened.

Whatever the cause, I remember clearly waking up one morning unable to move my neck. No injury had immediately precipitated it, and I was upset primarily because for most of my life I rarely fell ill. If I had problems they were mostly in my head, and if those also caused suffering then at least I could take pride in the mechanics of my body, in moving the sadnesses in my head from place to place with ease.

In bed that morning I tried to stay calm. I tried to imagine the inside of my body, wondering what gear had slipped and ground the whole mechanism to a halt. For a few days I moved stiffly and robotically and soon a strange and piercing and pulling pain burrowed into a place between the back of my neck and my right shoulder, the place where a devil or an angel might appear to convince you of something.

The pain sometimes made it excruciating to look to my left. But then occasionally the pain would appear on the left side in the same place, as a mirror image, and I couldn't look to my right, and I imagined someday it—whatever it was—would encircle me entirely, and what would happen once I was entirely encircled?

That was when the newspaper bought me a standing desk, because with pain the first order of business is to make it bearable. The newspaper also bought me a headset, the kind telemarketers use, because it hurt to tilt my head one way or the other to hold the phone against my shoulder when I took notes. My editor was sympathetic; lots of people had neck spasms, she suffered them occasionally, though she noted she'd been much older when they began, and they weren't painful enough to make her change anything. I felt a bit like a spectacle, standing there so upright wearing my headset. Every day I tried to keep my body perfectly symmetrical. I was aware of my body in a new way, and I wondered if I'd ever find the perfect position, the perfect arrangement of my body.

My Boyfriend and I Went for a Hike

My boyfriend was planning a long weekend of backpacking up north. He said he wanted to clear his mind, to return his mind to the state it had been on his previous wilderness retreat, clear and empty, though I suspected he wanted also to overwrite what had happened on his retreat; he wanted to walk alone into the woods and not get lost. He must have really needed to get away, I thought that morning, because he was usually reluctant to take time off work, to forgo a lucrative weekend of tips.

He wanted to go foraging for his trip, to get provisions to the backcountry, and also to add to our—he emphasized *our*, almost romantically—reserves in case of emergency. I considered not going on the hike. I wanted to work on a story about the anniversary of a major fire from some decades ago that was coming up, and I needed to go digging through property sale records to see if there were any leads on Mona's tip. But it would be good to clear my mind. If my mind were clear I'd work more efficiently. I'd been more anxious recently and my usual tactic for alleviating stress—my special mantra: *I am not me, I am not me*—wasn't working as well as it used to. Maybe the worksheets were getting to me more than I'd anticipated. Maybe it was hard to not be me with thoughts of certain past events swirling in my mind . . .

Anyway.

We went foraging, although really he took me foraging, because he knew more about plants than me.

It was the middle of winter but there was always something to forage. That was, allegedly, the beauty of this place, it was mild and always greenly lush, the kind of place you could garden all year round if you wanted. I figured we'd mostly scour for mushrooms in the chilly air, which would have felt tolerable except for the way the dense fog always penetrated my thick woolen sweaters to impart its wet chill. But somehow there were some ripe berries that day. It wasn't their season, they were usually withered when mushrooms arrived, but unusual things were becoming more usual. We went first to one of his berry spots, an hour-long uphill hike into the piney forest. Once we whacked through a few thickets of what I would have assumed, were I alone, to be impenetrable brush, we reached the sprawling patch. We went quiet because it was a quiet kind of place, and we started picking huckleberries and blackberries to dry.

It took hours to accumulate even a few quarts because the berries were tinier than normal and I kept eating them. The skins of the huckleberries were almost black and the juices stained my hands purple. They were tart and bitter and bracing. They tasted dark and confidential. I hadn't managed to collect much before my fingers started to burn a little. I was clearly going to exceed my daily limit for fine manipulation. I kept going but eventually the back of my neck, a little to the right, started to burn or maybe ache. I wandered around pretending to look for another bush to harvest while I prayed for the pain to abate, and I wondered again if they were connected, but if they were really connected the neck pain would have come first that day, right? I slid one of my hands slowly inside my collecting bucket and watched my hand disappear into the particulate darkness.

After my boyfriend was satisfied with the amount we harvested, he wandered around looking for some wild herbs for tea and I followed. He found mugwort and yerba buena and other herbs I didn't know. As he picked them I took pictures with my phone and he looked at me, annoyed. He asked archly if I wasn't supposed to limit my fine manipulation, and he was right but it was annoying of him to point it out. I said it didn't bother me, that I wanted to remember what we saw in the forest. We had good reception at the top of the ridge, and I started looking up mugwort on the internet.

"I can always get some for you," he said. "Come on. Put it away." Slowly he took my phone out of my hands and I was upset but let him. He saw what I'd been searching and said I didn't need to always look everything up, he said again that I was supposed to limit fine manipulation. But he hadn't said anything when we were picking berries because touching a plant didn't register as something that could be harmful. He put my phone in his pocket and crouched down, looking for more herbs.

"Well, what do they know, really?" I said, and complained that at first they thought I had that certain syndrome, but now they didn't, though they weren't totally sure, and had they ever even truly examined me? And what if something was *really* wrong with me, something fatal or maybe slowly degenerative, I went on, though I amended that no matter what it was, something *was* really wrong with me. Even if it came from nothing, even if it came from nowhere, even if it was just some error message sent from my mind, it was real—isn't an error message a real thing?

"And anyway, I'm just—" I said, and then broke off, absentmindedly dragging and digging one of my feet into the dirt as I tried to find the right word for how I felt or at least one that would help him understand how I felt. "I just like knowing things. I want to know what I want to know, when I want to know it. I don't want to rely on someone else. And on the internet everything is as up-to-date as it could ever be."

His attention was split between me and the earth and he crushed something between his thumb and forefinger to smell it. It was a plant, he said, that people could use as an abortifacient. It wasn't the best idea, he said, because it could make you extremely ill. "But you can also use it to kill fleas and treat skin sores. You don't need to be on the computer all the time to know stuff like that. It's in books too, if you don't want to ask me."

And, he went on, tenderly harvesting, giving me a piece of the potential abortifacient, which I crushed and smelled, that I could easily learn so much if I considered what he'd said during the awkward conversation with my father, if I would consider making a real life, which to him meant finding a way to live more sustainably, a way we could homestead, living in community, a phrase that seemed awkward in his mouth, dreams he'd thought would entail moving elsewhere, farther north, somewhere less populated and therefore to him more true, but maybe it was possible to do it here.

"You don't even like people that much. Or being around them," I said.

He was quiet.

"Are we close," I said, feeling a little combative, "to where you took me that time, when I interviewed you? When you blindfolded me?"

He never did tell me where he'd taken me, not even after all this time.

He always said he needed to keep some things for himself.

But if he couldn't share something like that with me, what hope was there for his communal rural fantasy?

I said I would have told him if the situation was reversed.

That got him to look at me, eyebrows raised, and I knew what he was thinking: I'd never told him about my bonds, which, even if we didn't tend to talk about our finances, was clearly emotionally fraught baggage I'd never shared with him.

Then he sighed and said we weren't anywhere near that mushroom spot. He'd never found any mushrooms there again, actually—someone, or maybe one of those horrid mushroom touring vans, had clearly found it. He plopped down, as if in defeat, in the pine duff. "Maybe that's my problem," he said. "You know, when I—when I maybe ate something that I misidentified. When I ate it, I wasn't far from the group. I could have asked someone. But I didn't. I just wanted to be alone. And look what happened." Maybe, he said, he was too in love with the idea of self-sufficiency as a solitary practice.

"So then, who are these people we might live in community with? And where, exactly, would we live?" I asked.

I thought he plopped down in exhaustion from my questioning but then I saw he was holding a huge bulbous porcini. He took out his pocketknife. As he tenderly peeled the dirt-crusted stipe, he laid out his vision in more detail, at least a little more detail.

We—the composition of this *we* wasn't clear but perhaps thirty or so people—could inhabit a big beautiful property, ideally with a source of water and land that could be cultivated, land that wasn't teeming with tourists tromping around on hikes not even knowing what they were looking at and stripping the land of the choicest mushrooms in fields they had been shuttled to by some stupid tour bus. In this vision I wasn't a reporter. In this vision I was gardening, which I often said I'd like to do. I was too stressed and busy here, in this life, but in this other life it would be different. I'd be me, he said, but a less anxious me, eventually a me with a baby. He could see me very clearly, he said. Instead of being cooped up in a room staring at a screen and talking helplessly to my computer, up for hours at night, drinking wine and reading through the wormhole of the internet, news stories about horrible things, half of which I couldn't even remember the next day, instead of some other future where I'd get another degree that would leave me, in his mind, unhappy—instead of all that I was in a well-tended vegetable bed, kneeling in loamy dirt and weeding rows of big leafy rainbow chard and juicy bulbous tomatoes and shiny, inky-dark eggplant, while a baby crawled and tried pull itself up on a bean trellis to take its first steps.

As he talked I'd continued, unconsciously I think, to crush the bit of abortifacient between my fingers into a rough paste. I smelled the funny mint and would even have tasted the tiniest bit but it would have given him the wrong idea, or maybe it would have given him the right idea. Not that I needed an abortifacient. I was on birth control, not a pill or a patch but a tiny piece of copper implanted in my uterus that made it inhospitable to sperm. I plopped down onto the pine duff and looked at him carefully, or at least for a while longer than you usually look at someone, and he let me, or at least he didn't look away. Did he really love me? Was it love if you sometimes wished the other person were just a little bit different? Not that it was crazy to wish that the person you loved were less anxious. And perhaps my job wasn't really compatible with some fundament of myself, maybe the effort to change myself was doomed.

I wondered, as I kept looking at him, if he would have ever suggested us moving in together in the first place, if he'd known about the parts of me he didn't like. I didn't like them either sometimes, although I also did like them, trawling the internet late into the night, following grooves of information.

But he had known what I did for a living, and still it was he who originally suggested we move in together.

When I had to vacate the small room I first rented because the house was selling, he asked me to move in with him.

But he didn't exactly word it like that. He didn't say *Will you move in with me?*

I remember clearly we were at his table, in his cabin; we'd finished the dinner he'd made us, each of us our own little roasted quail and morels he found on a trip in the mountains, a trip I'd hoped he might invite me on but he didn't, which wasn't really a surprise because our relationship wasn't too serious, or it was somewhat serious but there was still some small but seemingly unbreachable emotional distance between us. But he invited me over to eat the precious morsels, and it was dark and he lit candles so each of us saw the other in the gentle fiery glow of their light, enhanced by the darkness of early spring, by how cold and foggy yet rainless it was outside. In the light of one candle I started reading him the sheriff's calls from the paper. *A cow was in the road. A man was irritated at the sound of whistling. A motorcycle had* crashed. Someone said their neighbor was slandering them. Another cow was in the road. A woman died semi-unexpectedly. Another cow was in the road. Then suddenly he said, *What if you moved in with me?* as if something caused him to consider how the plot of our relationship might change, as if, just like how the sheriff's calls could move from tragedy to comedy to dullness without warning, it was possible for our relationship to suddenly change too, and perhaps he saw us moving in together as something that could fit into the log of life here.

I was surprised because we hadn't been dating long, though how long had it been exactly? It was hard to keep track or maybe it made us uncomfortable to keep track, since we never were that couple with some instant mystical passion for each other. He seemed surprised at what he'd said, yet he didn't take it back. He didn't want to edit it.

At first I thought *no*. It was a little frightening, to be with someone else all the time. But when he said *what if* I'd started to wonder. In that moment in time I was thinking I might stay a while and I was also thinking I might leave in a year or two—but for a year or two I could more truly be part of this place, with this person who had roasted each of us our own tiny bird, this person who I felt would inevitably leave me but whom I still wanted because I loved him and because we weren't done yet, there was some exchange underway between us that had only just started.

In the present of the hike he held my hand and it was nice, it was comforting, and yet more and more whenever my hands were in any position, I was attuned to them, waiting for something to go wrong. I squeezed back. I could have said many things, like I wasn't sure I wanted a baby, or I kind of did and kind of didn't want a baby, or I could have said I didn't want to give up on urbanity, but it was easier to ask how exactly he was going to fund this venture, which sounded like a pipe dream and therefore didn't merit deeper questions of whether I wanted any of it, although again I kind of did, I did and I didn't.

Maybe, I said, shifting the subject, he could take some of the plants we'd gathered and make some unique cordial, he could use some for his weekend trip but also use his knowledge of the forest for cordials that he could mix into cocktails at the bar. Maybe they would give him a raise or promote him if he concocted things that would elevate the place. But he only responded with a grunting laugh. He wasn't interested in developing anything for the bar and he didn't want to profit from what he gathered and he didn't care much for alcohol. Though he did sometimes steep his foragings in brutally high-octane alcohol because he recognized how useful it was in stripping all the essence of whatever was sunk down into it. He never bothered with the careful management of flavor though. He made tongue-wilting tinctures he took by the precious dropperful. Since the disorder arose he'd convinced me to take a few of them—dandelion, chickweed, elderflower—but except for a minor buzz if I snuck an extra dropper, I never felt any different, though he said recently he was working on something more sophisticated, more potent.

Then he pulled us back to his own train of thought. "There might be people willing to invest in it. In the vision," he suddenly said.

"Invest?"

He didn't want to explain just yet, he went on, but he'd decided to help a bit with the volunteer coordinating effort for the practice emergency evacuation, so that he could practice being part of something greater than his own little self, get comfortable organizing a larger *something*. What sort of *something*, I wanted to know but didn't ask.

It was a dizzying amount of information. I already knew who was coordinating this practice emergency evacuation. They were people who'd spoken at the sewer meeting and the bridge meeting, people interested in growing the town so there would be more places to live and maybe bring down the cost of living, and my boyfriend's vision didn't seem to quite align, so I assumed he was not really involved. Maybe he just wanted me to believe in him, that by displaying his minor allegiance to something I wouldn't be so judgmental about the fact that he was usually completely disinterested in doing anything about the world at large.

What he meant about investment I had no idea, but I didn't ask him then; I was more focused on the story I was supposed to write. "Well, I mean—that's fine. But I'm going to that meeting and I'm going to write about it for the paper. So as long as you're not—you know, deeply involved."

"I—I'm sure you'll be able to write about it," he said, and perhaps he was telling the truth in that moment, perhaps it was only later he decided to become very involved. Or perhaps he was already very involved, and his responsibilities included making sure I would be the one writing about it, to ensure that he could influence what went in the paper!

He got up and started walking back to the trailhead, clearly a little frustrated that this was the piece of information I'd latched onto. I got up and walked behind him and kept talking and it was frustrating, talking while I was walking behind him and staring at the back of his head. "I'm writing about everything related to fire, you know," I said. "I'm writing about that, and the anniversary of the fire twenty years ago. It's my—it's important to me."

"I know," he said.

"It's not the kind of thing you usually do," I said.

"I'm sure it'll be fine," he said.

The trail wasn't usually the quiet part of our excursions but we were quiet all the way back, in a kind of digestive silence, working out the weight of our separate desires.

A Doctor Listened to My Nerves

The next week, in addition to two-hour round trips for physical therapy and acupuncture, adding eight commuting hours a week to my life, as if driving to treatment were a whole new day of work, I traveled yet another hour on a different day to a new waiting room. I was finally going to be truly examined. The worker's compensation clinic sent me to a special doctor to see once and for all whether I had that common syndrome, or if something else might be wrong with my nerves.

I filled out another medical form, and I was tired of forms, on which there is always a long list of unfortunate conditions with empty boxes to mark or not mark, conditions like diabetes, night sweats, high blood pressure, heart arrhythmia, nausea, unexplained vomiting, tremors, sleep apnea, arthritis, conditions that always seemed a little more real than mine. I left them blank since they didn't apply to me, though as a teenager I briefly suffered headaches that sank down into my stomach and made me nauseated, like I was on a boat at sea, rocking sickly. When they appeared, I thought: This is it, this is when I turn into her. But they went away after a few months, and at the time I thought: Of course, the body knows how to fix itself. But now—well, maybe the truth of the disorder is that my mother wanted to get back at me for being a not-great daughter and the way to get back at me was by turning me into her, but she had to wait until she was dead to do it, she had to make herself dead to do it, because how can anyone become someone who is still alive?

The form wanted to know the details of my symptoms, using the back of the page to elaborate if necessary, but I didn't want to be that person, the person who can't stop describing what's wrong, especially after I read a research paper the other reporter forwarded me, after I mentioned something like *Maybe I should keep a journal about my issues.* The research concluded that a pain journal, which some people had suggested to me as a way to shed light on its cause, actually made people experience even more pain.

And yet that's what I'm doing right now!

Maybe by writing it all down I'm making it all worse. But maybe it doesn't matter now. Maybe that's what I want now . . .

The last section of the form included something I'd never seen: two outlines of a person, front and back, with instructions to mark the sites of pain. Sharp pain was an X and numbness was O and an ache was +. I considered the two simple figures, thickly bordered and hollow and splayed out like stars. Eventually I put a modest X over the neck and two big Xs over the hands on the front and the back, digging the pen deeply into the page.

After a short wait, I was admitted into an examination room in which a medical assistant asked me nicely to lie down on the sea-green bed covered in that toilet seat cover material. She asked where I was from and I told her, and she was surprised because I didn't have that accent. She had an accent, though, from a state that bordered my old one. "Do you think you'd ever go back? . . ." I asked, but she was distracted by the equipment she was setting up and didn't answer. Soon she was at my right side placing pieces of silver tape along my fingers and my right forearm like I was coming all apart and not even at the seams where it makes sense to come apart but just everywhere. The tape, she said, was made of the same electrically conductive material used in defibrillators to shock hearts. She clipped a tiny jumper cable to the piece of tape on my pointer finger and another jumper cable to the tape farther up my arm.

"So how much will it hurt?" I asked, laughing nervously but with the kind of self-awareness you want the other person to be aware of.

"Well, people experience it differently," she said a little formally, clearly words she'd recited a million times before. "But any pain you experience is nondangerous."

The first part of the test was the nerve conduction test, a series of electric signals sent down nerves in each arm. Against my arm she pressed twinned metal prongs that looked like electric plugs from a foreign country, midway between the two jumper cables clipped to the pieces of tape. I was about to become a conduit of sorts, and all the cables made me think of Lee, whom I'd still not heard back from, not that I cared, not that I cared! I wondered if what I was doing now was more or less weird than her weird gray box with the lights and the headstrap, but I didn't have time to mull that over because the assistant pressed some button and suddenly the inside of my arm lit up like a horrible horrible light and my hand popped open and I groaned in pain and I understood how a heart could be surprised back into beating. I watched her press the button each time so I'd know when it was coming, but still each shock was like a physical nauseating click, or like something tight popping open over and over. After each shock she gently laid a wooden ruler on my arm to measure the distance between the two jumper cables, and looked at her computer for how many milliseconds it had taken the shock to travel. Then she'd switch the cables to different pieces of tape along my arm, though there were some sections she had to do over again.

It was a whole new feeling, that clicking-shock like how a half-broken machine might feel if someone was trying to fix it, and with each shock my hands kept opening like a gesture of acceptance and in retrospect I could have kept my hands splayed open instead of curling them back inward each time but I didn't, or they didn't, my hands didn't do that and I don't know why they did what they did.

She went to my left side and began again. I reminded myself that I wanted to be measured, that the pain was nondangerous.

※

Dr. W came into the examination room after the medical assistant finished the nondangerous shocks. The second part of the test, which I only knew involved a needle, had to be administered by an actual doctor. He wore a blue button-up shirt and khaki pants just like the other doctors, as if in abstract representation of earth and sky, perhaps to suggest to us patients something of their own comprehensiveness. But his manner was different. Dr. W spoke quickly and flippantly, like someone outside the frame of the office needed entertaining. Maybe he was bored of listening to nerves and needed to entertain himself, or maybe it was a way of disarming patients. He began without the pleasantries I'd grown accustomed to. "So you're at your computer all day, I'm sure. What field are you in?" he said. "Writing? Data entry? Graphic design? It's really everything these days . . . accounting? You look like you could be an accountant."

"Um. I'm a newspaper reporter," I said, sitting up.

"Wouldn't have guessed. And what's your pain like? You're a writer so you should be good at this, right?"

"Well," I said, and commenced my usual stumbling description.

He raised his eyebrows. He cocked his head. He looked down at some sheet of paper in his hand, which I realized was my intake sheet. "For a writer, you don't describe it well, in any particularly evocative way, do you? You're not giving me the best starting point. We're trying to help you here, see? And it says here you have pain in your hands, but also in your neck? Have you tried getting that checked out?"

I felt embarrassed but also enraged somewhere in my body that I pushed down down down, fearful if I let it loose I might scream or those shocks recently coursing through my body might reappear of their own accord. "Yes, I did. I mean, as much as I could. I guess it's just some kind of crick, or whatever," but even as I talked I faced straight forward, for fear that even talking of it would bring out its occasional acute pain if I turned my head. "But my hands—it's like a light turning on, then it's gone, then it's on again. But even when I'm not in pain . . . my hands never feel normal."

"Okay, we'll do the test, but you should think about this more, maybe do some word association! Could be fun. Maybe if you described it better you wouldn't be here. Lie down, on your side. Are you afraid of needles? Some people get needles stuck in them—acupuncture. Have you done that? Some people find a lot of relief, allegedly."

I lay down and faced the wall with his medical certificate and its fancy calligraphy and embossed golden stamp. "I'm not afraid of needles. I just like to see what's happening . . ." But I could kind of see a faint reflection of him in the glass protecting the certificate. "Anyway . . . what does the needle do?"

"The needle *listens* to the electrical stuff inside you. The screen over there—see it?—will translate the activity of your insides into waves. You've likely seen something similar on a medical show. So I see the waves, but I'm also listening. I get a visual and an auditory reading. Neat, isn't it? But I shouldn't hear much. Muscles at rest don't really have electrical activity. I'll ask you to move a few times so I can hear how well your muscles respond to what your nerves are saying when you move. That's a lot of dialogue going on inside you, you might say. Okay. Going in now."

I strained to watch his translucent image in the framed certificate as he slid the needle into me behind my neck. He was suddenly quiet and serious. He was listening. I liked and didn't like the idea of someone listening to me in that way. But I hoped he would hear or see something to reveal to me. He pulled out the needle but then slipped it into my upper arm and I closed my eyes and I felt him moving it, listening, and he asked me to squeeze my biceps and I groaned as I watched the oscillations of my electric innards on the screen, and I wondered if my groan, which I tried to keep quiet, contained electricity, and if he could hear it or see it translated into waves, and I was certain Lee's machine couldn't be any weirder than this.

He did everything again on my other side, then told me to get up.

"All sounds good," he said brusquely, patting me on the shoulder as I rested briefly on my back. "Don't look disappointed. It's a good thing!" He smiled down at me, and from my supine position his face was in shadow and his grin looked almost maniacal.

I kept lying there. I didn't move for a bit.

"It's over!" he said as if I didn't understand. "You can go!"

Dr. W sent me home with a laminated index card titled WORDS FOR PAIN. "I give this to everyone, almost everyone," he said as I gathered myself and left the office.

In the car after the appointment I looked them over.

burning
tingling
sharp
numb
aching
mild
intense
piercing
tearing
pounding
knotted
tender
tugging
lacerating
pressing
crushing

pulsing
stinging
sharp
dull
sore
electrical
warm
shooting
cramping
heavy
radiating
constant
occasional
cutting

But still I was certain there was some better word to describe my disorder, something less specific. The pain was like the Platonic ideal of pain, but I couldn't say that to a doctor or really to anyone.

⁓⁑⁓

It didn't take long for the worker's compensation clinic to send the full official results of both parts of the nerve test.

I guess nothingness is quick to diagnose.

I opened the piece of mail in my car, outside the post office, so I could be really and truly alone while reviewing the three-page document which was in a weird typewriter font that gave the information a distant air as if this had all happened a long time ago.

The report cataloged each nerve evaluated during the test and the muscles into which the shocks were administered and the number of milliseconds it took each shock to travel. Each sentence began with the word *NORMAL* in all caps, *NORMAL* in stupid tilting italics as if the best way to emphasize something is for it to be frozen in place almost falling over.

I wasn't exactly surprised.

I read it a few times, scouring for at least one *ABNORMAL* to appear.

Even if I didn't have that specific syndrome I could have had some other nerve damage, a provable problem with my nerves had always been possible, and now I'd lost one possibility, though after you encounter one dead end, you know they are waiting for you everywhere, all the little dead ends, and then you worry that someday you might find the last little dead end and that will be the big dead end. I needed more possibilities, so there was always something it could be.

But I also thought: I just have to get rid of it, to get it out of me or make it disappear or at least make it bearable, even if it remained nameless forever, because I didn't want to be in pain—did I, did I?—and because I wanted to do my job—didn't I, didn't I?

My Editor Made Me Write Obituaries

Eventually I emailed my editor to let her know I allegedly didn't have the common syndrome and this was good news and I'd already started acupuncture on top of the physical therapy, and therefore I was doing something healing almost every day. I probably just had repetitive stress injury, which didn't sound that serious, did it?

My editor was glad to hear it. She joked: Who hasn't been stressed by repetition at some point? She sometimes felt she was living the same week over and over. *I don't know, Kim*, she wrote, confiding in me in a way she hadn't in a while. *I've been thinking recently I might just sell the paper* . . . She was exhausted and approaching the age that a person would reasonably retire, and she could barely afford her own rent; even the small sum she would get for the paper would help. But she'd said all that before. People just say things sometimes, just to figure out if they really want that thing, or to draw out a plea from the other person: *Don't do it!* Of course this time her comment didn't involve me and a passing of a torch. Not that I wanted the paper, because I still believed or hoped I was going to find something else, something Important with a capital *I*. Or maybe my reasons were starting to shift . . .

But she could have at least asked!

But she didn't ask, because she saw me now as weak, a fact confirmed by the main thrust of this email. She wondered, she said, about my expectation that I'd feel better soon; it had been months and I'd never mentioned feeling better, at all.

Not that I had to tell her anything, she added.

But she was worried. She was concerned.

In the meantime she had a number of obituaries to assign me.

I wrote the occasional obituary, but around this time there was a small flurry of death and I was assigned at least five obits over some weeks. *Maybe these pieces will take the stress off you*, my editor wrote. *Your obits are always so beautifully written. And they can be on the shorter side*, she added, as the other reporter was happy to write more so I could write less.

Obits were pretty straightforward: the whole life of the subject was in the past, they couldn't do anything out of the ordinary at the last minute, and as opposed to the conflict in many stories, obituaries tended to focus on the positive qualities of the dead.

I wanted to write back: no no no.

I had plans to dig into the archives for a long piece on the twentieth anniversary of the biggest fire in the village's history.

And in that week I'd also discovered an intriguing lead, or I thought it might be a lead, on the potential increase in home sales in our town, a story I hadn't much pursued since reaching out to a few real estate agents who had all either not responded or given bland responses about a generally hot housing market. The lead was born of my own procrastination. I'd been at the office late to finish a story, but instead I started searching for random things on the internet, and randomly I wondered who had bought the cottage I'd lived in before moving in with my boyfriend, a cottage that had remained, as far as I could tell whenever I drove by it, unoccupied. So I searched for the house number and *Madrone Street* although Mirror kept writing *My Drone Stream*, and I ultimately had to spell it out, though I also wondered, again, if there was something to what Mirror was saying, maybe I was droning on, a stream of drivel about nothing. But I pushed the thought away and clicked many links and eventually one real estate website had a history of owners, the newest owner being a blandly named corporation that seemed vaguely familiar. Eventually I saw the name on a piece of paper in my mind's eye and then thirty minutes of sifting through the totally unorganized documents on my desk finally unearthed it: an old permit application for clearing trees from the property Lee now lived on, which had been bought by that same corporation.

I felt the long-dormant jolt of adrenaline that accompanied the uncovering of potential news.

I thought about refusing to do so many obituaries and sharing what I found.

But what if she saw my nugget of information as meaningless, just a rich person buying another home, what if she saw my refusal as a sign I couldn't practice self-care. Or worse: she gave the story to the other reporter! And anyway, in the end I liked doing what she asked; I liked to please her. So I wrote back: *Sounds like a plan. Except you can't sell the paper! At least while I'm here.*

I'd take the time to gather some more information for my real story, I told myself.

And anyway: I did like writing obituaries.

The obituaries we wrote were different than obituaries families wrote themselves and paid to have printed. We had discretion in our subjects. We focused on active members of the community, including some people of only modest significance or who for one reason or another we found interesting, and then sometimes we wrote an obituary simply because a family asked and we had space to fill. I preferred to write obituaries for people whose lives contained an arc of forward motion, and clear accomplishments, the kind of person I once thought I could be.

I liked writing the obituaries with clear arcs—I wanted to like the more difficult ones, I wanted to relish the challenge, and yet I struggled without the scaffolding of a clear narrative.

One obit I wrote during this flurry of deaths was about the wife of a rancher who worked at the local pharmacy. According to her children and friends, she was nice and lovely and made casseroles and tended to a garden of marigolds, and I thought her obituary would be simple; her life didn't seem to have multiple tangents and tentacles that would be challenging to contain. But I struggled to write the piece, to find a nerve of real life in it. Sometimes the dead woman went north to a casino, which interested me, but the more I pressed for information about her impromptu gambling trips, the quieter people became; whether she had a secret addiction or they found it an inappropriate topic for an obituary I wasn't sure. I pressed for adjectives. What was she like? How did she dress? Did she travel beyond the casino? But no one could summon any revelatory anecdotes or illuminating adjectives. It was too bad, because with the right friends and family, the most boring people can have a good obituary. The most interesting thing about her was perhaps how she died, a heart attack in the supplement aisle, knocking over adaptogens and sending bottled extracts of ashwagandha and ginseng and reishi to the floor, where they leaked their health benefits all over the linoleum. But they asked me not to mention that. They didn't specify that it was off the record, but I agreed because I didn't want to focus on the way she died and I didn't want to upset them, which was maybe part of my weakness as a reporter. I wished I could find some new revelation about her. Sometimes all sorts of things are discovered about a person after they die, which, even if the new information is devastating, can keep the connection with the dead person alive. Months after my own mother died we found a key to a safe-deposit box in her name, which was a little thrilling and a little frightening. I imagined all sorts of terrible things we might find. But it turned out to be empty, and maybe it's also true that you might not ever find out anything else about someone after their death.

Anyway.

I was working on the obit, repeatedly saying *adaptogen* but Mirror wrote *adopt a djinn*, when Mona came to the office even though it was Friday. The other reporter was there too, at his desk, behind me. In her hand was a copy of a recent newspaper, its edges in tatters. When she saw the other reporter, her eyes took on a backward-searching aspect to them, as if she were trying to remember if he was one of her enemies. I hoped she would never look at me that way. I suppose she decided she had never met the other reporter because she approached my desk. She was in distress. She was often in abstract distress but this was more focused. She was clutching the newspaper tightly at its fold, and the ink of the front-page picture, of an infected pine tree, was all smudged up and the picture was beginning to look out of focus. She started shaking the paper in the air.

"I read your article," she said. "About the trees and how they're so sick. Someone has to do something. Trees give us the *breath of life*. We have to *honor* them, Kim."

"It's bad, yeah," I said, trying to summon the specifics of the article because I hadn't thought much about the trees since I'd written it. I was busy thinking about other things. "But the experts don't even know what to do . . ."

"But what should *we* do?" She smacked the paper again down on my desk and pointed to it. "This is serious! Serious enough for you to write about it! Wasn't it to get something happening?"

I tried to think of something she could do but I could only think of donating money to the university researching the disease and that wasn't something Mona could do. I thought of telling her what not to do. For instance she should not touch a canker on an infected tree and then touch another tree, and perhaps with more research I could have come up with other things to tell her not to do, but Mona would be disappointed in the idea of negative action and I didn't want her to think I was useless or that I didn't really care. I didn't want her to turn on me.

"I read," the other reporter interjected, and we looked at him, "that since beetles are responsible for a lot of the disease's spread, we might need to kill a lot of the beetles. Teams of people going out and killing them by hand. Or foot, I guess," he said.

Mona covered her mouth with her fingers in dismay, which is a typical though funny way to react to upsetting information, as if a person needs to cover herself to allow time for an appropriate emotion to gather on the face. "But what about the beetles?"

she said through the gate of her fingers, forgetting to move them away.

"Sometimes there has to be sacrifice," he said.

"He's just joking," I said.

She looked confused and sad and shook her head and picked up the newspaper and walked slowly out of the office, muttering to herself. But then she returned and asked me to buy her some groceries from the food cooperative. Before she left she asked if I'd done the worksheets. When I told her I had, she got excited, she seemed happier than I'd ever seen her, until she asked how long ago I'd finished and I explained that I wasn't even halfway through. Her eyes grew wide and angry. She said it was no good to drag it out, to drag out the *processing* of the *past*, she said, emphasis apparently needed to penetrate my simple mind. She'd already finished; so much of her pain had disappeared! When I said I'd been busy, she rolled her eyes. I promised to start again soon. Her face calmed a bit but retained a measure of suspicion and disturbance, muttering the word *ungrateful* and *I had more very important things to tell her* to herself, although we could all hear her, as she left with bread and carrots and apples and a jar of local honey.

I sat down again at my desk, unsettled and embarrassed at the mention of the worksheets in front of the other reporter, although increasingly any mention at all of my unnamed disorder embarrassed me. In some ways *embarrass* seems like a funny word when someone is in pain, but it's hard to overstate just how embarrassed I felt all the time, to have a weird disorder with no name, with no clear cause, with no known remedy, something I was sure every single person must believe to be my mind's creation. I looked at the handwritten draft I was struggling to dictate. I'd made it longer than usual, as if this might prove something. I tried to make it lively and describe the pharmacy in excruciating detail and invoke the heady smells in the dead woman's garden and the flavor of a hot sauce she had made, the last batch before she died, which her daughter let me try, each drop singeing my tongue while her daughter silently wept.

"Well, she didn't like that idea," the other reporter said.

"She's sensitive—she takes things seriously."

"She wants to do something. I was just trying to help," he said, and sighed but also kind of laughed. "I don't think she likes me."

"Well, for her to really not like you, you'd have to cross her," I said.

"So you buy her vegetables."

"She needs some help. And she's not going to accept the kind of help she needs."

"Well, maybe she knows what she needs. Or at least, wants or doesn't want."

"I don't know," I said to end the conversation. I looked down at my notebook and the inky words on the unlined page, where line by line the letters became more and more out of sorts, each one looking as if it were about to fall apart entirely, and the sentences sloped downward and then veered back up, trying to straighten themselves out but in the end just undulating. Ansty, I went to my computer and said *Mirror on*. I looked awkwardly behind me at the other reporter, who looked engaged with his work, and briefly I didn't half hate or harbor a fiery jealousy of him, briefly I found the scene of connection with his journalistic work moving. I asked what he was working on. He was still typing but said he was researching a piece for next month, about the twentieth anniversary of the fire in our village that killed four people and destroyed fifty homes. This startled me because I was supposed to write about it. I hadn't discussed it with my editor but I'd been writing about fire and about trees and so I thought it hadn't needed discussing. I said these things aloud and then his typing paused and he said, "I thought she emailed you already. It's only one article."

I checked my email and saw a message from my editor from about ten minutes ago. But it wasn't just about this anniversary piece. My editor also realized it wasn't a good idea for me to write about the meeting regarding the potential practice emergency evacuation. *You don't handle stress as well as you used to,* she wrote. *And your boyfriend is involved in this meeting? That's a no-go.* But he's barely going to be involved! I thought. I wanted to write back but I didn't write back. I didn't want the other reporter to hear me fighting back, because I knew that aloud I would sound pathetic.

"And this meeting," I said aloud.

"It's not really a big deal," the other reporter said. "Most meetings and plans—they don't go anywhere anyway."

I turned around to look at him and his face was full of pity and concern.

It was disgusting to me and I wanted to scream.

I said of course he was right.

I went home to work in a place that wasn't the office.

I managed to finish the obituary after dinner. The next morning, I saw that my editor had emailed me back in the middle of the night. She said the details were nicely rendered but the piece was long-winded and the threads of the dead woman's life seemed frayed like I hadn't really tied anything together, like I was losing my ability to focus on a story. But she cut it down to a manageable length and smoothed things over. She said it reminded her of my early, juvenile writing. I told myself not to cry. Why does it hurt so horribly to write a bad draft, when the story isn't even about you at all?

I collapsed on the couch and stared glumly into my mug, trying to finish not my usual black coffee but a milky earthy beverage my boyfriend had concocted from some herbs he'd picked the other day. I watched him measure out in precise proportions each of the dried leaves and roots down to the tenth of a gram, trying, he said, to find the perfect proportions for my body, and I bit my tongue to stop from asking how he could understand what to give me if no one knew what was happening inside. But I let him make it for me before he left for his weekend excursion. I promised to finish it. I was about ten minutes and two sips into that bitter viscous slurry, about to do another worksheet, when the phone rang: *Caller Unknown.*

I stared at it for five or so rings, then answered. *If you're ready, press one. If you're not ready, press two. If you'd like a callba—*

I was already pressing 1, perhaps even multiple times: one one one one one! Within minutes Lee called. "Just give me thirty minutes," I said, and rushed to do the next worksheet, piling treatment on treatment.

Worksheet 3

*A*re *you reaching the most painful part of your memories? Is the pain getting worse? Push through! It's a good sign, like pressing a blade to an abscess before the relief of rupture. Remember that your pain is real, created in the aftermath of traumatic experiences. Don't shy away from painful memories; this will delay recovery. Remember: you can do whatever you like with these pages—frame them, burn them, put them away for safekeeping. And remember:* I Am a Good Person! I Deserve Love! I Love Myself!

※

One day I decided what my mother's problem was: she was taking too many medications. If everything has a cause and effect and each problem she had was caused by another problem, then perhaps she needed someone, and the someone she needed was me, to reverse the course of her life, define every effect and eliminate its cause. Eventually I'd reach the first problem, which was to say the real one, and then we could fix it before it could cause all the others.

She had many problems and therefore took many medications and so I had to consider which medication would be best for my mother to stop taking first. It came down to the medication she took for her migraines and the medication she took for her depression, both of which were often changing. Initially I thought it should be the medication for her headaches, because I read that one of its side effects was depression, and so this might be a good starting point for reversal; although her headaches might increase, her depression could lift, I thought, and then I could reason with her. But then I found that a side effect of the depression medication was headaches, and so I had to consider if it would be better to eliminate her depression medication to cure her headaches or to eliminate her headache medication to cure her depression, and to me either of these seemed justifiable, since at the time she was taking medication for both things and yet still had both ailments, so anything I did to help her would be an improvement.

⁂

My mother kept all of her medications in her purse, which was usually on the kitchen counter. In retrospect it's a little strange that they were in her purse, as she rarely left the house and purses are for leaving, although she was the kind of person who believed that terrible events were always around the corner, and maybe she thought someday she would have to flee and she wanted in her own way to be prepared.

The day I took one of my mother's medications from her purse was a day she had made a rare trip to the pharmacy for some refills, and when she walked in the door she was also holding a package. I asked her uneasily what it was, though I already knew. Packages had been coming every few weeks. "More newspapers?"

She gave me kind of a rueful smile and opened the package. She said yes, it was from later in the war, and she pulled out the big broadsides as well as green stamps the color of clover, each one bearing an eagle perched on top of a swastika, and as I looked I leaned back, not wanting to be close to it. "You know, it's just a little . . . weird," I said.

"Well, the world isn't a rosy place," she said.

"Okay, but—that doesn't mean you need . . . that stuff?"

"Sometimes the bad stuff gets a little too abstract," she said, and drew the newspaper and the stamps slightly closer to herself, protectively, then placed them back on the table and looked at them steadily, searchingly. "I think I saw this image somewhere else," she said, tapping the eagle.

I asked her where.

She sighed. "I . . . let me go see," she said, and gave me a look. "I'll be back in a minute." As soon as I heard her footsteps on the stairs, I went to the kitchen counter and unzipped her black leather purse, which contained so many bottles, I sank my hand into it and it was like a ball pit; although a ball pit is fun, it almost completely subsumes you into bright atomic homogeneity. I could sink my hand so far into her purse it disappeared at the wrist. I rifled through the bottles, telling myself to focus, focus, to not fall too deeply into it, and in about fifteen seconds the medication I was looking for surfaced and I quickly pocketed it into the cargo pants I wore especially for this task and sat back down. Soon my mother returned with one of her old Nazi newspapers and she showed me the image from the stamp in the newspaper, and then she looked at the newspaper for a while and I looked at the stamps. I didn't ask her any questions. Eventually we switched. I didn't really want to be looking at any of it but it was nice to spend some time with her. We hadn't spoken in a week, not for any particular reason but she'd locked herself in her room for some days. At the table she reached over and gave my hand a little squeeze.

Over the course of the next week my mother deteriorated, not completely but strangely quickly, and also publicly, at least in the public places of the house, which was odd because she usually retreated to her room when she had an episode of whatever it was that went on inside her. On the first day I thought she would say something to me, perhaps accusing me or at least mentioning that important things had gone missing, but she was silent. This confounded me until the fourth day after I removed her medication from her purse. She lay down on the couch in the living room, and except to use the bathroom and at one point to try to make us dinner she didn't get up.

I realized then that she probably suspected I had taken her things.

I realized she was putting her suffering on display for me.

This went on for days.

"How do you make it?" I asked, frightened of her.

She turned onto her back to look up at me, and for a few seconds the muscles around her eyes tightened as if she were trying to reach a particular part of her mind, the part with instructions and guidance, but then her eyelids drooped somewhat self-consciously as she gave up and turned onto her side and dry-heaved before she said, "You've watched me make it a million times. Go figure it out."

I cooked the meatballs and then poured the cans of tomatoes on them but I didn't use the wine and somehow the grease, which my mother's sauce always had in just the right proportion, overtook the sauce like a maritime disaster and afterward my dad and I rubbed our stomachs uneasily in the dining room.

A few days later I was in the kitchen and heard my father finally speak to my mother. He hadn't said much to her, at least that I'd seen, and he was probably hoping to let whatever was going on in her run its course, but eventually he asked what was the matter. She said she'd lost her Zoloft and he said *Again?* And I noted this.

"I don't know," she said.

"Why didn't you say anything?"

"You gave me shit last time."

There was silence.

"You really lost it?"

Silence.

Then she said, "My whole body feels like shit. Even my . . . skin," and though I was in the other room I imagined she clutched her head because I heard her horrible moaning.

"I mean, where could it have gone? It's gotta be in the house . . . I just have to ask you: you're not holding on to . . . extra, are you?"

Silence.

"I'm trying to help you. I mean . . ."

"I lost it," she said.

When I heard his footsteps going up the stairs, I went into the living room.

"Are you okay?" I finally asked her, after all those days.

She looked up at me and her gaze narrowed like she wanted to squeeze me dead.

"I didn't . . . lose them," she said, as if she had to squish down her nausea to get from one part of the sentence to the next.

I didn't say anything.

"What did you do?" she asked.

"I flushed them down the toilet," I finally said, even though I hadn't, because I didn't want her to go looking.

"So now on top of my normal headaches. . . . I'm having these fucking withdrawal headaches . . . and I'm nauseated and I can barely walk ten feet without feeling dizzy. So this is me . . . underneath that stuff," she said.

Silence.

"Do you get that? Do you get it, Kim?"

"I—No. No. It's—if—there has to be some way. Something had to have—you know—or there's something happening inside your head or whatever that could be—I just don't believe there's no way to somehow figure out what is causing your horrible headaches and . . . your, you know, all the rest . . . I mean even when you take that stuff, you're not happy. There has to be some way to just—even temporarily to not be on anything but not be having all these symptoms, the withdrawal or whatever . . . I mean maybe something is wrong with you that you and no one else even knows about, and if someone could only figure out what this thing that no one knows about was, and . . ."

"And . . ."

Her eyes were closed.

"I'm . . . going upstairs," she said. "And when I open my eyes in thirty seconds, you need to go somewhere I can't see you. I can't fucking look at you right now."

I went to my room and closed the door and opened my sock drawer. I found the sock with the bottle in it and sat on my bed the way I saw her sitting on her bed all the time, cross-legged, and considered the bottle. I thought about how she opened her bottles, the way she stared straight ahead as she pressed down and twisted on the white cap and let a little capsule slide into the center of her palm and brought her palm right to her open mouth, and her palm always lingered on her mouth just a few seconds longer than it needed to. I looked straight ahead like her, although what I saw sitting on my bed was completely different than what she saw—she had a TV but I just had a blank wall. I twisted the white cap and tilted the bottle, but too many slipped out so I had to put some back, and it wasn't as elegant as her, and I brought my palm to my mouth like her, and the pill went in, and I held my hand there just a little too long like her, but my tongue pushed the pill back out so when I pulled back my hand the pill came with it. I threw that pill away because it was contaminated with my spit. I put the bottle by her door.

I Submitted to the Axon

That morning I again went up the winding roads and their changing names and past the main house, which had grown yet another appendage: a detached little building close to the driveway. As my car crawled down the gravel drive I saw through the window a few easels and blank canvases, an artist's studio for someone, or maybe no one. Maybe the owners hoped the creation of an artist's studio might cause an artist to appear. When I reached the cottage, Lee's windows were glowing with that seductive amber light. I didn't hesitate this time. The minute I parked, I was out of my car and knocking at her front door.

I was excited.

I was a little giddy.

It was a giddiness that comes with trying something that is, for all intents and purposes: a joke. I mean: old cords wrapped around someone's head and a gray plastic box that looks like an old video game console!

And yet—who knew? . . .

The placebo effect hadn't yet worked but maybe I just needed the right placebo.

Or maybe—

Could there be something to it? Might the Axon recalibrate my insides?

Lee had consulted it and it knew, somehow—I didn't want to think about how it allegedly worked—that I was ready. Maybe it sensed my desperation. Which seems a bit manipulative. And yet desperation can be a useful portal. Maybe reason and cause and effect only get you so far.

Anyway.

Submitting to the Axon was like a joke I was telling myself or telling the disorder. *Isn't this hilarious?* I asked the disorder. *Should we play along and pretend it's working, that crazy shit is going on inside me while I'm hooked up to her weird boxes?* The disorder responded by causing two long bolts of pain through my forearms. I took this, eyes closed and breathing hard, as agreement, as if the disorder were some paralyzed patient inside me that, surprisingly, had thoughts to communicate, if it were asked the right questions. *Okay*, I said to it, *so we're both in on the joke*.

But *can* anything ever be only a joke? I asked it, because there was a place in my mind that it wasn't a joke. The disorder was silent on that.

When Lee opened the door, she looked again different. The pale linens that had draped her body were gone. Now she was wearing all black, as if she needed for some reason to absorb all the light around her. Her clothes were cut more closely, slim trousers and a tight-fitting sweater embellished with a decorative crystal pendant hanging on a long chain around her neck. The whole temperature of her had cooled, and rather than properly greet me she nodded slowly and seriously as I entered the cottage. I sat down in the chair clearly prepared for me, the pristine wingback beside the foldout wall desk where an entire desktop computer had appeared. Beside it was the gray box, with the tiny red lights in the outline of a human form and the other lights atop a line of numbers.

Lee's tiny cabin looked the same: the pale ceramics lined on wood shelving, beautiful and perfectly uniform jars filled with nuts and flours and honey, and on the edge were tiny tincture bottles like the ones my boyfriend used. But there was one difference: a cat, which curled itself around my feet as Lee picked up the thick black strap on the desk and pulled it tight across my forehead, Velcroing it together at the back. Lee clearly didn't want to say much and break the moody spell of the room, but as she adjusted the black band she quietly said, "That's Anita. She's here to help my clients relax."

Everything began to darken. Lee was turning down the lights in the room, claiming the Axon worked better that way, and then she sat in the office chair directly in front of the computer, the screen at an angle so it was just out of my sight. She turned on the computer and into the silence came its electric hum, dull and droning and yet like a meditation. It's a joke, it's a joke, I thought, but I couldn't help but feel or hope that some shift might be possible in that space.

She pulled some other strap across the crown of my head and adjusted that too, and my head felt pressured and contained, which was comforting. I closed my eyes briefly, relaxing into it, when Lee asked me to put out my hands. I accepted an object, feeling a strange shape as a heady aroma filled the air around me. I opened my eyes and saw a citrus, but it looked like the Medusa, or in fact maybe like some fucked-up hand, with its many long pointy fingerlike sections.

"What the hell is this?" I asked, and she looked at me as if on the brink of scolding me for departing from the mood of the healing evening.

"It's a Buddha's hand. It's citrus. But there's no juice. It's all aroma. I like to have it around, to open up the senses." She paused. "Close your eyes and gently scratch at the skin with your fingernails, and slowly inhale."

I closed my eyes. I scratched. I sniffed. I put down the citrus and opened my eyes and saw Lee sitting at the ancient computer, looking assured and professional as she checked the connections between her various pieces of hardware. Before we really began she needed one final thing, she said. She held out a thick plastic cup reminiscent of urine vessels in doctor's offices and asked me to spit in it. I hesitated as I looked into the clear empty plastic, unsure about offering up body fluid, but I'd already come this far and it was all part of the joke and so I sucked and collected a good amount of saliva in my mouth and spit. She asked for a few strands of hair, too. I pulled out about five and placed them into a Ziploc bag.

She sealed it quietly and sat back down and placed it under her desk. She said she needed to ask me a series of questions and she needed me to answer truthfully. She asked if I was ready. When I said yes, she laid her fingers on the deep keys of her keyboard and a little seed of jealousy germinated in me.

At first the questions were easy: my name, the day and the city and state in which I was born. She asked the hour of my birth and I had to say I didn't know. Then there were gentle questions about my childhood—what was my favorite cereal? What did I dream of becoming when I grew up?—questions I couldn't quite determine the point of except perhaps to warm me up, or maybe there was some way in which my self needed to be drawn out into the room so the Axon could better diagnose or cure me. Quickly we moved into the present and she said I needed to answer these questions as quickly as possible, to give her the first answer that came into my head, a request that infuriated me because I didn't always think the first thing was the true thing but still I tried to comply.

"Why did you come here?"

"To get away."

"And why did you want to be a reporter?"

"To be a better person. Or just a different person. To be engaged with the world and not just in my own head."

I looked over at the gray box. A few lights were flickering.

"What made you fall in love with your boyfriend?"

"His knowledge. The way he knew so much and so differently. Sometimes I wish I could be him instead."

"Do you want children?"

"No. But yes. But no."

"What do you think is the true root of your disorder?"

"I—"

But my mind was blank.

"What do you think is the true root of your disorder?"

"I don't know!" I screamed. "It could be so many things! It must be typing. Right? But also, couldn't it be anything? Couldn't it be stress over having to interrogate people each week? Or stress over fires and the climate and everything? Or some bullshit repressed trauma? Or something I haven't even thought of? Or nothing, nothing at all?"

The lights on the body were going haywire.

I started crying.

Lee was quiet for a second.

"Does it embarrass you to talk about it?"

"Yes."

"Why?"

"If I were anyone but myself I'd think I was having an extended anxiety attack."

"Do you like your job?"

"I love my job. But I hate it. And I wish I never had to ask anyone another question ever again. Even though all I want is to know what's going on. In someone else's head."

"Do you think you should quit?"

"No. No. No."

"But don't you? Isn't that what you really want to do?" she said in a whisper, and a whisper really is the best way to infiltrate another's mind, maybe because another's voice made quiet enough starts to feel like it could be your own consciousness talking. "Don't you want to find what truly makes you happy? Can you imagine what that looks like, your own personal vision for the future?"

"I don't know. I don't know. I don't know," I said three times, as if it were a spell that might reveal something to me. Nothing came though. Lee was quiet, she didn't respond, and so I felt compelled to keep talking. "My boyfriend, you know—he has a vision for the future. A community. A farm or a garden or something in between. A baby. I don't know what I'd do. What my real purpose would be. But—I don't know. Maybe that's not a bad thing. Maybe it could be a good thing."

Maybe it could.

People always talk about the benefits of leaping into the unknown, of leaving open a big blank that the world or the universe or whatever will fill in for you, since the universe knows things you don't, since the random universe might make a better choice than you ever consciously could.

"Absolutely," she said, typing typing typing.

"So how is your work with this machine . . . how is it going?"

"Let's stay focused on you," she said. "Although actually, I think we're about done with our session. But just stay still for a little while."

I think I was still crying a little bit.

I wondered if there was still time to grab my spit and hair and run.

But the thoughts in my head began an argument among themselves. Some said I needed to see the joke of the machine through to the end, I should finish at least one thing I started, even a scam. Another contingent of thoughts said: Right! And what harm could it do anyway? And who knows—maybe . . .

Perhaps that was the disorder. Maybe the disorder itself didn't even know why it was there, inside me!

The red lights of the figure outlined on the gray box began to light up again, first the one denoting the head, then one foot, then a red light on each hand began to flicker excitedly in unison. I was entranced and tried to commit the pattern to memory: head, foot, hands. But the lights moved so quickly around the outline that it was impossible to track it. The lights along the numbers remained dark. Pain popped into my fingertips, and I made a little pathetic sound and squeezed my hands but then Lee told me sternly my hands needed to remain open, I needed to remain open. I obeyed. The lights seemed to respond, although I can't remember quite how.

I thought about Dr. W sticking the needle into my neck and listening to the electricity of my muscles. If I could believe that then maybe I could believe this, maybe it would know something after all, maybe I could believe in the Axon.

Then another group of thoughts fought back. They said: Come on! This is ridiculous! How many people has she duped? Do you really want to be one of them?

Finally there were those thoughts that were always there: Could I write about this? Research the Axon and report on it, mixing my own personal experience with interviews of other people who tried this weirdo treatment, maybe that was what the universe wanted me to fill in the blank of the future with?

But then I wasn't so sure.

I wasn't sure I wanted to ask anyone any more questions.

I just wanted to be better.

Lee was still sitting at the computer, her eyes closed and her clothes somehow slightly disheveled, her hair a little unkempt even though she'd barely moved. She seemed drained of energy as if the Axon had taken things from her too.

"The results are going to take some time," she said. "I'll let you know when I have something for you."

⋙⋘

I went home. I collapsed onto the couch and chugged the last dregs of the earthy brew. It's always strange to be drained like that first thing in the morning. It was the weekend and I was alone since my boyfriend was gone camping, a perfect time to work, to catch up. But instead Lee's words swirled in my mind; she had drained me of everything but her words. Instead of doing anything productive in my solitude, instead of even enjoying it somehow, I puttered around the cabin: washed some dishes, did the laundry, chopped onions for a pasta sauce that would incorporate no wild ingredients and no deer fat and absolutely nothing bitter, just canned tomatoes and imported anchovies and glugs of imported olive oil. And I noticed or thought I noticed that my hands felt maybe a little calmed, a little less of that background humming feeling that could spark to pain at any moment. They didn't feel normal, but did they, I thought as I chopped, feel a little closer to normal?

It was hard, as I've said, to even remember what they were supposed to feel like but what if, I thought, the Axon was . . . working? Would that mean she was right, about everything, that in my heart I wanted to quit? Maybe I'd wanted to quit for a while.

The Practice Emergency Evacuation Meeting

When I arrived at the church space for the practice emergency evacuation meeting, on the early side, as was my wont as a reporter even though I wasn't the reporter for this meeting, I saw my boyfriend in a dense circle with the organizers. He'd only returned to town a few hours ago; I hadn't talked to him yet or told him my pain maybe—maybe?—had ever so slightly started to abate and maybe in a few weeks I could try to type again and that would probably make him wish I'd never gone to Lee.

My boyfriend and the organizers were in front of one of the many informational posters, this one showcasing the blackened shell of an A-frame, its façade gone and rubble everywhere and yet the fireplace almost perfectly preserved. I was startled to see him looking so intimate with them. He'd been to an organizing meeting a week or so ago, or something, and he'd told me about the organizers: around his age and in the similar semiprecarious circumstance of being renters in an increasingly expensive and desirable place while working jobs that would never amount to the cost of a home or even undeveloped land. There was a farmer of a tiny organic plot, and that person knew a woman who worked at the grocery store and was also a low-key prepper, and she knew a carpenter who grew mind-altering mushrooms, and the last person was a teller at the local bank, a bit the outlier, but perhaps the practical, organized one. There had originally been a few more, but in recent weeks the group, my boyfriend said after the meeting he'd attended, had whittled down a bit. So you learned a bit about . . . organizing or whatever? I'd asked, and he said yes and I hadn't asked more questions because I assumed there was nothing more to it or I didn't want to believe there was more to it, since I didn't want anything to interfere with my job, with my stories. You would think if you lived with someone you would know all the particulars of their life, but it's easier than you'd think to avoid information you don't want to know simply by assuming things or leaving questions unspoken and unanswered, or not allowing those questions to bubble up in your mind at all. But there was something very focused about the conversing circle, a special energy gathering in the hollow of it, as they perhaps discussed the details of this night's meeting and how exactly they would convince everyone to participate in this evacuation rehearsal. My boyfriend clearly hadn't stumbled into the conversation; he seemed as excited and engaged as the others, although he was slightly offset from the circle, like he was trying to get a little bit of perspective while remaining part of it, which gave me a little hope that maybe he wasn't really involved after all. I kept watching them out of the corner of my eye.

When I reported on meetings I always arrived early if there

was something for the attendees to be doing or discussing, because then the story could include a scene of it, since there was little drama in people sitting politely in folding chairs. Of course I wasn't writing about this meeting for the paper. But maybe, I thought, maybe in a few months I could write about the practice evacuation for some other outlet, a magazine or an important website. The evacuation could be construed into something grand and not granular; I could add all sorts of interesting details I couldn't include in the paper because the people reading the paper already knew those things. And that was what I'd meant to do all along. I'd never meant to stay in this place. I'd meant to move up or at least along.

Except I'd agreed—had I agreed?—to build a life here or somewhere with my boyfriend. But maybe I could do it all from here, if I had just one good idea.

And maybe all of that or one of those things would soon be much easier. All weekend the pain in my hands had been almost nonexistent; no sudden bolts of pain had shot through my fingers since visiting Lee, though it had only been a few days, and I'd been minimizing my fine manipulation, perhaps more than ever. Yet the ready hum of it—was it maybe quieting? Maybe it was. Or maybe I just wanted to tell myself it was. Maybe I was trying by the force of my mind to make Lee's treatment come true. All weekend I asked myself: *How did my hands feel before?*

But I didn't want to think about it all anymore.

I didn't want to get too anxious, in case it really was dissipating.

So I looked around the room again. Other people were arriving and milling about and looking at the posters, each one stationed below a stained glass window. The posters looked hastily made, but clearly some thought had been put into their emotional impact. Multiple photographs were of the very deadly fire to the north of us in the previous fire season. Being so deadly and destroying a small town, it was a logical source to draw on, although it was ultimately just one of many fires. There was one aerial photograph of a fire itself, although the flames were hidden beneath gargantuan billows of smoke. Another was of a single home burning from the inside, its façade somehow still intact, and one photo of a burned-up tree reminded me of those commercials to fund orphans, as if a photo of something singular and specific might disturb us into action, in case we were the kind of people unmoved by abstract information and larger scales of destruction.

One poster explained what fire was exactly and how it functioned. I went to it because it made sense to know, first, what fire was.

Combustion, another name for fire, is an energy-releasing chemical reaction that, once initiated, can become self-perpetuating...

Since fire breaks complex molecules down to simpler forms, it is a type of decomposition, releasing and recycling nutrients...

Very large fires can create their own winds and local weather...

There were more people crowded in front of other posters, ones with more dramatic pictures, and they said words like *horrible* and *terrible* and wondered whether that was possible here, which of course it was, and whether every autumn the smoke would trap us inside for days at a time. Some people were discussing who or what was to blame. Other people were looking quietly at a photograph of charred automobiles, which to some was more disturbing than the charred trees and the charred forest. If I'd been writing about the meeting for the paper, I would have considered which attendees to approach for comments about whether they thought a practice emergency evacuation would be worthwhile or give them peace of mind or just be useless. It was difficult to be at a meeting without my role, without being a recorder and digester and explainer of occurrences and perspectives and predictions and debates, so I started taking notes on my phone, just for me and not for the paper. It was less noticeable than using my notepad, and I didn't want to be too noticeable because the other reporter would arrive. I tapped away on that screen with my thumbs. I'd been so good in the past few days, hadn't I built up some credit, I thought, and are thumbs really fingers anyway?

The organizers had migrated to the back of the church, near the little stage just a foot above the rest of the space. The circle had tightened, as if to ensure what they said could not escape the group. I started to make my way toward them as unnoticeably as I could, although I'm an uncouth person, but then they suddenly broke apart, perhaps because the other reporter had arrived. The other reporter looked trustworthy, at ease, in his nice button-up shirt with the top button undone, chatting with people in front of the poster with the cars that weren't cars anymore, and the people he was interviewing looked at ease too. He was doing a good job. I couldn't imagine anyone ever thinking such a thing about me.

Not everyone is meant to write about disasters, I told myself. Maybe I wasn't meant to write anything at all. I had long wanted to be a kind of prism through which substance could travel and be clearly elaborated upon. But maybe it was more like human digestion. I thought it was good, to digest information for people. It was a metaphor we used all the time. But what was digestion but swallowing a substance from which your body absorbs into its secret self what it can, and ejects what is useless?

Maybe I should inhabit my boyfriend's fantasy, I thought. Maybe I should just reproduce. Still, when I took a seat in the last row of chairs, I pulled my phone out and started taking more notes, the slim, wide body of the phone resting gently on my fingers.

※

One of the organizers of the meeting, the grocery store cashier and low-key prepper, took to the lectern and waited for the fizz of the crowd to come to a complete quiet. I remembered that she had, not long ago, belonged to the town's village council, volunteers who made unenforceable recommendations to the county government. But she quit before her first term ended, grumbling to me for an article in the paper about both the powerlessness of the council and their almost total opposition to any further development.

The other organizers took their seats in a row of chairs behind her, including, at the last minute, my boyfriend. My stomach dropped a little. I wanted to drag him off the stage, to remind him that he hated groups of any kind!

But I was not the kind of person to make a scene, and I needed to take my notes, even if the purpose of them was unclear.

After everyone at the meeting was sitting and quiet, the woman, who was wearing what appeared to be a very new and bright white T-shirt, looked out and considered us, and she seemed a little taller than I remembered, as if buoyed by the crowd, and yet also a little unsteady. She was young, younger than me, and the audience was mostly older and retired and I wondered if the attendees came just to see such a person trying to do something useful.

She started by leading everyone in a chant that it wasn't if, but *when*, not if, but *when*, and she passed around a handout that contained page-sized reproductions of the fire posters along with a wire service article about how towns in our state were unprepared for fire. A fire might, she said, move slowly and allow us all time to gather every precious thing, and yet, if strong winds were pushing a fire quickly in the direction of homes, and flinging embers so that it spread ever more quickly, we might barely have time to grab our go bags. Even with the best preparation people might die, and yet their small group felt it would be good to practice, to rehearse the leaving of this place, to strengthen communally a feeling of resistance. We could even practice a few times, a route over the little yellow bridge and also a route that circumvented the little yellow bridge. And then if, and really *when*, a fire happened, everyone would have a good chance of making it out safely—although there were no guarantees.

Then she said something that was actually news: there was going to be a prescribed fire, anonymous donors were helping the county match funds for it, and the practice emergency evacuation would occur on the day of the fire, to make it feel more real.

Around this point, the edge of my hand began to hurt like I was being painfully outlined or traced. I froze. *No no no.* I slid my phone into my back pocket and told myself to leave it there for five minutes.

Before the low-key prepper was done with her passionate speech, hands started going up with questions, which clearly annoyed her—and maybe it was when the hands went up that my pain appeared, or maybe that's too silly a memory to be real—and I sympathized because it's difficult to have an orderly meeting if people interrupt with tangents, or worse with a question meant to display their own intelligence. But she hadn't told the audience to hold their questions until the end, and if she couldn't plan ahead even for that then how could they get even a small group of people to practice evacuating? Still she took questions. One person asked what the point was if we would never know where a fire was going to start or what direction it would go, and another person pointedly wondered if they had any real expertise, and whether professionals shouldn't be in charge. Perhaps, she admitted, the group would not be qualified to organize the emergency evacuation of a large town or city. But this was a village, she said, a small village, and it could band together, couldn't it? It was about time, anyway, she said, with all the frustration over rampant tourism and the clogged streets, for people to come uncontroversially together for something.

I took my phone out because she was making important points and I wanted to write down some details, especially details the recorder wouldn't capture like what she was doing with her hands and her growing frustration with these questions, but the minute my thumbs started moving the pain spread from the sides of my hands along my pinkies into all my fingers including my thumbs, and every time my thumbs pressed down on the little icons of the keyboard it was like something ricocheted or echoed back into my fingers, a ping of pain but also a horrible ache in the meaty muscles of my hands.

No no no! I thought. Don't come back!

If it ever was gone?

I put the phone back in my pocket again and started squinching my hands again just like I did the first time, even though it wouldn't make a difference, but still I felt I should keep my fingers or the muscles in my fingers moving, or maybe it was those muscles themselves that wanted to move.

I took a breath. The worksheet! *I'm a good person! I deserve love! I love myself! I'm a good person! I deserve love! I love myself!*

A thought came to me: Could the Axon have done this?

Maybe the Axon had actually made it worse.

Maybe it made it better only to make it worse, because—well, for some reason I couldn't yet divine.

No! I thought. No. Because the Axon can't do anything! It's a scam!

Sometimes disorders just get worse, I thought in a weird attempt to comfort myself. Sometimes disorders appear out of nowhere and sometimes they get worse for no reason. Or not even no reason. I was, of course, engaged in fine manipulation.

I was trying not to panic but panicking a little bit, because touching my phone had never hurt. I was only half paying attention to the low-key prepper's reassurances that they would contact experts who researched fire patterns and evacuations. Then yet another person stood up and interrupted, without asking for permission, and started on a diatribe against the group, because he'd heard the organizers wanted to convince everyone to support the proposed sewer system, to overturn the ban on new water connections, so the village could grow and grow, become not just a town but a city, changing the entire character of the place.

The low-key prepper's eyes widened, either in true surprise or to create a look of surprise to give herself more time to respond. She turned briefly toward the other organizers seated behind her, and it became clear she had been chosen as the speaker for her enthusiasm but not the ability to respond to hostility. Eventually my boyfriend came to the fore. He said, very calmly but also with a low, authoritative voice, that the rehearsal, as it were, had absolutely nothing to do with the sewer system, it was only about safety.

I grabbed my phone again and took a deep breath, but even before I tried typing a single word, my fingertips exploded with little starbursts of pain. I put the phone away again and became just another member of the audience and I listened and tried to hold on to what he was saying, so I could write down some notes of it later.

We're not some secret pro-development group, he went on. However—and it seemed he was seeding something just as he was rejecting it—however, was it really such a horrible idea, to create more places for people to live when so many were struggling to find homes, or paying astronomical prices to rent little rat-ridden shacks in this very bucolic place? When the little housing that was available was slowly lost? Although it wasn't so slowly being lost, was it, since it seemed, at least anecdotally, that people were cashing out faster and faster, and more and more housing was being left utterly empty, the more beautiful the house the more likely it was to be bought and left empty, for the owners to vacation every once in a while or turn into rentals for tourists or perhaps just to leave it to accrue more market value.

"But what use is it," the man in the crowd persisted, someone who probably owned his home and could live there comfortably till death or till he himself cashed out when he liked, "what use is it to bring more people here, with the fire danger, and all the smoke that's going to blow over to us? That's maybe going to get worse every year?"

My boyfriend took a slow breath, took a moment to either genuinely consider the point or pretend to. "There aren't a lot of good options, are there? The smoke will be everywhere. But at least it's a little less risky here. Unless everyone just wants to leave entirely? And—I don't know. Maybe—maybe most of us will decide leaving is best . . ." he said, perhaps a little surprised at what he was saying.

※

Eventually the meeting disbanded and people milled about, but I didn't observe or take any note of anyone or anything. I just sat there for a minute, trying to be calm and hoping I could be calm enough to make my hands calm and comfortable. Then my boyfriend sat beside me and put his hand affectionately on my thigh and asked me hopefully and anxiously what I thought.

I squeezed my hands. "Well. I didn't realize you were—well, that you were so involved."

He looked at me a little confusedly. "But didn't I tell you that?"

"I—well . . . I don't know. Maybe you did. Maybe I just—misunderstood . . . I mean, anyway," I said, seeing that he really cared what I thought, "I think it went well. Although—growth doesn't seem like your kind of message."

"Well. We'll see, we'll see. Anyway. Maybe you could help out. With the practice evacuation at least," he said. "Maybe it would be good—practice, you know. Being part of a group. Good practice for the future."

"But—well, I don't know if that's a good idea, with the paper."

He sighed and looked at me to make clear he was frustrated. "You're not even reporting on this."

"Well, still. I've always tried to remain separate from that kind of stuff, from things the newspaper writes about it."

"Just think about it, okay? Please tell me you'll think about it. Maybe it would be good for you. To help people."

"I do help people. Don't you think what I do helps people?"

"Of course I do. I do. I mean in a different way. Maybe a little more concretely," he said, patting me again before getting up to convene with the organizers.

The Pain Was Worse

When I mentioned to my editor—I don't know why I mentioned it, since I didn't want to appear weaker, but maybe I made a confession of vulnerability to reforge a weakened bond—that my phone was causing some additional pain, she pulled the last obit she'd assigned me. Maybe writing about the dead hadn't been a good idea, she mused. Maybe obits weren't as stress-free as she had hoped. She mentioned again that she was seriously considering selling the paper in the next year or so. After mentioning it to me she'd put the idea out of her mind, but then she got an email, out of nowhere, asking if she had any interest in letting it go. She didn't want to in her heart, the paper was her baby. And yet she hadn't taken a vacation in a decade, and she felt not quite obliterated but so emptied of something she was at times on the verge of mental collapse. She said in some subtle way she didn't want to end up like me, even though that didn't seem possible, because she was older by some decades and already way ahead of me. But she was exhausted and felt there were stories she wasn't finding; perhaps a new owner would have a fresh passion for local news.

I tried to convince her to give me the last obit back even though I didn't want it. I told her I was soon getting an MRI, maybe I could get a blood test, to ensure that she understood there were places in my body still to be searched. But she wouldn't budge.

At least she responded to my message.

Whereas I'd reached out to Lee a number of times asking if the results, or whatever they were, were ready, but she hadn't bothered to respond—not even to say she wasn't ready!

Even though I didn't believe in any of it, I wanted to ask her about each thing happening to me, the pain maybe slightly abating and then roaring back even worse, triggered by even more subtle fine manipulation. I wanted to ask her what it meant.

Because what had it meant?

Maybe all it meant was that I'd been very good at moving very little, at being almost like a statue of myself, but then at that meeting I'd given in to note-taking, to my little phone screen, to the pleasure of fine manipulation.

But maybe I didn't want to tell her too much anyway.

Maybe it was best she hadn't responded.

If someday I might write about the Axon, if someday I might investigate her and her stupid machine, maybe I should hold back. Then again, writing about it someday, someday, required playing along. . . .

It was so easy to go back and forth and back and forth about what I wanted.

In lieu of the last obit, my editor gave me a positive story about turtles, or at least the story held the possibility of positivity. An environmental group was working to rehabilitate a certain species of turtle that had become extirpated from some faraway lagoon. I hadn't known what *extirpated* meant when I started researching the turtles, but a kind scientist explained it: the turtles no longer existed in the lagoon, although they still existed elsewhere, including in the ponds in our town, where they had managed to survive if not proliferate; perhaps the turtles knew this protected landscape was safe but circumscribed, and if their numbers rose too high there was no place in which to expand. The project involved taking turtle eggs from near us to a special hatchery and once they were born and not quite babies anymore putting them in the lagoon, which was far away in a different part of the state. They would hopefully repopulate, and that would be nice. The lagoon was once polluted with trash and light but was now dark and clean. It was a story about hope, at least hope within certain limitations, and that had to be good enough.

 I worked on the story first at the office, but I was frustrated at working near the other reporter, thinking of him listening to me dictate and repeat myself, because Mirror kept getting me wrong: *turtle* turned to *girdle*, then *eternal*, then *maternal*, then *terminal*, and I had to stop myself from asking myself or the disorder or Mirror: wasn't it a beautiful iteration of words and did it mean something, doesn't it mean something?

 Bad thoughts! Psycho thoughts! I told myself. Focus on the article!

 But now working on articles was even worse, because now every click of my mouse made me more and more worried, each click like some horrible painful countdown to something. Meanwhile the other reporter was working on his fire meeting story. He was nice enough to take some phone interviews outside so I could keep dictating, or that's what he said, but maybe he didn't want me listening to his reporting.

So I went home a little early and worked on it more, though when my boyfriend came home he made dinner and pulled me away from my makeshift standing desk to eat, a porcini soup, or some kind of mushroomy, brothy soup with all sorts of herbs and greens and flavors from his foraging, its surface dotted with a few dandelion flowers. He had started around this time to make more soup than usual. I'd never much cared for soup, and this spring season was turning out to be an usually warm one, but he was getting some alchemical urges, and maybe he also thought of me like some convalescent who needed warm healing liquids, though I don't know if you can really convalesce until you start to get at least a little bit better. But I ate the soup anyway.

He asked hopefully if I liked it, that he'd put some adaptogens in it that were supposed to be good for stress and nerve function. Adaptogens, a word he'd often disdained when it started appearing on every tea box and supplement bottle at the store!

But I didn't critique his language. I said it was delicious. I didn't say it was strong and bitter for my taste, and there was a new off-putting flavor I hadn't tasted before that reminded me of ripe compost. "But my nerves aren't the problem," I said glumly.

"They don't know everything," he said. "Not everything can be measured."

"I'm going to have an MRI soon," I said. "It might find something with my spine. It might find some kind of strain or tension. Or maybe something really horrible."

I ate the last spoonful of my soup, trying to suppress a grimace. Later on the couch he covered my forearms with pieces of cloth coated in some special poultice he made that day from wild mustard seeds. It burned a little and my skin reddened as he applied the pasty squares to my forearms and hands. There was a pungent smell, too, as he wrapped and wrapped, like this was the beginning of my mummification. "I hate mustard," I complained. But he told me to leave the poultice on for at least fifteen minutes. The plant was supposed to be good for arthritic pain and overused muscles, and perhaps I had some mysterious arthritis, and I had definitely overused the muscles.

Eventually I was back to my computer. I had a new email, from a local man who said at least four of his neighbors had sold their homes in the last six months. He was worried they were all going to be turned into vacation rentals. I was a reporter—could I look into it? He chose to email me because he had liked my story about the dangers of wildfire smoke, a compliment that gave me a brief moment of pride. I could look into it, I thought excitedly but without responding. Once I finished this stupid turtle article and found some time I'd go down to the county headquarters and look up the property records. I didn't want to go to my editor without proof, though what it was proof of, except perhaps some small-scale short-term rental scheme? Perhaps she would find it boring, just like my boyfriend did, just a repeat of an article the other reporter had already done.

I turned my focus to the turtles for a while. I tried to share some interesting turtle facts with my boyfriend, since he liked nature.

"The sex of the turtles depends on the ambient temperature," I said. I read aloud a quote from the scientist: "'The female turtle urinates to make the ground soft, and she digs a hole and lays the eggs, and plugs the hole, and leaves. At that point her job is done.'"

"Hmm," he said, and I knew he was intrigued because he was interested in animal behavior, but he was also typing again, in his own world, which was kind of annoying but the clicking soothed me, the ambient noise of letters accumulating and lining up one after the other, the sounds of searching or creation. I turned my head slightly to look at him and saw the focused posture of his body, neck reaching slightly forward in communion with his laptop, the posture of absorption. I would have liked to take a picture of him in that intensity but he would never want to see himself like that, so in love with his computer. He was a person who did not want to think of himself absorbed like that, but I could see in his body that he loved his computer just as much as I did. He had his books but he spent hours at the screen, not as many as me but still, hours researching what plants he could eat or crush and rub on himself, because it changed, sometimes people figured out you could eat something they had thought you couldn't, and he looked for obscure routes and trails on websites with pictures of all the wonderful things you could see, and I know he looked at the pictures carefully to decide if it was worth going to see those things in person.

"Most of them don't make it, though," I went on. "The coyotes can smell the pee sometimes and they dig up the nests and eat the eggs. It's sad. I know you're not supposed to say that with stuff in nature. But it's sad, isn't it?"

He was quiet for a moment. "It is sad. But—maybe focus on the positive side . . ."

I sighed and turned back to my computer. I wanted to describe a broken yolk I had seen in the field, but Mirror kept writing *yoke yoke yoke*, so many times that I got distracted musing on the nonmeaning meaning of it, substituting the beginning of life with something that restricted you or slowed you down or tethered you to work, but it was random, it didn't mean anything for one to be substituted for the other, and looking for meaning in frustration was just a way to feel better, or perhaps just procrastinate. I turned the dictation off. With the mouse, I started clicking and cutting and pasting letters together into words, like a criminal collating a ransom note to hide their identity. But this method of composition was slow and I knew it was bad, it was fine manipulation.

As I was standing there I started to feel a horrible contraction, a crushing cramp, not in my hand but my lower abdomen.

It was unsettling because my period wasn't supposed to come for at least a week or two, not that I kept great track. Maybe it was early, I thought—oh, if I'd only known what was coming!—though I'd never felt anything so intense, like my insides were being compacted. But I was practiced at this point at keeping my face blank in the face of pain, and I breathed through my nose and in thirty or so seconds it passed.

"What are you doing over there?" I asked my boyfriend, trying to distract myself from feeling frightened about a whole other bodily issue.

"Evacuation group stuff," he said. "Do you think it went well? The meeting?" he asked, and I looked over and he was looking at me and not the screen.

"Yeah. Yes," I said. "It was—professional. So what are you doing there?"

"Just—just this and that, emailing people and trying to figure a few things out." He was quiet for a minute and then he said, "I mean, this is also—maybe the kind of thing you could help with.

Like I said before. A little bit of research help, and then writing things to, you know, help people get behind it."

I said I'd think about it but reiterated it was a little strange because it was being reported on in the paper, and even though I wasn't the one doing the reporting, I shouldn't be an advocate for anything. And what would happen if I learned something from his group that the paper should report on?

"Hmm," he said, back to typing. "I don't know. You seem more unhappy there than ever. How long are you going to be there, anyway? Especially with . . . and, you know, our future. Living in community. Having a—family. Maybe here."

"Well, don't you think that's a ways off? And how could it really be here?"

"Maybe there's a way. Maybe a ways off. But who knows?" he said.

"I—I need to think about it," I said, and turned back to my notes. What had impressed me during the conversation with the turtle expert was just how passionate he was. Could I ever be as passionate about anything as he was about these reptiles? I'd happily followed him on his tangents and kept asking questions to feed his excitement, because he'd made me excited about his project and I needed his emotions in the story.

"Dictation on," I said, but then my boyfriend was behind me, snaking his arms around my waist and resting his head on my shoulder. He started miming typing. He said he'd be my hands and laughed a little but I didn't think that was funny, especially when I saw on the screen his words perfectly rendered.

He saw his words there and said it looked like my program worked pretty well.

And I thought then the problem with Mirror really wasn't that it was a shoddy program, but that for some reason it understood everyone but me.

Just then my phone beeped. I asked my boyfriend to see what it was, and he checked and told me Lee had texted. She wanted me to come over very soon, that night if possible. She was ready to see me. She had some results from the Axon.

My heart leapt, from excitement or revulsion I don't know. I looked at my screen. I wanted to be a turtle that could retract into the shell of its own body, into a body that was also an impenetrable home. I didn't want to go. What I wanted wasn't clear—I wanted physical therapy to relax me, I wanted the stupid worksheets to process whatever needed processing, I wanted my boyfriend to research what kind of pains can arise in hands and what kind of pains can arise in lower abdomens, I wanted his concern to take the form that mine would have if he were in my position. I didn't want to go further down some absurd path.

Without looking at him I asked, "Do you think I should go? Do you trust her?"

He took some long seconds to respond. "I—I . . ." he said, stretching out that pronoun until it turned into a meditation. I looked at him, wonderingly. "I—yes," he pronounced. "I do trust her. And you shouldn't be working so late. You should go, now."

Some Axon Results

I arrived at Lee's cabin in the last light of the late spring sun, a season that should have brought feisty winds from the churning ocean but instead the air was strangely still and dry and warmer than was normal for this time of year, little by little drying out the trees and shrubbery. I'm not always good at remembering the setting of things, even the settings of my own life, but I think I remember that unsettlingly still air because the eerie atmosphere seemed to evaporate once I arrived, because the mood in her home had changed yet again. My last visit had felt austere, Lee had made herself severe and cool in order to thermodynamically draw the hot truth out of me, but now everything was fuzzier and cozier. A big chair where she told me to sit was covered in a sheepskin pelt, and I'd barely settled in before she gave me a warm mug of chamomile tea and a light blanket. Lee sat across from me in an office chair, a notebook at a side table and a few stapled pages in her lap. She was wearing a light pink wool cardigan over a linen button-up and khaki pants as if imitating a therapist. Perhaps she was. Or perhaps she was vaguely imitating me and my bland taste in fashion, like she was a more tailored and capable version of me, and I could easily be fixed and improved if I just adhered to her instruction. Looking at her and around the cabin, I remembered that her landlord had bought my old cottage. I wondered what their plans were for it, if they would make it look so deliberate and precisely designed as this place.

Lee asked me gently how I was doing.

"Fine," I said, fidgeting, not sure what to do with my hands, which since the evacuation meeting were more and more easily set off. Or maybe it was the brief respite that maybe hadn't been a respite that made it seem worse, although I knew objectively it was worse, because I couldn't even use my phone, and it did seem at this point that there were more random shots of pain in my fingers. As I sat there all I wanted to do was hide my hands somewhere; I felt somehow they might give themselves away, that if she saw them she would know something had happened to them. I didn't want her to know they had been better after her treatment, even if there was no proof of cause and effect. I didn't want her to have anything over me. I thought of hiding them under the blanket, but given that they were the whole point of me being there, hiding them would make it even more obvious something had happened in them.

And maybe after all I did want her to know.

Maybe I did want to be seen by her.

She raised her eyebrows. "How are you *really* doing? I want you to really check in with your body. Close your eyes and take a deep breath."

There was something character-like about the way she spoke.

Not that it was fake, but maybe the opposite, that she was so completely immersed and utterly in thrall to what she was saying and how she was saying it. I went along. I closed my eyes. I took a deep breath. Following the order calmed me.

"Okay. I'm not great, I guess," I said, admitting that work wasn't going well. "And . . ."

"And . . ."

Maybe it was fine to trust her or to play at trusting her. Didn't I need to pursue each potential remedy through to the end, wherever the end was?

"And—after the—treatment, or analysis, or whatever, the pain in my hands—it felt like it was fading—maybe. It's hard to tell if it really was, or if it was just because I'd been good, and not using them. But then—the other day, I was using my phone and it all came rushing back worse than ever. But if the Axon was really curing me, using my hands, fine manipulation—that shouldn't have made it worse. Right? If it was a treatment . . . shouldn't using my hands have been less painful, not more?"

Lee's eyes widened a bit and she nodded in that way people do to convey thoughtfulness, to show they are taking you seriously. Now I wonder if she knew certain things in advance, if she understood that I would tell her anything, and maybe she only looked a little surprised I had given it all to her so easily. But even if you know certain things in advance it doesn't necessarily mean it's not real.

"I can see why you'd think that," she said. "It's confusing, isn't it? But it doesn't surprise me, based on the results so far," and she waved the stapled papers that were apparently the Axon's analysis like a victorious flag. "It makes perfect sense, actually. But don't worry. Your case isn't that complicated! This is one of the shortest diagnoses I've ever seen. Sometimes they're as long as twenty pages. This is only three."

"Oh . . ." I said.

Although it was all bonkers, I was annoyed. I thought I'd be one of those people requiring reams of pages because I was such a complex person, but maybe I wasn't complex at all.

Lee reiterated, looking over the pages, that the Axon didn't print clear diagnoses the way I might be expecting. "It takes careful reading and—interpretation to understand what the Axon's saying. But I can see you don't quite trust it."

"Maybe I don't," I said. "But—I don't know. Sometimes I even think the way Mirror messes up what I say—sometimes I find myself even trying to interpret that . . . do you ever . . ." But I trailed off because her eyes widened but in real surprise, then narrowed, like she was trying to decide how bonkers I was, and I quickly said, Never mind, never mind, I was joking, joking!

"Well—anyway. Do you want to look? It might not inspire much trust initially. But you like documents, don't you? That's what the Axon said, at least," she said with a little laugh, getting us back on her track, and without waiting for an answer she laid the printout in my lap as I felt another uncomfortable cramp.

It was one of the most bizarre documents I'd ever seen.

Each line of text was numbered twice, the first row of numbers a simple count. The second row of numbers seemed as random as a lottery ticket but that was by far the least of my confusion. The first issue was that half of it wasn't in English or any script I'd ever seen. And the English information seemed either meaningless, or potentially potent with meaning but without enough context to guide me, or just bizarre. Intermixed at random with text that was almost hieroglyphic were various foods or words related to food: TOMATOES (HAPPINESS) and ANISE and HARDBOILED EGGS (SADNESS) and PHYTIC ACID and MISC FOOD PRESERVATIVES. Then there were curious phrases like IMPONDERABLE HOMOPATHIC REACTS IMPONDERABLE and YOKED HELPLESSNESS YOKED. Then various diseases or health problems, only some of which seemed recognized by modern medicine: TOXIC SHOCK SYNDROME and URINARY RETENTION and NO 20 CONSTITUTION DISORDER. Then random words here and there, between symbols: ANTAGONIZE and BLOOD and EMPTY.

After a few minutes, she very slowly took the papers out of my hands.

It had taken her longer to decipher the diagnosis than she had expected, she said, because although my case wasn't complicated once she unpacked the most important parts of the printout, the printout itself was a smidge more enigmatic than normal, perhaps reflecting an unconscious—or conscious—resistance on my part to give myself fully to the energy of the universe, or whatever, during treatment.

She saw in these pages a few primary points of interest where she focused her efforts, she said. It seemed to her I was yoked and therefore unpleasantly tied to something, perhaps work—given that yokes were associated with working animals—that was not my life's purpose. The hardboiled egg—well, eggs were often related to childhood or one's child, and this was perhaps both. I'd thought about having children and yet worried I'd thought about it for so long that the dream of it would soon be cooked, so to speak. And yet it also called back to a childhood in which I felt a distance from a parent, perhaps I'd betrayed them, I'd failed as a daughter, like an egg cooked instead of incubated to full life, and of course the relationship was irreparable because my mother was dead. And I was scared, perhaps, that this would happen if I had children, I wouldn't know how to properly care for them?

Her analysis was disturbing and dizzying and insane, although it was true—it was true—I did feel certain things she had mentioned . . .

"That's quite a lot of analysis from one phrase," I said.

"The symbology of the words points me to the most—potent areas," she said.

According to the document, she went on, I was trying to cure myself in some way. Cure myself of myself. But I didn't *really* want to be the person I was trying to be, and maybe what I really wanted—what I couldn't tell myself I wanted—was to be a mother. "But you're too ashamed to admit it?" she said. "Maybe that's what the Axon's picked up on. Maybe that's what the disorder is trying to tell you."

Wasn't her analysis a little boring?

And yet the Axon seemed to know things.

Maybe I was just boring, boring and uncomplicated.

Maybe it was operating on the same principles as psychics who use a smidge of information to formulate vague and common predictions. I had never told Lee my mother was dead. But perhaps my boyfriend had mentioned it.

And yet what if he hadn't? What if the Axon did work? What if my inner turmoil was actually extremely boring? What if, in my secret heart that was secret from even myself, I wanted, just like my own mother, to be a mother?

"I won't pressure you to agree with me," Lee said. "But think about the Axon's assessment. There might be more here to unpack, but I need a little more time."

I was quiet for another few moments.

"What about everything else? Like . . . the tomatoes and whatnot?" I said.

"Like I said, I'm not totally sure of everything. But there's a lot of—noise in the universe. Some of it appears in the results, but the symbology helps direct my focus to what matters. And I think you're catching on to something, because the tomatoes do seem important. Tomatoes often point to gardening," she said, leaning forward toward me. "They're often one of the most bountiful plants in a garden. And they're one of the easiest to preserve. For the future. For one's own nourishment. It's a sign of—fortitude and self-reliance," she said in a way that I almost wondered if she was making it up on the spot. And yet there was a real passion and excitement in her voice, her eyes almost sparkled, although perhaps that was the fake fire in the fake woodstove reflected in her corneas, but still her excitement reminded me of uncovering some covert connection between things that would help a group of occurrences become an actual story.

And maybe what she was saying really did make sense.

I was about to ask her about my disorder's increased sensitivity but she seemed attuned to my mind's movements. "And as for your experience of your disorder—as for what you described as the improving, then worsening pain," she said. "So it got better, didn't it—until you overtaxed yourself at work. I think the disorder is telling you something. I think it's been trying to tell you something this whole time. But you haven't listened, and now it needs to speak a little louder. It's true, maybe the Axon strengthened its voice. Is that so bad? The question, ultimately, is: Are you going to listen?"

The longer she talked the more jittery I felt. I drank my now-cold chamomile tea. I didn't really want to believe the Axon. It was completely insane. She was the one who was bonkers, not me! But maybe it wasn't insane. Maybe I didn't know myself better than anybody or anything else.

"Your landlords bought my old house," I said suddenly.

She shook her head. "You really don't want to engage. With the Axon. I think I was wrong . . . maybe you weren't ready. But the Axon's not wrong, so maybe it just needs time to sink in," she said. "And as for that—well, they've bought a place or two. It's not like I talk to them often, but obviously they're wealthy. It's an investment, I guess. Though they've also talked about starting an artist's retreat. You know how the rich are. They have all sorts of ideas."

I Visited My Dad and It Was Mostly Fine

After I told my dad the results of the nerve test, he suggested I come to the doubly panhandled state to visit him.

At first I said: no no no.

I suggested he come to me instead.

He'd always wanted to visit in the spring, when it was more lush and green than usual, though this spring wasn't exactly the way spring was supposed to be; it had rained in the winter but prematurely stopped and on top of the previous year's drought, the landscape was a struggling kind of green. But still it was nice. I said I didn't want to interrupt my physical therapy, I had an MRI scheduled soon, I didn't want to take time off work. But in the end I agreed to a long weekend, to reassure him I was all right, although I wasn't all right, especially after the mindfuck that was Lee's Axon analysis and especially as I neared the end of the number of therapeutic hours the worker's compensation clinic had allotted me, and the MRI might be the last service they provided.

Anyway. I agreed to go but I was worried. It felt dangerous to go home with the disorder. What if being in that home with the disorder, with something mysterious and ineffable wrong with me, elicited some new extra-potent grief over my mother? It was dangerous. Sometimes an extra shot of grief for someone can be curiously addictive, because although grief is painful it also connects you to that person so viscerally. I even asked the disorder: *Do you want to go there? Do you want to be in that house?*

But it was silent.

Still, maybe something would be revealed to me at home, I thought. Maybe in a new place I'd learn something about what the disorder wanted. It was complicated trying to consider what it wanted, whether the disorder just hated computers like my boyfriend thought, or hated the news, like perhaps my editor thought, or wanted me to be a mother like the Axon alleged. On the phone my father implied that perhaps—not that he was saying the disorder wasn't a real physical phenomenon!—even he was starting to succumb to psychological explanations when he implied that perhaps I was unhappy out west, perhaps I wanted to come home and pursue a stable life, perhaps it was getting worse because I didn't really want to *homestead or whatever—or is it some kind of commune he's thinking about?* He was concerned I was preparing to go whole hog in throwing away my life. And it wasn't that he didn't want me to settle down and start a family, he clarified. He'd like that very much. But wasn't that more prudent in a pleasant midsized city rather than starting a whole new community, or whatever, from scratch?

Anyway. My boyfriend didn't come.

I'd wanted him to initially. Together we could explain our plans for our future, after the awkwardness at the end of my father's visit. I needed my boyfriend to explain the vision coherently. But he was busy with the practice evacuation. I tried to argue that it was only a few days, but he said things were proceeding quickly, he was more optimistic about the group than ever. I asked if there had been disagreements between then, but he brushed my question aside; there would always be disagreements in communal planning, but they were more and more seeing his point of view, about what he didn't really say.

In truth I thought my boyfriend didn't want to come because he didn't want to face additional interrogation over the life he wanted. He didn't feel the need to defend his life to anyone, something I envied but could never absorb from him. Still I kept pressing, I pressed hard for reasons I can't quite comprehend, and before I left I blew up and screamed that he needed to have a passable relationship with my father if we were going to have a child, and if he couldn't come for a few days then how could we have a family?

On the plane ride I worried about leaving in anger, although he'd seemed calm, quietly giving me a few tinctures to take with me, the ones I'd been taking for a few weeks now. But a part of me was relieved to be on the trip alone. I wasn't sure what the disorder wanted but maybe it wanted me to go home alone. Maybe there was something in the house it wanted me to see. At the very least I could go into the attic, where my father stored all my mom's old possessions. I liked to roam about the cardboard boxes of her old books and plastic storage bins of her old clothes and even the horrid genocidal paraphernalia she had collected and collected and not dealt with before dying.

I got there in the evening, having lost some hours in the sky, and my dad took me to a new restaurant. In my childhood we went almost exclusively to chain restaurants and ate chicken tenders and mozzarella sticks. But now there were independent restaurants, this one featuring local meat and mushrooms and dishes inspired by the traditional cuisine of the region. The town was becoming a whole new town, my father said, more than once, a town I might find more interesting than I had in my youth. Maybe next time I could bring my boyfriend, he said pointedly as we sat down, and we could all visit one of the many beautiful rural regions of the state.

When the waiter came my dad ordered a dozen raw oysters, which seemed odd since I lived in a place famous for oysters and we were in a landlocked state. But they came with a mignonette with local ramps and my dad wanted me to try these oysters, which came from the southeastern coast of the country, which wasn't too far away, which was another desirable place to live, he said, with oysters and nature and nice restaurants just like where I lived. The oysters came served on beds of coarse salt in their little open caskets. But my dad only ate a few, slurping three in quick succession and encouraging me to eat the rest. At first I ate only a few, and they were delicious and easy to slurp because it was a nice restaurant so they ensured that the muscle of the oyster was detached from the shell, free to slide into your mouth along with the savory liquid it had once lived in. But I could see that my dad wanted me to eat all of them, as a treat, and so I did, and for hours after it was like a gelatinous sea had settled in my stomach.

"You know I read about something pretty interesting this morning," my dad said after we ordered our entrées, chicken and morels over dumplings for him and some fancy heirloom beans and cornbread made with heirloom corn for me.

"Oh yeah?" I said, and was relieved he wasn't asking about me.

First he talked about an experiment mentioned in an article in some online magazine, where researchers tricked subjects into believing they had been burned, and many actually suffered second-degree burns even though it was all in their heads. But he quickly saw I didn't want to talk about that, even though I recognized that it was interesting. So he switched to something else he'd read about, a computer experiment in which people attached to nodes were instructed to think of a letter. A computer read the person's brain waves and almost always displayed precisely the letter the person had conjured in their mind. "If you had a program like that, you could write without having to type or even move!" he said, and I knew he was trying to make it lighthearted.

"Right. It would be a little slow, though," I said, and laughed a little to go along with the jovial nature of the conversation, but I was nervous he might start talking about my disorder and I didn't want to with all the oysters there in my stomach.

"But soon it'll be entire sentences. I mean, this isn't just about people who can't—for whatever reason. This could be for everyone. We'll just think our texts or emails or whatever and the computer will, you know, manifest it on the screen. Or maybe there wouldn't even be a screen anymore."

He didn't seem to find it very disturbing. But I did because I loved typing.

Our food came. I tore a piece of cornbread with my hands and dunked it into the soupy beans and took a big savory bite. My mother never cooked beans or cornbread. She would have hated this restaurant.

"Maybe you wouldn't have even developed your—thing, if we were living a few decades in the future," he went on.

"Right," I said again. "I guess it's too bad we're not in the future yet . . ."

Then he brought up something else he'd read about: some recent study or poll found that newspaper reporters were some of the most unhappy people.

※

I thought in coming to my dad it would be easier to ward off his questions about my life and my disorder, but I was wrong. He knocked on my bedroom door early the next morning, asking if I wanted to help with his sourdough for pizza he would cook that night. Before my mom died no one ever cooked but her, but now my dad made pizza. I could tell he wanted to have a conversation. I said I needed more sleep because of the time difference, but once he left I lay awake for a while in my childhood bed. I looked at the drop door on the ceiling, which could be pulled down to release the stairs to the attic. I decided to wait until I was alone in the house to ascend.

So instead I got up and looked through the things in my room. Whenever I came home I looked through everything, things I didn't want but also didn't want in the garbage, or precious things I thought would be safer here. There were pictures on a corkboard of people I no longer knew, and a spelling trophy that once felt like my greatest accomplishment, after my mother had spent hours drilling me, her reading words out of a little booklet and me breaking them apart into their letters. In the closet I considered each shirt and dress and coat. So much of the material was stretchy, I noticed, so much of my old clothing contained stretchy unnatural fibers. But I'd learned on the other coast that clothes shouldn't stretch. Pants should be broken in through brute force and linen button-ups should soften over time, since time was the natural catalyst, since the combination of time and repetition was the natural and best way to make things fit right. Although I still never felt I looked quite right. Not like Lee, in her linen pants and the balloon-sleeve cardigan, not like Lee who, inhabiting so much looseness, managed to look so elegant, like she knew just how to navigate such spaciousness. And not like my editor, always in her uniform of neat, slim, dark-wash jeans and loose black pullovers.

My dad knocked again. He heard me walking around. Downstairs, the kitchen smelled like butter and sugar and cinnamon and cooked fruit, unfamiliar scents in the house, to me at least, since my mother hadn't been a baker. She liked sweets but she stuck to ice cream and chocolate bars from the freezer. She preferred sweets extremely cold, and she rarely ate fruit and didn't care about cinnamon. *Unfamiliar* isn't really the right word for the smell of the kitchen, though, because she has been dead for a while and my dad picked up baking years ago. But still it was disorienting. I foraged fruit and baked in my new home, but I didn't want to like those things here. Yet there was my dad handing me a blueberry muffin he made. He was proud of his blueberries. It was too early for fresh ones but he kept a huge store in his freezer, which he proudly showed me. Then as if it were totally natural for one subject to lead to another, he casually asked to see the report of my nerve tests, and we again went over my symptoms, and what the nerve test had found, which was nothing. My dad read, nodding his head the way doctors are perhaps taught to nod affirmingly like that, like a boat bobbing on a sea with the tiniest of waves. I sat quietly and ate the buttery muffin.

"Well, okay. Okay. This is a good thing, Kim. You don't want injured nerves."

"I know, I know, I know," I said.

He took me into the backyard and showed off his garden. It was still early in the season, but he had kale and peas and even asparagus. He showed me his prized garlic. Somewhere between the garlic and the showcasing of his blueberry bushes, he pressed his case that I could come home, perhaps using the garden as enticement. I wouldn't have to pay rent, which was obviously important, he said, since I couldn't have much saved given my salary. I could rest and be away from everything, maybe that would ease my symptoms. He sighed for what seemed many reasons. He said it would be nice, to have me home for a bit. He knew therapists, cognitive behavioral therapists he could contact.

I said vaguely I would think about it. I took my phone out of my pocket and looked at it, if only to look at something, if only to break away from the pressure of his gaze. He backed off finally, wondering if some areas of the garden needed more amending. It was still strange, to see him with a garden, to listen to him talk about sourdough, things he had never done or even talked about doing until my mom was dead, when he was spurred into life in some way.

Maybe I could come home, I thought briefly. I could garden. No! No! No!

I couldn't. I couldn't go home and do nothing, because I had seen what doing nothing was and when you start doing nothing it turns into a hole you never get out of.

I asked if he had other ideas, besides coming home and therapy, though still I didn't look at him, still I kept looking at my phone, scrolling through old emails, thinking maybe I'd find one that would remind me of my job and my life and why it was important. "You're a doctor . . . Don't you have any other suggestions?"

He went into doctor mode. He elaborated on a medication historically used for seizures but sometimes now used for pain because it slows nerve function, though he admitted it could affect my mental function. Then he said that, although he didn't think I had an autoimmune issue, he'd gotten me a prescription of steroids, though there were side effects. "You might have a hard time sleeping, or get pretty hungry. But it's just a ten-day course. It's like a little test. If you take them and your pain goes down, that says your immune system could be . . . Are you okay?" he said, because I'd put the phone down and started squeezing my hands into fists and closed my eyes and groaned a bit.

"Yeah, I'm fine. Just—it's tough, now, to use the phone . . ."

He watched my hands for some seconds as I kept squeezing them and rolling my wrists around. "Well, that's no good. Not good."

He liked to repeat things.

"Let's go to the store, get stuff for dinner," he said, and I was glad because my dad and I used to go to the store every week, both of us trying to decipher my mother's horrible handwriting. It was a different kind of bad handwriting than mine, which was uniformly tiny and sharp, and different than his, which was airy and dilated with letters that all seemed to want to be the same letter. My mother's handwriting had a half-cursive loopiness to it with huge capital letters followed by thin tails of the rest of the word.

We went to the store and walked around downtown. That night we made sourdough pizzas on his new pizza peel, and I made a salad, and we opened a bottle of wine. I thought maybe there wasn't any grand reason for this visit but it was nice to be here. After the store I'd scoured my room to see if a scrap of my mom's handwriting might be somewhere, maybe an old grocery list. It wasn't but it was okay; even if her handwriting was gone there were traces of her in the attic and maybe I'd take something and feel a little closer to her but not in a bad way, not in a way that would catalyze me into her, just something to hold close to my heart at times. Next time I'd bring my boyfriend and we would have a good time, and although I couldn't live here maybe there was a way to be closer, even though it was difficult to imagine leaving that other coast. But then very late, after my dad went to bed, I pulled the cord hanging from the ceiling in my bedroom, which released the stairs, and I climbed up to find the attic of her things completely barren. I walked around anyway as if something might suddenly appear, but there were no hidden corners in that attic. It was clear every last box and plastic tub was gone, the container of empty jewelry boxes gone, the remaining mysteries gone, the old clothes gone and definitely the paraphernalia of the midcentury European genocidal regime gone. Later my father said he and my sister had cleaned it out some months ago, I never mentioned wanting any of it, it had been there for years. He said I didn't even read mysteries. He said all the things I said to myself as I walked and walked and walked and walked the perimeter of the emptiness.

I Decided to Obey the Pain

The other reporter's article about the evacuation meeting was long, so long that my editor put off one of my short assignments that week. I was grateful because my trip to the doubly panhandled state had put me more behind, and anyway I didn't even want to write that piece, about a new art exhibit featuring smudgy painted landscapes of this place, as if my editor thought writing about peaceful paintings might bring me solace or perspective. In fact landscapes of this place exasperated me. They were always bleary and benign, even though the land wasn't really like that. This painter stripped even the barest hint of menace from the precipitous crumbling sandstone cliffs and the sea below, which in real life foams like some rabid hungry animal.

When I read the other reporter's article on a Wednesday afternoon as we all proofed the paper before it was sent to the printer at the end of the evening, I worried at how my boyfriend would take it. The lede positioned my boyfriend and his comrades as *an inexperienced group of locals trying to organize a series of practice emergency evacuations in case of fast-moving inflagrations like those that took lives in other parts of the state in last year's record-setting flames* . . .

It wasn't fair to prejudice everyone against them, I thought at the time, at that point in time, though I wish he'd prejudiced people even more against them, I wish I'd been paying more attention to anything beyond my own stupid body!

Anyway.

I was starting to feel more defensive, even protective of them. Or perhaps I was forcing myself to take their side, starting to see that things with work were moving in an inevitable direction.

I went back to the other reporter's story. He had accidentally invented the word *inflagration*. I circled it with my red pen and wrote in the margin CONFLAGRATION! But then I crossed that out and rewrote it because it was almost completely illegible. My handwriting, though I used it more than ever, had gotten not better but worse. Maybe it was becoming more itself, or maybe it was becoming resistant to communication even though my handwriting was usually trying to communicate with my future self.

The article referenced a poorly publicized meeting and critiques from officials who weren't sure that practicing evacuating would do much to help people, because residents would receive robocalls and texts with information if evacuations truly came for us, that there was no formal evacuation plan from the government because there were too many variables, there was no way to know exactly what to do until a fire actually happened. We needed fuel breaks and better technology, not a *false sense of security*, the officials said, though they offered modest support and they would give the group radios and advice. The volunteer group pushed back in the article, arguing that official communications hadn't always come through in other fires, and that part of the importance of practicing was that at the very least we'd be a little more calm and collected in a real emergency. Their message was a bit scrambled at this point, because some of the organizers, including my boyfriend, were quoted as saying they hoped a practice evacuation would help but emphasized there were no guarantees, that practice could help but it would be safer to live somewhere with less danger of fire. The other reporter quoted various residents, some of whom supported a practice evacuation, but others agreed with the officials, and then others grumbled that all the media attention about a practice emergency evacuation might somehow spur more insurance companies to withdraw fire coverage of their homes. Some grumbled that maybe it was time to leave; it was getting more dangerous and yet they could still get a lot of money for their homes.

I worried that my boyfriend would be upset, but then I was upset that I had to worry about his reaction when he was part of the reason the story was taken from me. All I'd wanted was for the story to be mine, to bring disaster close but also distance myself from it by writing about it.

But how much did I really care at this point, that the story had been taken from me?

I'd been thinking more directly about what the disorder wanted since returning from my father's. I told my boyfriend about the empty attic, how in seeing that emptiness it felt that nothing of her was left, and somehow this catalyzed my desire to be myself a mother, and I didn't care what my father thought of our lives, I wanted soon to start a family. Soon, but not quite yet, maybe. Maybe I could finish one more important story.

But my boyfriend even pushed back on that *soon*.

He said while I was gone he too had been thinking about the disorder, and that, as I had offhandedly mentioned, I should consider what it wanted, and maybe instead of fighting it I should obey it, now. When I pushed back that I didn't have money saved up to let me let go of everything, and I wasn't going to ask my father to help, even the bonds wouldn't hold me over that long given our rent, he said not to worry. He had money saved up, though when I asked how much he was vague, clearly uncomfortable, he only said it was enough before finding his track again. Wasn't this what the Axon had said, in the end—I should listen to my body? Not that I needed the Axon to tell me that, it was clear the disorder wanted me to get away from my computer, and that particular pair of words had echoed in my head afterward: obey it, obey it, obey it.

Since that conversation I'd started to care a little less that my story had been taken. When I first started working at the paper I'd been so hungry to know things, but now I wasn't sure I wanted to know anything at all. Sometimes I wanted to be empty. Maybe the desire to be empty was another form the disorder was taking . . .

In the office, I circled a *TK* in the other reporter's story in my red pen and swiveled around in my chair to face him. "Forgot something," I said, tossing the printout onto his neatly organized desk, all his documents in neat stacks and every piece of paper held tight by a clip or staple or folder, and it looked so nice, to be stapled together, to be stacked and pressed so neatly. I swiveled back to my own desk. "Didn't realize you talked to my boyfriend," I said.

"He didn't mention it? I interviewed him after the meeting."

I turned back around. "Do you think this whole idea . . . I

mean you're skeptical, right? I'm reading between the lines here and . . . Maybe you think this idea is just silly."

"Hmm," he mused, pursing his lips and tapping his fingers. Finally he said he didn't think it was silly. It was only that something seemed funny about the whole thing, something he couldn't quite put his finger on. In interviews the organizers kept undercutting their own message for the evacuation, harping on the danger instead of how it could be abated, even though that was the whole point. And one of the organizers had said—during an interview, off the record, which in retrospect the other reporter regretted agreeing to—perhaps if anything there should be fewer people here, not more.

"Well," I said, wondering if my boyfriend was responsible for the change of heart, "people change their minds. I don't know . . ."

"Maybe I'm just overly suspicious," he said, though he didn't sound too convinced. "Anyway. How are your hands?" he asked, still typing. "How was the MRI?"

"My hands are—you know. The same." I held the pen more firmly. I started proofing one of my own stories, about a woman who won a Good Samaritan award from a local nonprofit, but I bored myself. The Good Samaritan hadn't been driven to good deeds by something interesting or specific, like a personal tragedy. Her desire to do good seemed to arise out of thin air.

"And the MRI?" he asked again.

I had kind of enjoyed the MRI.

I enjoyed the idea that someone was looking deeply inside me without needling me or pushing or pulling me or touching me at all. Instead my body was thrust into a big white vault of a machine and the main rule was to not move for about thirty minutes. The machine made interesting sounds, at first like industrial electronic music and then like the shooting of a laser gun, and then like the staccato of a jackhammer. The worst part was when my mouth started filling with saliva, a problem I hadn't anticipated. Eventually I swallowed. "Don't swallow so hard!" the technician immediately cried. I was so still for so long I felt my pulse in strange places in my body: my forearms, my toes, my mouth, it was as if my skin was vibrating on some strange frequency, begging me to do something. I felt distorted and explosive. In every part of my body I started to lose my sense of that part but was also somehow more attuned to it, like each part was begging to move so that I would not forget about it, as if I might leave behind a few body parts in the machine.

"It was fine," I said. "Didn't turn up anything. And then I got a blood test too, which was normal. Whenever they find nothing, they say it's a good sign. Anyway, I'm trying alternative treatments, too. Some new modalities. One's called the Axon. It's cutting-edge."

I don't know really why I told him that. He quickly started asking questions, and as I imagined trying to explain it, as I remembered how totally crackpot it had all felt, I put him off. I'd tell him after work, I said, with no intention of doing so. I took back the printout and read the other articles. The other reporter had another important piece about the sale of the local water company, which I'd totally forgotten was for sale. A cohort of locals, he reported, had formed a corporation to buy it, a list of people that included a familiar name that I realized was Lee's landlord. The big news was that they immediately, for the safety of the water supply, implemented a moratorium on new water hookups, effectively prohibiting new development, and I wanted to think about that, if it meant something, but then another painful cramp struck me, like my insides were being crushed as if in a trash compactor, and it was all I could do to breathe through it and read the rest of the paper.

When the cramp subsided and I was done, I handed the proofs to the editor, who was at the main computer. Its screen was wide in a way that always cowed me a little, though it was necessary for the toggling of text and photographs and advertisements. My own laptop was about the width of my shoulders, a size I found comforting. My editor stood before the broad screen engrossed in the layout of the ads, the grocery store that always ran big half-page ads with sales of the week, and real estate ads with bucolic descriptions of so-called country estates for millions of dollars and even listing the ones that had already sold, of which there were many this week, and then little ad boxes for restaurants and gift shops.

I liked to watch her gingerly tug at the edges of text boxes and delicately move ads one millimeter this way or that to ensure everything lined up just right. She was on to fiddling with the font size of headlines when I handed her my corrections.

"Thanks," she said, seeming a little tired, complaining that ad sales had been slow.

Then she added that she'd left some mail on my desk.

I found the envelope under loose piles of paper all mishmashed around the composite wood of my standing desk. I tore it open and laid the letter in my lap.

The letter was from the worker's compensation clinic.

It started by saying the clinic appreciated the opportunity to assist in my healing journey, that it had provided me with dozens of hours' worth of health care services, though I'd not taken advantage of the last few hours. The clinic said that since my workplace was accommodating my condition and I'd used most of my allotted hours and since I'd ceased to make progress and since my nerves were healthy and the MRI had found my neck and spine to be totally and completely normal, the clinic considered my case closed.

I folded up the letter and put it back into the envelope and stuffed the envelope into my backpack, where I knew it would become very crumpled and eventually mashed up with all the other bits of paper I didn't want or need.

After the paper was put to bed and the file emailed to the printer, the other reporter left. It was just me and my editor, and I sat down at my desk as she wheeled her chair over to me, as if it were clear to both of us what was about to happen.

She sighed a big sigh and ran her hand through her gray hair, still thick but losing some of its earlier bounce. For all the time I'd been at the paper her hair had been luxurious and airy, but these days it seemed flat and crushed. She was about to speak but then got up and pulled two bottles of beer from the mini-fridge. We hadn't had a beer together in a while, and it was nice, although I knew it wouldn't restore the mad energy of my early days. We both took big gulps. It was malty and comforting. She finally said she got a letter from worker's comp, that my coverage was considered complete.

I nodded. "Yup."

We were both quiet for a minute.

"What is that?" she suddenly said, looking under my desk.

She was pointing to a box containing a new piece of equipment I'd brought in that morning but hadn't yet set up, something I'd bought before deciding to give up or give in or whatever I was about to do. The box contained a mouse I could operate with my foot, to reduce even more the fine manipulation of my hands and address the fact that there was increasingly when I used my mouse that feeling—a pain in my fingertips like burning or maybe smoldering or maybe just heat. I searched for a mouse that didn't require hands, so my hands could just hang limp beside me. There were some devices a person could control with their tongue or mouth or eyes. There were many parts of the body that inventors put to use to control a computer. But I wanted something less noticeable, and many of those devices were marketed to people fully paralyzed, without any other means of communication, which made me feel like a fraud. I wasn't paralyzed. My limbs were all present. My hands were right there. Eventually I stumbled upon a foot-operated mouse, which worked poorly. When I moved the cursor it was difficult to place it where I wanted on the screen. I felt like an avian predator unsuccessfully trying to scoop up prey.

I took a sip.

She took a sip.

I looked at her more closely than I had for a while.

"Are you all right?" I said.

She put her bottle down on my desk, in the perfect center of one of the old indentations. She looked up at the skylight. It was now completely dark. "Yeah. No. I don't know. There's an offer for the paper. Way more than it's worth . . ."

I asked who it was, if they had offered details of why they wanted to buy it, but the offer had come through a whole series of assistants and representatives, promising good intentions but not willing to disclose their identities. She'd tried to find out more information but kept coming up empty, which was perhaps the biggest reason she hadn't just said yes. But maybe, she went on, even with more information she wouldn't give it up. Sometimes you're just doomed to love and hate the same thing, she said, though she wasn't quite sure whether it was the hate or the love keeping her there.

She went quiet and we took more synchronized gulps.

"I tried steroids recently," I said.

She raised her eyebrows. "Did anything . . ."

"No. Another dead end. Just like the MRI."

My father's theory seemed plausible: something in my body attacking itself. When you googled autoimmune disorders there were so many people who had them. It was becoming increasingly common for the human body to attack itself. Maybe the immune system was bored because our world was becoming cleaner, somehow even as the world fell apart it was also cleaner in certain ways, and the immune system needed something to do. Like all of us it just needed something to do, it needed to feel useful. But I was on day seven of the steroids, and nothing had happened. My pain felt the same. The warnings on the package had been numerous: possible side effects include extra energy and insomnia and the potential for unspeakable hunger, things that to be honest sounded at least useful. I could stay up working on my stories, and maybe an increased appetite would help me eat more of my boyfriend's nourishing cooking. But it gave me no extra energy or appetite. My body seemed unaffected by anything, as if whatever had caused the disorder was the last thing it would ever respond to.

I finished the rest of my bottle, holding it upside down for a moment to let the last foamy drips escape. We stared at each other for a few seconds, and then I asked, "Do you think this is all in my head?"

She looked down at her half-drunk beer, about to take another long gulp, but thought better of it. Maybe she didn't want any more. Maybe she was trying to become one of those people who could easily leave a drink unfinished. Instead she looked back up at me. "I think, for whatever reason, you are very, very stressed."

"I think it's time for me to take my—sabbatical," I said.

⁂

I stayed a little while after my editor left. I told her I wanted a little alone time in the office, which was partly true. But I also took a deep breath and opened up my laptop again. There was a moment of hesitation at what felt like betrayal although I wasn't sure if it was to myself and my ambitions or to my boyfriend, although how could it be a betrayal of him, unless it was possible I knew something without knowing it?

Anyway.

I emailed the other reporter that I thought there was an increase in home sales, that Mona was pressured by someone to sell her home and she believed there were others, that Lee's landlords had bought my cabin, and about the man who'd emailed me about so many homes on his block selling at once, and maybe it was all nothing, and yet someone who actually wanted to know things, which perhaps was no longer me, someone who still had that drive to put the pieces of things together, should look into it.

⁂

At home that evening, my boyfriend was making more soup, standing at a pot sipping and tasting the broth from a wild turkey he'd managed to trap in our backyard. I didn't say anything about the other reporter's article at first but announced I was officially taking time off. He hugged me. He said it was fortuitous timing, my sabbatical and the catching of the turkey, which he'd been trying and failing to do for weeks.

While he finished making dinner I placed my laptop on my makeshift standing desk. This is our last night together for a while, I thought. I wanted to cry. I wished we could be alone, without my boyfriend, and I could look up all the last things I randomly wanted to know before putting the laptop away. I turned on Mirror, but I couldn't think of what I wanted to know and I was tired of having my words mangled. I sat at the table and tried to let my mind go blank and calm. This should be easy, I thought, since I don't have a job anymore, I'm not a reporter anymore, I'm not a reporter and therefore there's no point to me at all. *You are not you.* Maybe it was better this way. Maybe it was better, to stop pretending I was someone I wasn't, to stop pretending I thrived on the absorption and creation of stories and information. Just smell the savory bird broth! I thought.

Soon he placed two steaming bowls of soup filled with chunks of squash and beans and bitter foraged greens on the table. I sighed. I hated those greens but when I brought up their bitterness he said they contained important compounds the body needed.

I took a first slurp from a wooden spoon. The broth was warm, with shiny slicks of bird grease on the surface. He'd made the stock last night, simmering bones and bits of meat for hours. My boyfriend said boiling the bones of the bird would transfer nutrients good for my own bones into the liquid. Maybe we should consider your bones, he said, maybe stronger bones would ensure your muscles and ligaments and nerves aren't overtaxed or compensating for the weakness of your very structure. Whatever, I'd thought at the time but didn't say. But maybe he was right. Or if not, then at least he'd made something delicious, because I hadn't thought I was hungry but then I was picking up the bowl and chugging the savory liquid. My boyfriend commented happily that I must like it, but then something in me concerned him. "Aren't you excited? To be free for a while? Sometimes it's so hard to read you," he added with a little nervous laugh.

I put the bowl down. "I don't know," I said. "Maybe this is all stupid. How can I obey something that doesn't even make sense? It hurts to use my computer, but also sometimes to fold laundry or wash the dishes, but then sometimes it doesn't hurt to do those things, and every once in a while it hurts when I'm not even doing anything . . ."

He shrugged. "Don't worry about that," he said, touching my cheek with his thumb in order to show tenderness, yet the contact made me realize he was slightly shaking. He was somehow both happy and nervous, or maybe he was hopeful but frightened. I asked if he was stressed. I finally mentioned the other reporter's article and how the other reporter had characterized them as amateur, and what he'd said about my boyfriend's stance and the shifting opinions of the others. My boyfriend didn't seem bothered. He was dismissive of the impact of the article, but asked if he and the others had been quoted, and I said yes, but that the other reporter had relayed how they amped up the danger of fire, and they were perhaps undercutting their message by focusing on the fact that nothing nothing nothing could make one truly safe. My boyfriend wasn't bothered by that either. He seemed relieved.

"Is that what you want?" I asked. "It just seems . . ."

"People need to know the truth," he said. "And that's the truth. Anyway, we don't need to talk about it now. Tonight's to celebrate a new chapter in your life."

After dinner I wanted to go for an evening walk, alone, to wrap my head around the idea of leaving my job but also because I was cramping again, the worst one yet, and I thought maybe I could walk it off. So I left and walked up the hill of our street, and tried to think about a new life. I thought, between cramps that had me bent over on the side of the road, about what other job I might do after my rest, if I didn't somehow decide to go back to the paper. Think about the future, I thought. I could start a family and live in whatever kind of happy community my boyfriend envisioned but it didn't mean I couldn't do something, eventually. Even at the paper I'd had all sorts of ideas about what other work might be fulfilling and meaningful, though it changed depending on who I was interviewing on a given week. I'd already considered being a baker of bread, studying psychology, working as a cheese importer, researching birds or maybe mushrooms, crafting unique preserves and jam and syrups, becoming a park ranger so I could walk around in the woods, applying to law school and working in environmental law. But I would be terrible at most of these things or maybe all of those things, I thought as I stopped once again and bent over and clutched my pelvis, and in reality I didn't want to really do any of them. I just liked writing about them. And I was doubtful the pain in my hands wanted me to do any of those things, given that most of them involved computers. Even park rangers needed sometimes to be on computers. I wished I could just explain to the disorder why I loved my computer, I thought as I breathed so hard, as if breathing could deflate the pain in my pelvis, and then the pain in my hands would have to give up, but the pain must have known these things, being inside me, and yet remained unconvinced, and maybe it was true that I just had to obey it.

I made it back to our cabin and ran to the bathroom and shut the door. My boyfriend asked if I was okay and all I could say was I don't know, and he asked if he should call an ambulance and I told him to wait, and I breathed and cried, and I unzipped my pants because the pain was clearly something about to exit my body, so I sat on the toilet and groaned at the tightening of my pelvis until I heard a little plop. Still crying, I looked down into the toilet bowl. There was a little piece of metal in there, the little piece of copper that had been implanted in my uterus many years ago, the little object preventing a pregnancy in me.

The Other Reporter Visited Me

A week after my last day at work and after the precious piece of copper dropped out of my uterus and my boyfriend said it was a sign, the other reporter visited me.

He had some questions.

Being interviewed made me nervous. I was usually the one asking questions. But in a way I liked being a subject, and I appreciated the skill with which he moved between asking questions and morseling out bits of information with which to goad me.

The other reporter texted beforehand to say he was coming, but I didn't see the message because, in trying to obey the disorder, my phone was in a black jewelry box. I don't wear jewelry, but after finding the empty attic at home and after crying and maybe briefly screaming at my father in a way that resembled my mother's screams, he found a few storage boxes in the garage he hadn't gotten around to dumping. I furiously excavated them. There wasn't much. One box contained only more boxes, specifically a cache of black jewelry boxes. Some were made of velvet and some of a strange fake leather, and some snapped open and shut with spring-loaded hinges and others had tightly nesting lids. But they were alike in one way: empty. That didn't matter to me, because as I said I don't wear jewelry and even my mother didn't wear most of the jewelry she bought. I did wonder where it had gone, though. Maybe she had sold it on the internet to buy the midcentury genocidal paraphernalia, or pay off some of the debt she incurred by buying the jewelry in the first place. Or perhaps my sister had pawned it in order to make up for the fact that she never found a savings bond for herself, and this thought, that she may have pawned it and maybe we were even, was comforting.

Something stood out about one box, a box made of soft velvet and sharp corners and embossed with a golden leaf. I liked the leaf. Maybe it once contained a leaf pendant to hang on a neck, or a bracelet to encircle a wrist completely in golden leaves. I stored the savings bonds and this velvet box in my bedside table, side by side, not one in the other, because the bonds couldn't fit in the box without being folded and I didn't want them folded, because even though they were thirty years old they were still so crisp.

After I quit the paper I found I needed both things, the bonds and the box.

I put my phone in the box and asked my boyfriend to check it every once in a while, because touching that screen for even just a few seconds left my fingertips feeling—maybe the right word is *dissolving*, though that wasn't an adjective on Dr. W's list.

I was alone when the other reporter knocked on my door in the late morning, three assertive and spacious knocks, perhaps a pattern he used on people who wouldn't respond to emails or phone calls. The other reporter had never been to my house and it was weird to see him outside the office, not dressed in his usual button-ups and khakis and loafers but instead wearing track pants and sneakers. Sweat peeled from his forehead and soaked the sternum of his shirt. He smelled like something left to ferment but forgotten. It was shocking to see him sweating so profusely, there was usually something cool and effaced about him, I couldn't believe he had that much moisture and stench waiting inside him.

"I jogged here," he said, smiling happily. "Did you get my text?"

I said I hadn't but he was welcome inside. As he made his way to the couch his eyes darted around quickly and efficiently, looking probably for illuminating details as if I were the subject of a profile he planned to write, assembling some version of my home in his head or at least some concentrate of it he could reconstitute later.

"It's not usually so messy," I said, picking up piles of old notepads off the couch.

"So that's how you spent your first free week. Going through your notes," he said in what I think was admiration.

"I was thinking I should clear things out. I won't need them for—a while. And I don't have a lot of storage here. I was actually keeping all this in the trunk of my car. But I think I'll put them back there, for when, or—if, I come back . . ."

I finished clearing off the couch and then cleared a wine bottle from the coffee table. It was the most expensive bottle of wine I'd ever bought. It wasn't right to be spending frivolously, but in a way it wasn't frivolous. I bought the bottle after going to the bank and depositing the savings bonds, which were finally matured in their entirety.

I hadn't known about the bonds until after my mother died, because she never mentioned them. In fact she had almost certainly forgotten about them or at least misplaced them; otherwise she would have made me sign them back over to her to pay off her shopping debt. It wasn't until my mother's room was cleaned up afterward of empty alcohol bottles and pill bottles and cigarette ash and piles and racks of stuff and stuff and stuff that my father discovered the bonds in one of her jewelry boxes. She probably bought the bonds and put them in the box and never touched them again.

Or maybe she hadn't forgotten or misplaced them. Maybe she wanted me to have some money, a means of being self-reliant, in case something bad happened to me, and she must have believed something bad would eventually happen to me. She was a big believer in bad things. Of course if she'd really wanted me to have a source of my own money it would have been helpful to mention their existence. Maybe she was planning to tell me but didn't get around to it. After all, whether a death is planned or unplanned or somewhere in the gray choppy middle you can't get around to everything before you die.

On the day I took the bonds to the bank, I spent a long time sitting in my car in the parking lot, looking at them. For a while I looked just at the envelope they came in, because bonds come with their own special envelopes or at least they did when she bought them. This one said A GIFT FOR YOU and PAYING BETTER THAN EVER. There was an oval hole cut out of the envelope so the man pictured on the bond was not hidden. He looked out through his window but not quite at me, like God. I wondered if there wasn't some way to keep the pieces of paper instead of exchanging them for money. But I didn't want to rely entirely on my boyfriend, and perhaps I could save a portion for some future baby, which now seemed imminent without the metallic protection to make my womb inhospitable. So I went into the bank and soon enough, instead of the man looking through his window, I had ten thousand dollars in my bank account. Afterward I wondered what to buy first with that money, and even though it wasn't a good thing, she did love red wine, or at least drank it regularly, which was close enough to love, and perhaps soon enough I wouldn't be able to drink, so I bought a fifty-dollar bottle and brought it home. My boyfriend rarely drank but we split the bottle, first a glass each and by the end pouring small sips into each other's mouths and laughing, me drunkenly joking that even while inebriated he understood me better than Mirror. I was grateful, I said as I took the last swig from the bottle, to be done with Mirror for the moment, maybe forever. The idea of never returning, of never having to ask anyone anything ever again, made me giddy. But then I cried a little, I cried and said, Why didn't Mirror understand me? My boyfriend grabbed my hands with a strange passion and said, It wasn't you, Kim, it wasn't you, it was about—it was about—well, who knew, he said, then sprang to assurances that this period of rest would be so good for me, and now that I didn't need the old tinctures—he was talking fast and I assumed he meant I didn't need them because I wasn't working—he'd make me a new one, a fertility tincture. The camping trip we were going on in a couple days, he went on, would jump-start everything. Without being on the computer and my phone for hours each day, my hands would heal in no time, he said, rubbing them with his hands that were always so much warmer than mine, rubbing and rubbing like friction itself was some special healing poultice.

The other reporter and I sat down, me in the one comfortable chair and him on the couch. We made small talk for a bit. I'd accidentally left my Axon printout on the couch, and he gave me a bemused look until I told him it was from that innovative therapy I'd once told him about. He asked if my sessions had gone well, if Lee knew what she was doing, and I was defensive but also wondered if I'd ever mentioned Lee specifically. Then he shifted gears—he wasn't ready to get into it, he was clearly warming me up as a subject, and I respected that—and asked if I'd be back in a few months. He said, in a way that seemed genuine, that he hoped I would. I said I wasn't sure, but maybe, maybe if my hands repaired themselves or rested sufficiently. My boyfriend, I said, had once talked of moving but now suggested he might want to remain here. The other reporter seemed about to say something but I talked over him, asking, if I returned, if he would be there.

He leaned back into the couch and exhaled as if unable to answer while maintaining good posture. It reminded me of his chair in the office behind me, creaking as he leaned back while he interviewed someone on the phone. Finally he said, "Well, I think," then took another pause, clearly considering how much to reveal. "I might—well, I was offered a job, at a different paper. Daily paper. Bigger city. Which is tempting—I miss that relentlessness. But that paper isn't doing well. They'd probably lay me off in six months. And—there's another option. I might try to buy the paper. Our paper."

I wasn't expecting that.

He went on, explaining that our editor was considering selling to the semimysterious cohort that had approached her over email, though she had asked him if he had any interest in making an offer. I tried to imagine him at the helm instead of her, everyone gathered around him instead of her, awaiting new stories. He was always so calm. Even at the office when I heard people yelling at him over the phone, even when occasionally people came to yell at him in person, he remained outwardly composed, as if there were some secret force field around him such that no one could truly touch him, and maybe in a way there was. Maybe that was the kind of person who should own a small village paper where everything was a little personal. In my heart I didn't want to own that paper, but I did want to be the kind of person who wanted to own the paper.

I asked him, as his eyes started wandering again around the cabin, if he might really buy it.

"I really might," he said, but he wanted our editor to string the potential buyers along, to see if she could squeeze any more information out of them. When I asked if he knew who it was, exactly, his eyes snapped back to me, lit up with new excitement, new intrigue and glee, and without him telling me I knew the answer.

It wasn't only Lee's wealthy landlords, he said, there were multiple people involved in the corporate entity offering to buy the paper, but Lee's landlords were the names he knew I'd quickly recognize. And that was why he'd come. He wanted to write a story about their offer to buy the paper and he wanted to find out as much as he could about them, and I'd written about that house they built, at least in the planning stage.

"You've obviously been there or at least seen it, since it was built, since Lee's been—treating you or whatever," he said.

"I—yeah, just once or twice," I said vaguely, not wanting to delve into the specific embarrassments of what I'd submitted to.

But the other reporter didn't seem interested in the Axon. He took out his voice recorder and a notepad. He wanted to ask me a few questions for his own story, about the landlords and the property, anything I might have seen while visiting Lee or anything I remembered from my story, maybe seemingly unimportant things I'd left out of the article.

I said sure. At first he just went over the details in my article and asked me to elaborate on anything if I could. He asked about the trees they cut down and the neighborly complaints and we laughed because neighbors getting absolutely enraged was always a little funny, but then he slowly pressed on how much reporting I'd done on those landlords, how deeply I'd investigated them. I don't remember, I said, and he gave me look, a look like yes you do, yes you do remember, and then I admitted perhaps I hadn't done much investigation into their background. I'd found out when they'd bought the property and how much they had paid and I had gone down to the county to obtain the records on the permits and plans for the property and I'd looked up the development rules for that area; the original plans had been massive and the project was scaled back and the affordable cottage added to appease county planners and the neighbors. But did you try to find out about their background, the other reporter asked, did you try to find, I don't know, past business partners? People with that much money must have fucked someone over at some point, don't you think? I don't know, I said, and the other reporter kept pressing, So you didn't look into how exactly they amassed their fortune? Or I don't know, anything they invested in, peculiar interests or obsessions? The rich often have weird pet projects. No, I said, but he kept finding different ways to ask the same questions, maybe he hoped I really did know something but I didn't know anything, and I wished in that moment that I had told him more about the Axon, maybe he'd ask me about that instead, maybe he would have pursued a story about the Axon instead, and I could have given him a potent scene about being in Lee's cabin and having a weird strap wrapped around my head and Lee's assertion that I wanted a child, that I didn't want a stressful yet meaningful career at all, and how I worried it might be true, that everything she said might be true—maybe I could have distracted him from my failures. He wasn't searching for my failures exactly but in his pursuit of knowledge they were there, I admitted I'd never even managed to meet the landlords, they declined all interview requests, I only talked to their representative, and he asked if I ever tried to show up where they worked, an office perhaps, and I said no no no.

But no one ever reached out? he went on. Because you wrote multiple stories about it—no one they knew ever reached out? And then I hemmed and hawed but he managed to extract from me that yes, one time someone had emailed claiming to know them, claiming the landlords were manipulators always framing themselves as do-gooders, just like this historic property they promised to caretake when really they just wanted a country estate, or . . . what had they said? I thought but didn't say aloud. And what happened? the other reporter asked, and I admitted it had been after the last story I'd written about it, when the whole business over the property and permits had come to a close, approved with the required amendments, and I never emailed that man back.

By the end I felt rawly open, freshly spliced. I was upset and yet jealous, of his skill, the way he'd drawn it all out of me, like how you can pull firmly at the gills of a dead fish to remove its intestinal tract in one fell swoop, the viscera clean and intact and easy to inspect before tossing it into the trash.

He could tell I was upset, my head was in my hands, and although I sensed he was disappointed at my lack of juicy information, he also said gently, "I'm sorry, I didn't know this would get so . . . but I think there's something important here. I do. I wouldn't press you if I didn't . . ."

He reached over and patted me on the knee, which was interesting because I wasn't sure if we'd ever even touched before. I looked up and suddenly wondered what might happen if I got up, and went around the coffee table, and sat down next to him, if I put my hand on his hand, on his thigh, if I crawled upon him, unbuttoned him, unzipped him and he unzipped me, skin on new skin, maybe he would respond eagerly, fall back easily onto the couch and hold the weight of me, me with my hands on his chest bracing myself against him, turning myself into a whole different kind of subject, and maybe certain articles on the internet were true, maybe it wasn't about whether I was good or bad at my job or did or didn't want a child or had spent too much time unergonomically on my computer or that the world was on fire or flooding or ecologically crashing, maybe I was just a tense woman in need of an epic fuck, maybe he could fuck me passionately yet precisely and it would be like a thorough chiropractic alignment, the climax one thunderous *crack* and then he'd buy the paper and we could run it together.

But he wouldn't do such an unethical thing, if I was a source. And I wanted to be a good source, and when I really tried to imagine it, not just in words but in images, it wasn't even possible. When I unbuttoned his shirt there was white space beneath like an undressed paper doll and under the zipper of his pants was somehow his voice recorder.

As he was leaving I asked then about the other story, the one I'd emailed him about, although whether it was a story wasn't clear. He said he was about to start work on it. He'd confirmed that at least half a dozen homes had been bought by one entity, though not Lee's landlords. But he still had a lot to do. He needed to look up records of all home sales in the past year or so, and it would take time but it shouldn't be too difficult. He said he might want to talk to me about that too, he wouldn't be surprised if Lee's landlords were in on it, maybe multiple people efforting to create a mini-empire of vacation rentals. "I think there's going to be a story. Maybe a multi-part story," he said a little gleefully. "Oh! And there's one weird little tidbit. The entity that bought those six or so homes. There's multiple investors, and the main one is—well, some rich guy. But one is part of the little practice evacuation group. I think the woman that works at the grocery store."

"But none of them—they don't have that kind of money," I said.

"Clearly they do. You know, there's something . . . well. Keep your ears open."

Maybe more should have been obvious in the moment, and not only in this recapitulation of potentially important events, and yet . . .

Anyway. I said I would.

The disorder maybe didn't want me to be on my computer or look at my phone or write stories, but what did it matter if I paid a bit more attention?

I said I wasn't using my phone for a while, but if he wanted to talk, my boyfriend was usually on a morning hike on this day of the week. Not that I didn't want him around, I said, but he wouldn't understand the difference between being the reporter and the subject, that it wasn't stressful to answer a few simple questions.

The Camping Trip

My boyfriend wanted us to go to a very different landscape for our camping trip. A trip is a way to mark a significant change, to differentiate before and after, and there were multiple shifts to mark: the decision to take my sabbatical and relax, the decision to obey the pain and not touch my electronics. And perhaps the mountain air would help me, like how people used to travel to far-off lands to take the healing waters.

There was also the fact that, while drunk on wine, we'd decided that on the camping trip we would try to conceive a child.

After my uterus expelled the little piece of copper, we had been careful, but on the trip we would not be careful because the timing of the expulsion right as I quit was a sign, though in some ways it seemed a bad time to have a child, I thought but didn't say. It would not be relaxing to have a person inside me. But he sensed my hesitation and said our child's future would be safe and secure, something he knew without being able to explain. I wanted to argue but I was supposed to relax, so I let my thoughts swirl alone in my head. My mother would be so disappointed, I thought, that I'd given up, that I was well on my way to depending on another person. Even though she was dead dead dead, I wanted to make it up to her somehow.

Anyway.

I was glad to go far away for the potential conception.

I didn't want to conceive a baby in our town by the ocean where it had been so windy and foggy for weeks, the blue sky swapped for a white-gray background that made it difficult even to tell what time of day it was. I always struggled to bear the fog but it was even more difficult to bear without my job, like blankness on blankness. Of course the fog was good, it meant moisture for the soil and the plants. My boyfriend liked the fog. He preferred it to the sun. He said it suited his mood. But although I too wished to be that kind of person, in truth I always wanted for the sky to be blue and for the fog to be something hovering over mountains far away, something beautiful at a significant distance. But instead we lived inside it, and on some days it chilled me so thoroughly it was as if I was becoming part of it, as if when eventually the sun burned off the fog's droplets, my cells too would evaporate away into the air.

For our camping trip we traveled to an inland landscape much more stark and dramatic. It was mountainous and exposed, with narrow valleys cut by glaciers millions of years ago. We were hundreds of miles away from the fog and thousands of feet above the sea. The sheer drop of the eastern side of a mountain range stood imposingly between us and the faraway coast. It was bright and sunny and dry. It was a little dangerous, it was again fire season, but it was early.

Our first stop once we arrived was a little convenience store a half hour or so from our campsite. Inside the store I wandered the aisles, assessing the snacks and gazing through a refrigerator door at the beer selection. The bottles looked so cool and bitter and refreshing but I looked away because we weren't drinking alcohol on the trip. I turned a corner and came upon half an aisle devoted to chips. The bags were all puffed up from the lack of pressure at altitude. They appeared filled with nothing and ready to burst. Or maybe, I thought, picking one up, considering the sunny yellow bag from all angles, touching the taut seams, maybe it was just a better and expanded version of its true being, proudly convexing itself, finally rid of its sad crumpled recesses. Maybe the altitude could help me, I thought, pressing gently with both hands on the tight air of it. My tissues would open up, my muscles slightly dilate, certain things inside me would move more freely. Maybe by the end of the trip I would be like the potato chip bag. I wanted to take a picture of the bag with my phone but of course I didn't have it. I hadn't touched or even looked at my phone or computer for many days.

I was proud of myself for obeying the disorder.

It hadn't been easy.

My hands felt nervously empty, they kept reaching into my back pocket for my phone. They missed my mouse and the scrolling and clicking and sinking into the internet. I wanted to look at a screen, to read the news from everywhere, I wanted to marvel at in-depth reportage because even if the specific facts quickly left my mind they lingered in my body, in my stomach like low-level food poisoning even if and especially if it was done well, and I longed for my email, even though most of my emails were work or spam and so without work it could only have been fraudulent requests for investments and enticements for increasing sexual pleasure and offers of cheap mortgages for a house I'd never own.

But it was also true I found some pleasure in my absence.

There was pleasure in the renunciation of my electronics and my job, both being temporary, I reminded myself. Of course it was early in my renunciation, but when I managed to bury the feeling that I'd become a pointless kind of person without work, a calm found its way into my shoulders and melted the tense muscles of my forehead. In the days after my last day of work, I sat each evening on my porch and stared at the trees and sometimes my mind could be, for some brief moments, still. Perhaps I'd just been waiting all this time for something to unthinkingly obey.

And if I was vaguely paying attention to anything I might pass along to the other reporter—well, that was barely doing anything at all.

In the little market my boyfriend came over to me from the spice aisle, holding jars of smoked paprika and cumin. He had been trying to liven up his cooking after I complained rather forcefully about the monastic quality of our meals. I'm not an invalid! I'd said the day after I left the paper, after he prepared for dinner another soup of bitter greens. He had nodded quietly and I felt guilty, but soon it sparked a flavorful fire in him, because though he typically tried to stick to herbs he found in the wild or at least herbs like rosemary and mint that had gone feral in our neighborhood, he recently started craving smoky profiles, buying jars of whole spices that he toasted and ground himself.

I was surprised because my complaints about his cooking had never gone far before. In retrospect—and I'm getting closer and closer to the present moment, the moment where I know everything or at least a portion—I wonder if he was trying to atone, since he accomplished what he'd set out to, succeeded in getting me to join him on a certain track, on a certain path, a certain kind of life even if he hadn't divulged all its details, and now he could relent in certain ways.

He tossed the spices into the basket. I added two inflated bags of potato chips. He picked up one bag and looked briefly at the ingredient list before reluctantly returning it to the basket. As we left the store and drove to our campsite I told myself to stop thinking of my phone and my computer. I needed to breathe the dry air and relish the heat and relax. I forced into existence the thought that maybe by the end of the trip, the disorder might really begin its fading, not the fake fading like before, if it had faded at all, but truly, maybe after all what I'd really needed was a break, a blank mind, and what better event than a camping trip, what better than the outdoors, what better than hiking until each contraction of my muscles burned in pain but for good and right reasons, and my thoughts would die down, and the concentrate of stress would flow out of my body, as if nature were a place where such a lack of anxiety existed, it couldn't help but pull it out of me to establish some kind of thermodynamic equilibrium. Maybe not working would really make my disorder go away, though I didn't like to think about what exactly that would signify. It wouldn't matter that worker's comp was done, and I could stop the Axon and stop with the worksheets.

Perhaps I wasn't going to have any more Axon treatments anyway.

After I quit and drunkenly agreed to pregnancy, I asked my boyfriend to call Lee and arrange another session. I wanted to see—even though it was a scam! even though I'd known it was a scam before the other reporter kind of confirmed it—what the Axon might say or sense about me in the aftermath, if it would respond to my decisions, if it might offer additional healing hocus pocus, since what could it hurt? He said Lee was busy, she didn't have time before our trip. But this is my health, I'd said to him—doesn't she care? She had previously been so invested in me. Hadn't she? My hands still feel weird, I'd said, and even in that very moment my fingertips burned a bit, even though I wasn't doing anything, and in my mind I said to myself: *You're not real! Go away! I love myself!* He just laid his head in my lap and looked up at me, a position we were rarely in yet a position he luxuriated in for that moment, as if there had been so many things recently requiring extra effort of him that was not totally natural and he would if possible lie like that forever. But then he sat up and held my hand and said not to take it too personally, maybe I didn't need the Axon or Lee anymore.

※

We decided to try conceiving a baby on the third day of the trip.

It was unfortunate it wasn't the day before, because then we might have conceived the baby before he found what he found, and I wouldn't have perhaps been so pressured into agreeing to his terms and not mine before the conception.

We were having a nice evening at our campsite, making burgers from venison he had harvested from a freshly dead deer on the side of the road a few weeks prior. As I formed the patties at the picnic table he looked at me more lovingly than he had in a while. When I asked what he was looking at, he said he liked seeing me relaxed in the outdoors, instead of in my little corner of the cabin at my standing desk. He noted, prodding the logs, unsatisfied with their arrangement, trying to perfectly position each one, that we hadn't been camping in a while. "Remember the first time we went camping?" he said, and looked at me, smiling but a little hesitant too because we didn't often bring up our past, the nostalgia of it somehow embarrassing. "And you ate a wild mushroom for the first time? I gave you those chanterelles before, when we met and I took you out, but you didn't eat them."

"I let you blindfold me. A person can only give up so much trust right away."

In fact, after that interview I'd gone home and eaten the chanterelles he gave me, but later I said I tossed them into the forest. You don't always want someone to know how quickly you let yourself trust them.

My boyfriend left the smoky firepit and sat next to me and kissed me on the cheek. He looked so genuinely happy, and the tenderness in his eyes seemed meant to literally tenderize its object, which was me. He then began detailing the hikes he'd researched, including a trail full of obsidian and very old trees and pictures he'd seen on the internet of exquisite alpine lakes. And I felt softened like butter ready to be spread.

But then in that softening, and in the empty clarity the forest was so quickly providing me, certain negative thoughts threatened to break free, to burble up.

Like why had he not spent hours on the internet trying to figure out what might be wrong with me, why had he not spent hours looking for anyone who might help me, scouring the internet for rare diseases and syndromes, or why hadn't he found out about the workbook, even if I might have been offended at my own boyfriend suggesting any form of psychoanalytic origin.

Why hadn't my boyfriend become obsessed with finding out what was wrong with me?

Of course he thought he knew what was wrong.

But why had he never become obsessed with trying to uncover every possibility?

I closed my eyes briefly and took in a slow breath because that's what people do, as if the mixture of breath and blackness were some dark hurricane that would make the bad thoughts scramble to hide themselves again. When I opened my eyes I felt better and saw my boyfriend, who loved me, and a new, pleasant thought arose. Trips were nice, it was nice to see my boyfriend not framed by the white and mostly plain walls of our cottage but instead against the backdrop of the aspen leaves and the special way they had of quivering in the warm wind.

After we ate and sat a while around the fire, we made plans to go for a night hike and find a beautiful moonlit spot for our first attempt at conception. I asked him if he would check my phone for messages before we went. I was still hoping Lee might send some sign she wanted to re-Axon me or had new insights. I wanted for whatever reason to be interpreted again.

So it was a bit my own fault when my boyfriend went to the car to check and came back with a somewhat horrified expression on his face. He held up a small piece of fabric and asked what the hell it was.

Oh fuck, I thought.

It was a weird and disturbing thing for someone to find.

It was a Juden star.

I wrote before that I hadn't found anything of my mother's at home except for empty jewelry boxes, but actually I'd found in one of them a stray bit of the midcentury genocidal paraphernalia she had bought so much of, and, wanting some last bit of her, I took it. During the packing for our trip I'd stuck it in the jewelry box that contained my phone, and then I took the box in case Lee texted but also because I wanted some piece of her around as I made a new person, as I possibly became a mother.

The situation clearly looked weird and psychologically unhinged, but the fabric, in a completely messed-up way, was the object I had of hers that meant the most to her.

I tried to explain in a shortened way, that I'd found it and had so few objects of hers, and the genocidal paraphernalia had meant so much to her even though it was very very very messed up, that I took it and just stored it there.

He was still looking at me hesitatingly but seemed willing to go along with it until the conversation turned into a question of whether I wanted to raise this child we were about to conceive in that faith, and the minute he asked it I realized I did, that it was the best way to remedy the disappointment my mother would surely feel in me, the disappointment over my canned career: to raise a baby in that faith.

"But you don't even practice anything," he said.

"Well . . . I could start."

His eyes looked about to burst out of his head. "That's not how faith works!"

I shrugged. I thought I could win if I stayed calm. "Maybe it does."

He took a deep calming breath. He was clearly trying to figure out how best to change my mind.

I asked him why he cared. He didn't have a competing religion. But he did, in a way, he said, not a religion but the community he imagined us living in, living in community with others off the land, or on the land, and the members couldn't have entirely different belief systems because it would create division, when really the community should—well, he didn't like the word *worship*, but in lieu of a less-loaded word, yes, worship the earth and soil and plants and live in rhythm with the seasons. And all that. I argued there could be both, that one didn't preclude the other. Eventually we agreed to talk about it later, that the night might not be ideal for conception.

"I wish I had a drink," I said, laughing even though it was kind of sad.

I wasn't drinking alcohol. It could contribute to inflammation and why would I ingest something that could be, if not the main culprit, an accomplice, and part of obeying the disorder meant being good to my body. He offered me a tincture, one that promoted relaxation, which he'd made because he knew that even without a job I'd find something to be anxious about. He joked that it was made with alcohol; I'd at least enjoy that. So he held a dropperful of hazy yellow liquid above my mouth, a tincture he'd made just for me, a mixture of St. John's wort and yarrow and other herbs he was too tired to name. "It's sweetened with honey," he said as he squeezed it, and I thought: Be grateful. Be grateful! But all I could taste were the musty vegetal compounds that the alcohol had stripped from the plants by force. I swallowed quickly before the bitterness fully set fire to my tongue. I started coughing violently but uselessly.

"Jesus," I said. "That's strong."

He rubbed my back. "I made it strong for you. It's a mixture of things—for inflammation, and to help you relax."

I looked at him. He wants to help me, I thought. He is being sweet. He is being tender. This could be good for me. He knows about things I don't, which is part of what I admire about him. Maybe he was right, I thought as I got into my sleeping bag.

All night my back failed to find a groove in the earth in which my body could fit, to find some way to be held by it, since we hadn't brought any inflatable padded comfort. My body turned onto each side, and onto my stomach, and then my back again. I couldn't understand how the arch of the human back was supposed to lie comfortably on the earth, though later my boyfriend said I'd get used to it, maybe that could help my hands too, the primal ground. When I finally fell asleep, I had a dream I remembered, which was rare. I dreamed I wrote the story of my disorder and that when I finished I had a great revelation. When I woke up I couldn't remember what the revelation was, but could it be anything other than that its cause had revealed itself to me?

⚛

The next day we decided to postpone discussing the future of our unconceived child. I was supposed to be relaxing and we would be in better frames of mind to talk if we enjoyed the natural beauty, if we let it seep into us and relax us the way online articles always promised it would. So for the next few days we went to see the sights. We walked the black perimeter of a caldera. We hiked a loop trail that passed a dozen scenic alpine lakes. We briefly swam in slippery alkaline water. We walked around our campsite and talked to people pitching tents nearby, including two men I'd seen the first night. A man coated thickly in sunscreen told us he had recently developed an allergy to the sun that made him break out in vicious, weeping hives, but he couldn't stop going camping, so he wore long pants and long sleeves and huge hats and lots of sunblock. I admired his dedication, which briefly made me want to find my phone or use my computer the minute I got home. Maybe perseverance was better than obedience. But I put the thought away. I'd barely started to obey the pain, so instead I tried to do as my boyfriend suggested and not think of medical things, not think of my hands, though they were always hanging there at my sides. The disorder was relatively quiet, except for the occasional—and were they, if occasional, a little more frequent than I would have expected?—bursts of sharp pain in a hand or forearm or even all the way in my biceps. *Don't leave me! Or wait, no, go away!* I kept thinking, starting to get a little mixed up. *I'm not real—or wait, you're not real! I hate myself! No, I love myself!*

⁂

I think I could have remained firm in my desire, or what I thought might be my dead mother's desire, if I hadn't accidentally—or was it accidental—consumed that substance that led to the mind-altering experience.

It's possible it was an accident, but when you write things down and pick out all the potentially important parts, more and more things are tainted with suspicion.

It happened on a hike in a forest of the oldest trees in the world.

Before the hike we went to the visitor center at the trailhead. The visitor center used to have a cross section of a very old bristlecone tree, with age rings that an informational sign correlated to historical events, like the reign of Caesar and the birth of Jesus Christ. But a religious zealot who believed no tree could predate Noah's flood had burned the visitor center down a few years earlier. So instead my boyfriend and I went over to the pine cone display and played a guessing game trying to identify the pine cones of various trees. It was something he usually would have dismissed as ridiculous but he was in good spirits. Before we left the center, I picked up a handout with twenty facts about bristlecone pine trees, each fact related to a numbered signpost along the trail.

The trail was cool in the early morning when we set out, and I was alert and carefully looked for the signposts to connect to the facts on the sheet. Most of the trees, the thicker ones at least, had shed quite a lot of bark from their trunks, the peeled exposure revealing striated wood that looked carefully painted. Many of the trees, short despite being so old, grew in great tangles of twisted trunks, as if they had been moving just before we came upon them. Signpost three explained that the bark peeled because the tree was killing off parts of itself to stay alive. There were few competitors at this elevation—in fact there were few plants at all, at least that we could see—but also few nutrients in the rocky spartan ground, in dolomite made from the bed of a very old sea. Signpost seven, at which point the coolness of the early morning had given way to a heat that was to me initially luxurious, said this species of tree might add only an inch of girth to its trunk in a century. I read each fact aloud as we came to each signpost, and my boyfriend listened attentively.

By signpost twelve, which said the oldest tree in the grove was 4,600 years old, the heat had lost its initial novelty and pleasure, especially at this elevation. I knew we'd be hiking at over twelve thousand feet, but still I was surprised at how I struggled in the heat, at the thinness of the oxygen, the way my muscles felt denatured and weak. Maybe I was weaker than I thought. Although this had been part of the point, to exert myself, to make my body exhausted and therefore softened, capped off each night by my boyfriend gently massaging my fingers and forearms and neck.

Even my boyfriend slowed down, although he liked his body's struggle, or at least the feeling of his body contending with a new environment.

I asked him for the big water bottle, and during the pause of our hydration he said he wanted to look for the oldest tree.

It wasn't really like him, to want to look for something like that. What did it matter that one tree was a little older than another, since they were all so so old? And the oldest tree wasn't along the trail and it wasn't marked at all, since marking it would draw people and probably lead to its quick demise.

My boyfriend said he knew it wasn't marked but he wanted to go wandering off-trail and maybe it was marked in some subtle way we could see.

He did like to go off-trail.

So halfway along the loop we wandered into an untrailed grove of old trees. I don't know how long we walked, maybe half an hour, although it felt longer in the heat, especially since the trees provided little shade. These were not trees of shelter. He kept stopping at each thicker tree, looking for some sign that it was the oldest one, talking about the minute differences he noted from tree to tree, although to me the more trees we examined, the more their swirls and twists and all the beautiful branches blended into each other.

Maybe I was like the tree, I thought, trying to kill off part of my extremities to survive, but it was probably a thought born of exhaustion and profuse sweating, and anyway a thought like that is anthropomorphism. Or would it be the reverse of anthropomorphism? Finally my boyfriend said we should stop to eat, and in the slimmest stripe of shade, we sat on a rocky outcropping for lunch: trail bars and jerky he'd made, and oranges, and a bag of chips I'd bought at the store, and two avocados that turned out to be rotten.

Then he said, starting to nibble on his overly dry jerky, which he somehow ate easily while I hopelessly chewed and chewed and chewed, that he wanted to talk again about our unconceived baby and the belief system in which it would be brought up. He was sure now that there was a way in which to remain in our little town without paying astronomical rent, without feeling like we were living in an overtouristed parody of rural living, we could reduce our impact on the earth, live harmoniously. And it seemed to him that bringing religion into it—a religion I hadn't ever practiced in adulthood, a religion I seemed fixated on out of a weirdo sense of guilt that had already led me to hold dear a piece of midcentury genocidal paraphernalia, itself a sign I was way way way off track, and here he really looked at me, trying to bore into me how truly alarming it was—that bringing religion into it would divide whatever community we might create.

I saw that it was important to him. But still I felt that what was important to me was more important than what was important to him. Perhaps it was the worksheets, which had so far done nothing to help but had me reliving a certain guilt and grief all over again, had me searching for a way to reconnect with her and wasn't religion really one of the oldest and most surefire ways to connect with the dead?

But he wouldn't see that argument as valid.

Instead I protested that his vision didn't seem possible—home prices were only going up and it was impossible we could have a place of our own, and what about his own assertion that the rise in home sales was probably a prelude to a community almost totally taken over by short-term rentals for tourists, so how was this now supposed to be a home for a small self-sustaining live-off-the-earth community?

I swallowed the still-not-completely-chewed piece of jerky and grabbed a trail bar, which he had made and which was not very tasty but at least was soft.

My boyfriend brushed it off. He said who knew how many houses had really sold? I'd never looked into it myself, had I?

Then he said he had been offered a new job. Not just a job but a livelihood.

He'd been hired, he said, by—well, some wealthy locals to be their private forager. They were paying a premium, a salary, the kind of money he'd never imagined he could make before, and yes it was a little gross, he could hear my arguments already, but this was the world we lived in, and why be miserable, and wasn't it yet another sign that it was the right time to have a family, since he could really and truly provide?

I barraged him with a string of questions, mainly: Who?

But didn't I already know?

He wouldn't answer. He said it was early and somewhat tentative and he didn't want to jinx it. What he really wanted to talk about, though, he said, was, again, the belief system of our future child.

At this point it was just a little bit hard to concentrate. "But what about—what about honoring ancestors, or whatever? Isn't that part of, you know, natural living?"

He stood up. "Kim, I have never once heard you even use the

word 'ancestor.' You just—you have an unhealthy fixation. You never should have started those worksheets. Given to you by a crazy person!"

"But you said it couldn't hurt! You encouraged me. Kind of. Didn't you?"

He was upset. He walked away. I quickly gathered our things and followed, even though he was walking even farther from the trail, which I could only see the last inkling of. I thought he would march quickly away in frustration, but he walked slowly and wanderingly. Maybe he thought finding the oldest tree in the world would help our situation. As I followed, one of the trees we passed seemed to subtly twist along its already twisted grooves. I stopped. Something in me gently started to shift. I looked at the tree. It too provided only meager shade, but I suddenly felt awed to be within its shadow.

"I love this tree," I said, then looked to my boyfriend, who was still wandering slowly forward. "And I love you!" I shouted.

He turned around very slowly, reminding me of the way the tree seemed to twist.

"I love you too," he said very tenderly but didn't approach.

Then I paused. I looked all around at the vast and rocky landscape. "Wait . . . why do I feel different?"

His eyes widened though perhaps not as widely as I perceived them.

"Did you eat a trail bar?" he asked. "I thought—I thought I said not to . . ."

"You said you didn't think I'd like them. And I was hungry. . . . Oh no," I said.

"Don't worry," he said calmly. "It's not very much."

"What?"

He had added a modest amount of mind-altering substance to the trail bars.

"I needed to get a little lost. Just a little. And then find my way back. You weren't supposed to—Don't panic. Just try to relax. You'll have a better experience that way. Just sit there by that tree with your pack. There's plenty of water in it."

I sat down beside the tree I'd fallen in love with.

"Or you can come with me," he said.

But I was tired and I didn't have the energy to get lost, and anyway I already was lost. I was turned around and didn't know how to get back to the trail and didn't know anything about using the sun or whatever to find my way back. I told him to go get lost and get unlost and then find me. He left me extra food, which he promised did not contain any more mind-altering substances, and wandered nonlinearly away.

He was gone for a few hours, though never really gone: the landscape was so open and barren save for the squat trees, and he moved so exquisitely slowly, so he was in my sight almost the entire time he was trying to get lost. I was grateful to be at a remove, so I had something to observe. I'd never taken a psychedelic. For a while I was able to focus just on him. I watched him curiously touch the trees' bottlebrush needles. He chose one tree to walk in circles around, but without quite looking at it, like it was a merry-go-round. Although he'd come looking for the oldest living specimen, he seemed drawn to the dead, which was no surprise to me because the dead ones, which had lost all their greenery and much of their exterior, looked in their death or dying like living sculptures. His actions fell into a pattern: he would interact with some element of the landscape—drop to his belly and gaze intensely at a prickly pine cone in the dirt, or roll a rock between his hands or fall into the hypnotic bark of the tree—and then suddenly remove himself, close himself off from it, only to interact again with that thing or maybe another thing. It was like someone in the throes of an internet failure who must turn their internet connection off and on and off and on and off and on in an attempt to reconnect. Watching this cycle, I felt cosmically webbed to him, or webbed with him in something greater. I'd never felt that connected to him or anyone. It was that kind of drug.

Yet at some point the feeling shifted, perhaps because I was still enamored with the tree I was sitting beside. I felt invisible roots grow outward from my fingers and toes all the way to him, directly feeding me all his experiencing. A few times I tried to get up to be closer to him. But each time a voice said: no no no! I don't know if that voice was the psychedelic or the real inner me trying to break through, although to say there was a true inner me is a certain kind of assumption I'm not sure I believe in.

On my last attempt I didn't listen. I stood up and started walking and immediately the feeling within me or around me darkened; the web, if I was still in the web, became a void, and I came to believe that moving had ripped all the connections, and I was dead but somehow still wandering, feebly carrying around my pathetic hands, broken roots dangling uselessly from my fingers, like some idiotic reformulation of Medusa.

"I'm unrooted!" I started saying or maybe screaming. "I'm unrooted!"

Suddenly my boyfriend was sitting beside me. My hands clutched his wrists, and I relaxed. He looked calm and happy. He had gotten successfully lost, he said, or claimed.

"Did you find the oldest tree?"

"No," he said. "But it's okay. It was stupid. I think I just needed something to look for, to help me get lost."

"I think I'm unrooted," I said.

"Drink some water."

We chugged the bottle and shared an apple. I felt the world or me or me in relation to the world start to return to normal, which made me panic slightly because I didn't want to return to normal in my unrooted state. I held on to his wrists again.

Then I said, "Okay. Okay. I was wrong. I don't—I don't need to carry things or my guilt or whatever from my past into our future."

He embraced me slowly and slothlike, his arms like a halo around me. We weren't completely back to normal yet but in some halfway place. He released me just as slowly, but then we were kissing, and I lay down in a patch of bare soil, although beneath the small of my back was an area of dolomite rock, which according to the information center was supposed to be relatively soft but it still scraped at my skin as we fucked under the meager shade of one pine that still seemed mostly alive, in the shade of its thick twirling trunk that reached up and out of the earth at a steep angle. The striations of its bark seemed at the beginning of our fucking to be fuzzy and mysterious, moving sinuously like a snake, but as we got toward the end of it, the bark's curling and coiling slowed and then was still, and I could once again see the striations clearly, and near the very end my boyfriend asked me to switch, he asked if I'd get on top of him, which wasn't ideal for conception yet he suddenly wanted to be the one fucked. But I was still too out of it and I couldn't, and I grabbed his hips and goaded him, because the mind-altering substance was almost done with me and in the last few moments I had left I wanted to be part of the earth, I wanted to be fucked into the ground.

※

In the middle of the night, while my boyfriend slept deeply and easily on the stupid earth, I quietly unzipped the tent and went to the car. I found the workbook and flipped to the fourth and penultimate worksheet, which I had been avoiding. But thoughts of sperm moving through my cervix to my now-hospitable uterus, that any day now I might be a temporary home for new life, and my boyfriend's horror over the midcentury genocidal paraphernalia made me manic to finish. Whether finishing would suddenly cure me was questionable. But maybe before a whole other life began, the worksheets could exorcise or banish whatever unprocessed grief was left in me—as if that grief were food that would spoil and sicken me or the potential child unless it was processed in some way, most likely with an intense heat that would kill anything living left in it.

But when I finished I felt unsatisfied. I wanted to write more. I wanted to expunge not just her but everything, the whole disorder, in order to understand what had happened and get it out of me. I told myself that's what I wanted, wasn't it—to get it out?

Worksheet 4

K*eep going. You know where you're headed, where you've been heading all along. You know what the terminus is. Don't stop. Don't think. Just keep writing.*

⁂

The day before she died my mother asked me to drive to the nearby gas station and buy her a full carton of Marlboro reds. But she asked me in a new way, not in the old way when always we argued into the air between us.

Instead she gave me a letter.

She came downstairs one Saturday morning when I was on the couch reading. It was the late morning but I had already been up for hours, since like I said before I had decided to be healthy, to ensure I was not and never would be my mother, to ensure that whatever I turned out to be, I was not-her. In my head being healthy involved the unteenage habit of waking up early, unlike my mother, who often woke up late. It's hard now to articulate exactly why it's so healthy to wake up early, except that somehow being as aligned as possible with sunlit hours seemed healthy, and spending so much time awake in darkness seemed bad, at least metaphorically. So instead of staying up with my mom watching bad and raunchy television, I occasionally fell asleep to the muffled sound of her in her bedroom talking and laughing with my sister on the phone.

When she came to me that morning and stood at the couch, I stopped reading, but I didn't put down the novel. I held it open in front of me, pinched in my right hand, my thumb pressing into the split of the page and my pointer finger curled to brace the bottom of its spine. I looked up at her. She held my gaze. Her whole face held me, her compulsively plucked eyebrows and her nose sharp like a vanishing point and her thin dissolving lips, and when she was satisfied that she had obtained something, she stuck those three printed pages into the split of my open book. The letter wasn't handwritten, which was good because her horrible handwriting was like some creature let loose that doesn't know where it should go. The pages were numbered, which made me for some reason uneasy. Maybe it was the idea that she was so worried about even a short document losing its order, or maybe everything about it was just a little strange, because her life wasn't one that often necessitated a word processor at all. In fact I don't know if we'd ever exchanged a document at all.

I closed the book on the pages.

She went back upstairs.

When I heard her bedroom door click shut upstairs, I pulled out the pages. They were holding my place but that really didn't matter, because only a real idiot can't remember where they left off in a novel, or that's what I thought in that moment—I don't believe that anymore, it's very easy to lose your place in a novel, especially to start reading only to realize you got ahead of yourself, but then sometimes you just plow on anyway—and then I read the letter. It took about ten minutes. The font was this same font I'm using.

The letter—in that moment I had a feeling the letter explained so much, almost everything, it laid out a case, it contained strong reasoning with citations, both medical and psychological, it contained new personal information couched in telling anecdotes, it was clear, or at least clearer, I remember thinking things seemed clearer about her but maybe it was too clear, so clear that you are certain you will always remember, if not the specific words, then at least the main arguments and examples, the flow of it, how one thing proceeded to the next. I remember now only bits of it, though, maybe especially the degree of her debt, all those sickening zeroes. So when an hour later she came back and asked me to return the pages I handed them back and said right away:

"I'll go get the cigarettes."

"Thank you, Kim," she said.

When I came back, I went upstairs and knocked but there was no answer, and I tried the doorknob but it was locked, and I remember thinking: I understand this now too. I left the carton at the door although she would never finish the carton. Then I went and removed from my underwear drawer the medication of hers I'd stolen, and left it beside the carton. A few hours later I left the house to do who knows what, but I do remember that before

I got into my car, I looked back at the house and she was at her open window with a cigarette in the vee of her fingers, and she exhaled through her nose a long long stream of smoke, and she looked down and smiled and waved, and that was the last time I saw my mother.

We Go Canvassing

Until now everything I'm writing about has seemed so far away!

Even the camping trip, which wasn't so long ago.

But everything that's happened since feels and is very close, perhaps because when we returned the weather had shifted, the fog completely gone, replaced by a heat wave that made me feel I was still far inland, and sudden gusty winds that would be perfect for providing a fire with extra encouragement. A few small fires had already started elsewhere. Smoke hadn't yet reached us but hearing about them made the practice evacuation feel less theoretical.

I need to do a better job of compressing time, I want to get to the end of this document, but it's hard, it's very hard because I want to stop and pick at so many little details, the ones that are important, and also inevitably ones that aren't important, I've tried to stick with what might be important but I'm sure things that probably had nothing to do with the disorder are here too, because once I start writing I can get carried away.

Anyway.

The other reporter came by again after I returned from the camping trip. He asked if I'd learned anything and I immediately and without hesitation told him my boyfriend was taking a job with Lee's landlords, as their well-paid personal forager. I didn't know much else. The other reporter didn't share anything he'd learned, if he'd learned anything new; he just told me to keep my ears open. I tried to comply because I wanted to be a good source, but it was difficult for a while—though soon enough I knew almost everything—because my boyfriend was suddenly reluctant to let me come to a meeting, of which there weren't many left because the prescribed fire and the practice evacuation were happening soon. He said I should relax, focus on the baby that may have been conceived. Watch the trees. Read a book. Go for a hike. All the things I was too busy to do before! He said the whole point of quitting was to relax, to see if the disorder might fade away in a calm body, though it had been weeks or even over a month and I knew it was still there. I could feel in my hands its sweet uncomfortable hum. During the camping trip I waited to see if the trees and the mountain air and then the unexpected mind-altering substances might cause some valve in me to open and the disorder to exit, which is what I wanted or what I should have wanted. I should have wanted it gone. And I did want it gone.

But I also didn't.

In the woods the idea that the soothing setting of the forest might fix me had made me, in certain moments, a little fearful.

It's hard to say why because I didn't like the disorder.

But slowly it had become part of me, and I was its home.

From my boyfriend I know some relationships in the fungal world are parasitic, when one life benefits to the detriment of another, and other relationships are saprophytic, one life feeds off the dead, but finally other relationships are symbiotic, when two living things exchange elements they need to survive.

I always thought the disorder was parasitic and I hoped it wasn't saprophytic but maybe it was symbiotic, or at least somehow it gave me something: it was intensely mine, with a namelessness that had developed an air of purity to it.

And even if it received more than it offered—sometimes it's difficult to let go of certain things, even painful things, and if it wasn't in me then where would it go?

After all, I wasn't in agony. I missed my computer and my phone, but the disorder had become a center around which I operated, and its disappearance might leave me spinning around an emptiness like a hurricane.

Or maybe the relationship was parasitic or even saprophytic, but maybe I was the parasite.

I felt—I feel—like if it went away, then it will never somehow have been real.

I wanted to talk to Lee about it, to be hooked up again to her machine. Maybe talking to her or the Axon could remind me that I wanted the disorder gone, but she wasn't responding to my texts, at least the texts I asked my boyfriend to send on my behalf. I thought about driving to her, cold knocking on her door like the other reporter would. But that wasn't the kind of thing I did. I was a coward. And my old spell—*I am not me, I am not me, I am not me*—didn't work or wasn't strong enough to overcome my revulsion at the idea of surprising someone with my presence.

And as for the worksheets, once I returned from the camping

trip, I struggled to follow the program, I kept mixing up what I was supposed to tell the pain, I would try to think *You're not real!* and instead think *Don't go, not yet!* and maybe that too was because I was no longer sure I wanted the disorder gone. I only had one worksheet left before my pain was supposed to evaporate, but it was the most difficult one: I had to compose an imaginary conversation with, in my case, my mother, and somehow absolve myself of crippling guilt, but I couldn't bring myself to do it.

And when I started writing about the disorder—when I took the notebook I'd started on the camping trip and started from the beginning about what had happened so far and everything that might be important—I told myself it was in order to understand and expunge it, but sometimes I wondered if instead I wrote about it because I loved it, because I wanted to be closer to it. Maybe that was dangerous, a way to ensure it never left. But I don't believe that's true. I don't believe in that at all. Because I know that loving and obsessing over something has nothing to do in the end with whether it will stay or go.

❦

Those were the kind of loopy bad thoughts I should not have been thinking.

I needed to get outside myself. I needed to think about other things!

Eventually I convinced my boyfriend to let me accompany him on a canvassing expedition of a small neighborhood. It was in a way a good day for it: it was hot and dry, and the risk was literally in the air, sucking all the moisture from the flora. On the drive my boyfriend noted that the woods around the area we were canvassing were not only near the location of the prescribed fire—though the fire was actually even closer to our own cabin—but also an area that had become especially dry, according to fire specialists the group had recently hired. We could mention that, he said, as we went from home to home—many of which were empty, which wasn't surprising except even more were empty than I'd expected—to collect information for the practice evacuation, such as what medications people took and if they had pets, so neighbors could prepare to help neighbors.

Although he asked other questions too.

I wasn't sure why he let me come with him, since I'd obviously want to know why he was asking the question he was asking.

But really he did want to tell me.

He wanted to tell me everything but he wanted me to be excited, to be happy about the life he was preparing for us, because he'd worked hard and he had, he later admitted, compromised certain values he held. But he could see the way the future would go, that he couldn't hold on to all his values, and so he decided which ones were important and what path would get us there, and if I could just accept it, we could be happy.

But he couldn't just come out and tell me.

In part it was because he didn't trust me completely.

He didn't trust me while I was at the paper and not even after, because although he didn't know about the other reporter's visits, he intuited, more vaguely, that I was still loyal to the newspaper, that I might run to my editor if I found out something especially untoward about the group.

But I think he also wanted extra time to ensure that he had commitments from Lee's landlords and the rest, since he was sure I'd try to talk him out of it, I would have told him it was wrong or absurd or far-fetched. He wanted to present it as a fait accompli, an accomplishment, an offering, the way an animal brings fresh kill to its family.

I think he let me come with him to canvass the neighborhood to gauge my reaction, to get a sense of how much he could reveal.

When we finally found a house with someone home, a woman with long gray hair who stood for a long cantankerous moment in the slip of her half-opened door, deciding whether she wanted to talk to us, he asked the questions I expected—whether she was on medications, whether she used medical devices or had pets, whether she had a car and if she could drive. But then he asked if she owned the home, and what it was worth, and how long she'd lived there, and what impact the danger of fire, the home being so close to the forest, had on her, if she felt safe. He asked if she knew how significantly the danger of fire was increasing, if she knew how dry things were, even along the coast, and if she'd lost her fire insurance, which many people had, and what if there were a program, or something, he asked, that bought homes in areas of significant fire danger, would she be open to moving?

She eyed him warily. "I'm in my nineties!" she suddenly exclaimed. "You think I'm going to move? I'm going to die in this house!" and slammed the door in our faces.

As we went back down the driveway, he asked me to wait to talk until we'd finished the neighborhood. So for a few hours we walked up the winding hilly road, and a few people who my boyfriend spoke to were receptive and many people were suspicious, suspicious but curious about how much, exactly, they might get for their homes.

Finally we reached the top of the hill, where the road ended and a trail began. I took a sip of water while he looked at his phone, texting someone. The trail looked vaguely familiar. My boyfriend put his phone away and saw me staring up into the trees and took my hand. "Let's go for a walk," he said, and so we kept going, walking slowly up switchbacks for a half hour or so before he led us off the trail for another five minutes, until I remembered this was where he'd taken me that very first time I met him, when he blindfolded me and took me to one of his precious mushroom spots.

We sat down in the pine duff and sipped some water quietly.

"Okay," I finally said. "Can you tell me what's going on? About your new job, and all the questions you're asking of people . . ."

He took a thoughtful sip of water like a man at a lectern preparing for a long speech. "Okay," he said. "It's good timing. It might be in the newspaper soon anyway."

"*What* might be in the newspaper soon?"

Maybe the most offensive thing is that he knew of something that would be in the paper before I did!

I was the one who was supposed to know what was happening.

My boyfriend proceeded to explain or try to explain.

Yes, his new job, his new livelihood, would be foraging for, well, hyperwealthy people who could afford something like that. Wasn't I the one, he said, who had told him time and time again that his interests and passions should align with his job, that he'd be happier that way? They would pay well. They would pay everyone well, everyone being the other members of the evacuation group, who had originally banded together to organize a practice evacuation they hoped would morph into a movement to grow the town. But my boyfriend had joined and eventually convinced this group, who all had various skills—growing mushrooms and hunting, for instance, that the wealthy could also fund—to convince people of the opposite. The few people who he considered useless had been, early on, nudged out.

Eventually they wouldn't need money, only their plot of land and a small hillside of cabins, which had been promised to them. It was a fair exchange, to live in a place that, at some point, perhaps quite soon, would be so very peaceful and quiet.

I was quiet.

"So they want to buy up—as many houses as they can? Is that it?"

He nodded. "And tear some down, except the ones they'll live in," he added, watching my reaction, but I tried not to let my face react. I wanted to keep my reactions to myself until I understood it completely, although who knew if even he understood it completely. It was difficult to think of clarifying questions in the face of such absurdity, but perhaps it wasn't absurd. He went on to say that the area we lived in, as I knew, was prized for its Mediterranean climate. It almost never froze. So much food—save for, lamentably, hotter crops like peppers, which didn't always fare so well, though they were doing better and better out here recently—could grow all year long, and although it would inevitably get hotter, it never got too hot, the fog helped mitigate the danger of fire, as I also knew, it was ideal in so many ways. Lee's landlords and the others, he said, were wealthy and lame and wanted it to themselves, as people with that much money want, and with the way things were going ecologically, it seemed an ideal place. Well, there would still be smoke, but they were rich, they'd be fine inside when it blew our way. They had good ideas, he kept going, becoming defensive of them even as he also kept saying they were horrible, as if he needed, in accepting what he had from them, to remind himself they were rotten. But still, they wanted to tear down most houses and rewild the place, it would benefit the place ecologically and also, he finally admitted, so there was more room for wild flora and fauna for them to subsist on as much as they could. That was part of why they needed—well, need, he said, ashamedly, then tapered off—they needed to knock down the houses, why others couldn't live in them, because the land would only support so many people, and these people wanted to live off the land. Except of course they didn't know how, which was why they had enlisted him. He knew what I'd say, he said quickly as he wrapped up his first soliloquy, it sounded like a conspiracy, or it was a conspiracy. But didn't we already live in a conspiracy? Wasn't it true that rich people were buying houses here anyway (not to mention the world in general and how the whole reason fires were more dangerous was because of the changing climate, which was a conspiracy of certain people and corporations to enrich themselves at everyone else's peril, wasn't it?) and if that was generally going to be the case no matter what, why not take the opportunity to remain and even possibly to live in a better version of it?

"But . . . but . . . how did they know about you?" I said weakly, a question I wanted the answer to but a question that wasn't really the point at all.

"Well, Lee, of course. She knew I could do it, and we'd always complained when we were volunteering about how impossible it would be to stay here forever."

I nodded slowly. Lee.

"And what will she do? She's . . . part of it? What skill does she have?"

"Oh, well. She's basically—their therapist. With the Axon."

Maybe the rich more than anyone want to believe in a scam, I thought.

"It's funny," I said slowly, "that I got involved with Lee—with the Axon, and Mirror—at the same time you got all wrapped up with her landlords . . ."

"Well, how are those even related? It's just—it's just a time of upheaval, maybe. Or maybe the timing—it just means you were coming to a shift in your own life when this—opportunity came along for me," he said, clearly with some distaste for that word, *opportunity*, a word that had clearly come from Lee's landlords.

"It seems she doesn't want to see me. Like she's done with me," I lamented.

"She's just been busy, helping with—logistics, or whatever. But you don't need her anymore."

"But what—what if I'm not cured?"

Not that I was totally sure I wanted to be cured, but I did want to know more about the disorder, I wanted to be closer to it, I wanted to hear what else she might have to say about it—it had given such a short diagnosis and yet there must be endless things to say about it, perhaps if I went back she or it could reveal something else to me.

"Kim," he said slowly, locking eyes with me. "It doesn't—you just need to rest. And anyway. Even if it's not—totally gone, you don't really need your computer or your phone, do you?"

We'd gotten off topic, and I wanted to get back to the crazy topic at hand, I wanted to ask so many questions but they all turned to mush inside my brain. I'd never interrogated someone over something so serious and so insane.

Finally I thought of something. "How will it be so quiet if

there are still a bunch of tourists? Isn't that what you hate most about this place, anyway?" I said.

He laughed, a little gleefully, clearly this was what he was most excited about, what he most approved of, perhaps he'd even given them the idea. They had bought, he said, many or most of the short-term rentals. They were trying to buy any other bed-and-breakfasts, and the hotels, and they were working on buying all the little businesses downtown, too. "They'll knock down the houses, shut down the businesses," he said. "I mean, there won't be zero tourists. People can camp. Or drive here for the day. But there won't be many amenities. There won't be much to do, or much to eat."

They wanted paradise, and paradise, according to them, was sparsely populated.

I grasped for language. I stopped and started and stopped and started like I was talking to Mirror but I couldn't think of another question, all I could do was look at his hesitant but proud face, relieved I think to have said it all, to have unloaded the offering, a dead meaty and nutritious animal, nutritious at least if I ate it quickly, if, instead of thinking about it too much, I ate it all up before it rotted before me.

"I need to be alone," I said.

My boyfriend nodded. He acknowledged it was a lot to take in. He agreed to walk back to the car and drive it to the other terminus of the trail, where I'd meet him.

I Ran into Mona, Maybe for the Last Time

On that hike I ran into Mona in the woods.

At least I think it was that hike, it was around this time and that's good enough because I just need to finish this document, get to the end of it, which is to say the present, and although the present is always on the move, it's fair to say I've reached the present I'm now writing toward . . .

You'd think I'd remember when exactly I ran into Mona because it wasn't that long ago, it's much closer to me now than the beginning of the disorder was when I started to write about it, and yet sometimes the near present is just too close and cluttered. Or maybe other things are affecting my memory!

Anyway . . .

I started my hike walking a little more quickly than I usually did. I was almost marching as if a regimented and energetic pace would organize my thoughts. It was dark, what they were doing, buying up the most idyllic land for themselves, giving a modicum of land and comfort to people who could serve up to them a fantasy of utopia. Or something. But if it was reported, people would understand, and people who hadn't sold their homes would refuse, people would do something, I thought, right? For a while I told myself I didn't care about certain things anymore, but I couldn't believe I'd let the story slip through my fingers, that the other reporter would get to write about something so horrible and nefarious and fascinating, something that could propel his career. Why had I been so distracted, I thought? Why had I let the disorder scramble me so thoroughly?

Maybe there were too many scrambled things in me.

I thought on the hike again about that last worksheet.

Maybe the trees could clear my mind of everything my boyfriend had told me and the potential life inside me. I needed to process things in the order in which they happened, I thought, so my mother should come first; if I could finish this last worksheet I'd be done with her! I needed to empty my mind of everything else, and then my mother might begin to speak. Hopefully my mind was like an internet browser that would work better once I closed enough tabs. But maybe finding my mother's voice in my head on a hike was a doomed effort. She had never been one for hiking. If I'd really wanted her to speak to me, I should have smoked a cigarette or gotten quietly drunk instead.

As I hiked, the brittle-dry pine needles crunched loudly, and I felt guilty relishing the hot dry breeze as I admired the dense stands of young trees, uniformly slim and tall, slivering the view. Soon though I started panting; I hated the uphill parts of hikes but I preferred to hike upward first, exerting myself, then give myself up to gravity at the end, though my boyfriend enjoyed hiking quickly downward into some deep gulch or valley and then pushing upward and out, so the end felt almost like an escape.

I tried to walk slowly. I worried a quick gait would cause my arms to swing too much and that might goad the disorder, but then I felt ridiculous, walking so deliberately, ready to scream *Go away! You aren't real! You aren't welcome!* But the other thoughts crept in again. *You don't want it to go away! It* is *real! You love the disorder!*

I hiked up and up, and breathed harder and harder. My mother was not going to say anything in my head, and even if she wanted to speak, my heart was beating too hard and too loud to hear her, and sporadically the disorder was going haywire in my hands, seemingly triggered by nothing, each time causing me to stop and breathe through my nose, and I was happy and angry it was there, in pain but relieved it was still there. Maybe it hadn't wanted me to quit at all. Maybe there was something else it wanted!

At some point along the trail I started to see huckleberry bushes, and I stopped to pick a few for a snack, but the berries were already desiccated on the bush. They weren't supposed to be dried up yet, barely supposed to be fruiting even, though it wasn't clear what *supposed to* meant anymore. The berries were still edible but it seemed pathetic or maybe even ominous to pick raisins.

Then I saw Mona.

She was sitting off-trail, stroking a tree, perhaps whispering to it. It wasn't like me to go up to someone in that kind of situation, usually I would have pretended I didn't see anything, and yet I was compelled. I found a narrow opening along the trail and began trudging and pushing through the brush. She stopped whispering. She looked around frantically for a second, hearing my stomp and crunch, before I emerged from the brush and she saw me. She snorted. "Oh, it's you," she said, a little annoyed.

She was wearing a muumuu like always, the skirt brown and the top green like she wanted to be recognized as kin to the forest. She looked at me, still stroking the tree. I didn't know what to say. "Hi," I finally said dumbly, but that didn't go anywhere.

I tried again, since approaching her required it. "Mona, I don't know what to do. I don't think I can finish the workbook. I can't do the final exercise. And it—well, it hasn't helped much at all anyway..."

She rolled her eyes at me. "The last worksheet—that was my favorite one," she said. "It's the most important, the one that sorts out people who truly want to push through from—well, some people are just weak." She shrugged.

I was hurt at her judgment. I'd helped her buy groceries. I'd listened to her woes. "Right, well... I'm having trouble. Maybe something will speak to me out here."

She rolled her eyes again. She had really turned on me. "Yeah. Go into this beautiful forest hoping to hear a human voice. Maybe listen to what's actually out here!"

I started tearing at a serrated huckleberry leaf in the discomfort of her final judgment of me. "Stop!" she scolded. "I don't know why people do that! Tearing leaves to bits and pieces. I sit here and see it all the time, all the time. Horrible."

I sat down, which drew another huff from her, worried I was going to overstay my welcome with her or the forest. I picked out thorns that had clung to my clothes as I pushed through the brush. "I guess it's good they'll clear this area," I said. "It really is thick. And those diseased trees—I guess it will make the forest healthier . . ."

I was curious what she'd say.

"I already know the fire's going to be close by," she said. "That's why I'm here."

"To see it off," I finished.

She shrugged. She was being difficult, yet I noticed then the new ease in her body, like some stiff internal scaffolding had been removed.

Then I asked her about whether she'd ever sold her home.

"I sold it all right," she said, and I was a little shocked. Then I was the one disappointed in her.

"They're not good people," I said.

She shrugged. "I want the house gone."

"Right. Because they're just—going to tear most of them down, I guess . . ."

Her attention drifted back to the tree.

"What were you—saying to the tree?" I asked.

She looked at me like I was an idiot. "That's kind of personal," she said. "You could have a conversation, too, if you wanted. But pick a different tree. Maybe that would help you. I always thought you needed some help! Just in your whole—" She waved her hand in the general direction of my being. "And in your writing. I could tell you didn't really care about those trees! Always on to the next thing."

I hated to keep asking questions, it seemed pathetic when she was clearly done with me, but still I asked her a final one: to describe what it felt like when her pain was cured or fixed, what it felt like when it left her body. At this she turned very still and actually looked at me, her eyes seeming to remember some moment of fearful joy. She said she had been talking about that with the tree, or trying to talk to the tree. But then she started to feel guilty, the tree couldn't move, and she didn't want it to be a prisoner of her story. Then she continued the story with me, and I froze, happy she was talking to me but terrified she would go on and on and I wouldn't be able to extricate myself. It's hard to leave a person telling a story, even a story that seems to have no trajectory or foreseeable end. Really the most frightening kind of story is one that doesn't end. But Mona was unable to talk for long. Her previous self could talk and talk and talk. But now she kept halting, trying to find words for the absence of her pain. When she couldn't find them, she started crying. Or maybe it was the other way, maybe she started crying and her tears and harsh shallow breaths buried and buried the words.

Worksheet 5

This may be the most important part of the program. The act of writing about your repressed trauma, and admitting to what extent this grief has affected you, began the healing process. But there is more to be done: forgiveness. It may be you need to forgive someone. It may be you need someone's forgiveness. It's often the case, though, that these people are no longer with us, or may be otherwise unable to engage with you in this process. That's okay—in fact, it's better for you to undertake this part of the journey alone.

In this worksheet, you'll do something different: create a dialogue between you and the subject of the previous worksheets. In this dialogue, request or offer forgiveness. Explain everything you never got to articulate to them when the trauma occurred. In this dialogue, allow the other person to offer or accept this forgiveness.

⋄⋄⋄

I can't. I'm sorry. I can't I can't I can't! No no no!

The Other Reporter Visits Again

When the other reporter came over for what would be the last time, he knew almost everything and had already interviewed one of Lee's landlords.

He knocked but opened the door and barged in excitedly without waiting for an answer, making his way to me wide-eyed, not carefully looking the cabin over like last time. He started talking immediately, with a sense of horror but also admiration at their sheer brazenness, revealing what I already knew: Lee's landlords and a few others had colluded to buy an unseemly number of homes, and they were well on their way to owning at least half the town.

"Of course you know that now," he went on. "Don't worry—they said they were sure you didn't know about it. That your boyfriend didn't tell you anything while things were—uncertain. Although . . . come on. Did you really not know?"

I sighed. I picked up the little tincture bottle and squeezed the grime-green liquid, meant to help me relax, into my mouth. My eyes squeezed shut and I stuck out my tongue as if hoping the bitter taste would evaporate away.

When the other reporter arrived I hoped he might have additional information about this alleged idyll, information to sway me one way or another. Maybe, I thought, he knew something that would cause me to see the landlords in a more benevolent light, or on the other hand something that would show that they were going to treat my boyfriend and the others horribly so I would know whether to leave.

But now it would be harder to leave.

My period was already late.

I know it only takes one time but still it shocked me. The scrapes on my back still hadn't completely healed.

"I didn't know," I said slowly. "Not until a few days ago."

The other reporter made a face. "That tincture looks disgusting. But whatever. I mean—you didn't know? Well, I guess you were distracted. Stressed . . ."

"To be honest, at this point you might know more than me," I said, still stewing a little that this story was his. "Tell me what you know, what they told you. And if I know anything more than that . . ."

"Okay," he said, and stood up and, pacing all the while, proceeded to tell me what he knew and how he'd come to know it. It hadn't been difficult, he said, after poring through property records to find that Lee's landlords hadn't been part of the first few houses he first found out about but they were buying up many others, and it wasn't just Lee's landlords, there were maybe ten or so groups, and it was clear something was going on. At first, when he contacted them or their liaisons, they played it down, questioned if it was really a story, that people with means were buying property, even many properties, they did that all the time! But the other reporter was persistent, even rabid; it was a story, he told them finally, and he'd publish what he knew whether they consented to an interview or not.

As the other reporter talked I tried to imagine myself in his role; I wondered if I would have pushed them hard enough, if I could have said to myself *I am not me* enough times to surmount my fear, my fear of being somehow wrong, of angering someone, or maybe just of being overpowered.

Suddenly, he went on, they opened up, or changed tactics. Maybe they realized that at this point, they were well on their way to accomplishing their idyll, the other reporter said, and their best course of action, if things had to be public, was to shape the conversation. That's when they said his assumptions, which he'd mentioned in many emails, were wrong; they didn't want to turn the area into a short-term rental empire but the opposite, to return the land to its more natural state, rewild it as much as possible, offering homeowners a premium for their property. So they funded the prescribed fire, to help restore ecological function. They were concerned about the human shit making its way into the waters, and to ensure that not a speck of their own waste ended up in the stream, they would scrap the sewer and each install composting toilets, the most ecological way to dispose of human excrement, and fish would flourish under their stewardship. A few less-fortunate locals, they told him, would remain to forage and help tend to the land. And there would be an application process for the artists' colony they were preparing, so people could still enjoy the area and be inspired by it to produce things of great beauty. Yes, they admitted, it did seem a little elitist that they would live here while most everyone else left, but again—

wasn't everyone being offered a premium, which was especially kind given there would still be smoke each autumn, since there would be fires elsewhere, since there was still risk, and people could find somewhere to live—the owners never defined this somewhere—with clean air all year round?

When the other reporter finished recapitulating what he knew, he sat down, exhausted at his own summary.

It would clearly be a big story. It more or less corroborated my boyfriend's story.

"I guess you'll stay," he said.

"Right," I said. "They—they already offered us one of the cabins they've bought. It's not just a cabin—it's a real house. We'll move after the practice evacuation, I guess. I mean, do you—do you think they're horrible people?"

"Oh, I don't know. Obviously the way they're framing things is self-serving. Craven. But evil? . . . I don't think so. Unless—do you know anything? That's really what I'm here for. I mean, I wanted to see if—you know, you knew anything else . . ."

I told him I couldn't think of anything.

"I will say—did I already say this?—it's pretty convenient Mona tried, in her own way, to tip you off, and yet you were so distressed with—well, mostly with your computer, really. I mean you were upset about your hands, and you were stressed, but—I mean, Lee sent you that program? A copy of it, so you wouldn't have to pay for it?"

"Well, she really did have some—issues. Which she told me a long time ago, long before all this. I'm not even quite sure what you're getting at . . ."

"I'm not totally sure either. I'm just saying—maybe there's something there . . ."

"I don't think so," I said quickly. "Or I don't know—I don't want to think about it anymore. I mean I do. I do need to think about it. I just don't want to start wildly speculating about this and that..."

At this point I just wanted to be reassured that staying, which I'd more or less decided to do—*decided* being a tentative word, maybe not the right word—was the right thing. I should just stay, I thought, more like an instruction than a free thought. What was so wrong with staying forever, anyway? My money wouldn't last much longer and I'd promised not to run to my father for financial help. If I stayed—well, I would be, in a way, dependent on my boyfriend. But if I was growing my own food, if I learned not to kill any seed I tried to plant, that wasn't being completely dependent on someone else. That was being self-sufficient, if anything!

Wasn't it?

Wasn't it?

And maybe there was a way to turn it into a meaning of my own making. I could become, without saying it aloud, a reporter again, taking notes, observing, someday pitching an exposé of a moneyed idyll or utopia or whatever it was, when it inevitably soured. Not that I'd tell my boyfriend; he wouldn't like the idea that I was, in some way, remaining an outsider to it. It would be like going deep undercover, deep reporting, the way people live as prison guards or inmates in insane asylums.

Which reminded me.

The reporting idea, not the insanity.

"And what about—are you going to buy the paper?" I asked.

"Well. That's an interesting question. I don't want it to be sold to these—well, we know what they are." The editor, he went on, was distressed by the idea of selling to them, since they would immediately shut it down, having no use for it, perhaps keeping some bare-bones newsletter among the select who would live here. "That could be you, actually!" he said. "Maybe it could be, like, homey and handwritten. Anyway. The thing is—they're willing to buy it. And if she holds on to it, eventually—I mean, if people are convinced to sell their homes, or they worry about not being able to handle the liability of a fire, especially with the issues around insurance, and if local businesses start shutting down . . . I mean, there might eventually not really be—a town. Even if they don't buy every single home—at some point there might not be enough people here to sustain the paper. It would go bankrupt, without people, without advertisers, without—everything. Anything. But I actually think she might go down with the ship, so to speak . . ."

"No paper?"

"Well, obviously it's devastating. It's not that unusual, though. Small papers like this shut down all the time. It's barely viable as it is, this place being so tiny . . ."

It made me sick to think about.

The Last Few Days

In those final few days together in our tiny cottage, which were very very recent, my boyfriend wasn't home much. The group was meeting regularly before the practice evacuation, and he went for long hikes each day. As the day got close and closer I struggled to imagine us together in a different home. When I tried my mind went blank. He on the other hand painted a very detailed picture of the new chapter of our life, and every day he added more and more details, a bit anxiously and sometimes to the point that they would contradict each other; one day we'd have such a bountiful food and herb and medicine garden we wouldn't care if local stores closed, but on other days we'd spend more time foraging and cooking for the others, who I suppose would now be our community, and maybe they would focus more on the gardening. Maybe he was creating slightly different versions of our future to see which one elicited the greatest excitement from me. He could tell I was hesitant, worried to move, to be beholden in such an uncomfortable way to these strangers. He asked repeatedly if I was still on board, clearly worried I might jump ship at any moment with our potential baby, potential because I hadn't taken any official test and because I hadn't yet mentioned my missed period.

"I'm staying," I said. "I'm doing this," but he kept pressing, hoping enthusiasm would suddenly burble up if he asked the right way, pressed the right valve.

⁂

Finally, the day before the practice evacuation, he seemed so anxious about me, about whether I was happy and whether I saw him as a morally compromised man, and so I told him my period was late, and it was never late, and it was possible we made new life on the very first try. I hoped it would get his spirits up and it did. That night he made for dinner a pasta tossed with a thick sludge of bracingly bitter wild greens he pulled from the depths of the freezer. Maybe he needed to fortify himself or else he was determined to start fresh and therefore use everything he'd saved in the freezer, a place he didn't respect for saving food because it wasn't a stable place, it was an artificial cool, but even he had his weaknesses. It was honestly the most bitter thing he ever made and I wondered as it burned in my stomach if he was trying to purify me, maybe for the potential baby. But he also made a huckleberry pie from the one bag we froze, the ones he didn't dry. The pie shocked me because he never used refined sugars, but he went all out, clearly in the mood to celebrate, sprinkling sugar crystals on the top crust to give it crunch and glitter.

I forgot all about the horrible pasta in the midst of that first bite, a big mouthful of tiny berries suspended in their own sweetened oozings, soft and dripping. As I chewed and some juices slid down my chin and buttery crumbs followed, I remembered when we had picked them, the berries he mostly dried, which when dried tasted bland and moral, nothing like this, nothing decadent and yielding like this. When I was eating the pie it became worth it, following in the footsteps of his new life for us. He didn't like it when I framed it like that, whenever I said I was staying to be with him. He said we were doing it together. But it wasn't true. I was following his lead. Of the two of us it was just a fact that he had a stronger, more concentrated aura, and so it made sense. At one point in my life, when I was alone and younger and the future was a hopeful blank, I believed it would be the opposite, that I'd be the one another person would follow. But maybe the newspaper had prepared me for this, since part of my job had been following other people and trying to understand them.

I scooped a big bite of pie for him, but paused as I held it aloft.

"I know I've said I'm staying, that I can be happy, doing whatever we're doing. But sometimes, I don't know how well I even know myself. So—you believe, right, that I'll be happy here, in this new way, with you?"

Before he answered he took the spoon from my hand and chomped down.

His mouth was bigger than mine, but still it was a big bite, and the syrupy filling spilled from his mouth. Maybe he needed energy from the sugar to answer my question. He chewed for a while, but even after he swallowed there was a space of time, like he was actually thinking about it, and I wasn't sure if it was good or bad that he was taking the question seriously, treating it as a serious something to consider. Finally he said, "Yes." But he looked a little nervous, like he'd never thought about it as deeply as he did in that moment. But then the doubt flickered away. "*Yes*," he said more surely.

"Okay, another question. Why doesn't Lee want to see me anymore? Why won't she do another session with me? I'm not—the disorder is still . . . there. But every time I ask you to get in touch with her, you put me off."

He held my hand. "Because it's not her!" he said eagerly, as if he'd been waiting for this moment to confess, proud, I think, of his caring subterfuge. "She'd do another session if you wanted. I lied. I don't want you to go back to her. You don't need some crazy computer to diagnose you! Or fix you. Or whatever it does. You don't even believe in it."

"So *you* don't like the Axon," I said.

"It's not—there's so many ways to take care of your body without going cyborg, or whatever."

"But why did you keep encouraging me to do it? More or less . . ."

"Because—I don't know. I thought maybe the placebo effect would help . . ."

"That's why?" I pressed.

"Yes," he said.

But that was not why!

Then

When I woke the next morning, my boyfriend was already gone. He went early to the meeting point, where his group would meet and talk and wait to greet the participating townspeople, the remaining townspeople, who, in addition to being briefed on what had gone well and how quickly people on each street had reached the meeting point and whether there had been unexpected hiccups or choke points in the road, would also watch a presentation highlighting the danger of fire in the area.

I was planning to be one of those people.

It seemed absurd to hold a practice emergency evacuation when the group responsible was now trying to convince everyone to leave. But the plans had been in motion for so long, and it was an act of goodwill, they'd decided, to help those remaining, even if they hoped the remaining would be gone in another five or so years.

The other reporter's article hadn't yet come out.

There were, I heard through my boyfriend, some legal wranglings from Lee's landlords and the others, delaying the publication.

But at this point people had heard that homes were being bought, and some were determined to dig in their heels, to stay, in the face of whatever danger or pressure to sell came their way. My boyfriend just shrugged when we'd talked about it; people change their minds, he said. It was never going to happen overnight but they were already halfway to their goal, he claimed, and when enough people were gone it might convince the remaining people to move along, to take the money and find some real town to live in. I nodded along, though he didn't understand, I thought, how determined, how resistant they could be—he hadn't attended hundreds of public meetings, hadn't documented them almost word for word like I had!

I got out of bed and made myself a cup of tea, an herbal elixir Mona gave me long ago, back when she liked me, an infusion of roasted roots and powdered mushrooms and unknown herbs, alleged to boost immunity or lower inflammation or act as an antioxidant or mysteriously increase energy or calm the nervous system, or maybe all of those things at the same time. I didn't know if it could help but maybe it could. I told myself: At least it couldn't hurt! Roots! Mushrooms! Subterranean filaments drawing sustenance from the earth, turning nonlife into life—who could resist ingesting a metaphor like that?

So I drank it slowly while waiting for the alarm in the air and the alert on my phone, which was still in its monstrously thick protective case but which my boyfriend had turned on so I'd hear it. I wasn't quite sure when it would go off. No one was. The prescribed fire had probably already started but they wanted the time of the evacuation to be unknown. It seemed important somehow that although people would know the day, they wouldn't know the precise time, to throw people off balance just a little. It wasn't really the best approximation of a real fire, since people would not be waiting for an expected alarm, but on the other hand maybe it did make sense, the fire season was becoming more and more dangerous and people were starting to realize that they would always be waiting for an alarm.

I thought I might read in this interim, but then I decided to open my journal and try to get to the present, and I wrote till I reached the night before. It would have been easy to get all the way to the present but I had the feeling something was going to happen, and I should wait for something—what it was I wasn't sure—before I caught my journal up to the very moment of now. I wondered what would happen once I reached the present. I'd have to dictate everything into the computer, I'd have to open Mirror again. The story of the disorder in the journal was so messy, my handwriting was so messy and I wanted it to be clean and perfect in the computer. And then what? Would there be time, before my boyfriend returned, to test my hands on my laptop? I knew the disorder was still there, perhaps stronger than ever, but still I wanted to try typing, just to see. Maybe I'd do that instead of going to the practice evacuation, maybe I'd ignore the warning.

The thought of reading over everything, especially the worksheets, made me a little ill. Maybe it would lead me to some revelation, I thought, but I expected the opposite, that it was all just nonsense, there was nothing to be learned or deduced at all. Maybe my boyfriend was right, I thought as I drank Mona's nasty elixir. Maybe the worksheets were psychobabble, tapping into a narcissistic impulse to plumb backstories for meaning and depth, so the pain had a narrative, a potent origin story. It not only allowed the person to believe their pain was meaningful but also circled all the way around, so the trauma, the source material, also carried more weight: it was so awful, so psychically potent, that it manifested physically, like when a god for very rare but important reasons deigns to take a human form. Maybe I should burn the notebook, I thought. Maybe I should never open my computer again!

I swallowed the gritty dregs at the bottom of my teacup. I thought about how my boyfriend would probably be gone all day . . .

I decided suddenly to open my computer immediately.

This didn't make much sense, since I was set to leave at a moment's notice when the alert sounded. But my urgency also seemed a consequence of the coming alarm, like the pretend fire might somehow become real, and creating the digital document of my disorder would be the ideal thing to be doing if I were trapped by a quickly raging fire. That would be the thing to do. Don't try to escape, don't turn on the hose, just speak speak speak speak into the laptop. It wasn't impossible for the prescribed fire to go out of control or for another fire to suddenly erupt, I thought as I opened the front door and stood for a minute on the porch. It was hot. It was dry, deliciously dry, and the wind was blowing, not just blowing but whipping, I saw as I looked around at the firs and the bays. The fire danger had stood at moderately high for the past week, the other reporter had written in the paper, and officials debated delaying the prescribed fire, but so much money had gone into it and it wasn't quite dangerous enough to be totally off the table, after all it was the coast and the coast was usually a little moist, and ultimately they decided to go forward.

I returned indoors. I built up again the towers of books for my standing desk. Before they had all been mixed up but this time I created an order for them: a stack of novels for the mouse pad, twin stacks of plant guides for the ergonomic keyboard, and a stack of dictionaries and reference guides for my computer.

I pulled out my laptop from under the bed. I placed it on the dictionary. A flash of fear hit me that perhaps my computer had died, like a plant that withered away without nourishment, and I suppose a computer's nourishment is its user. But it was perfectly alive. In fact I realized I never even turned it off. The last time I used it was my last day of work, when I brought it home afterward and wondered what final things to look up. Since then it had been sleeping under me the whole time.

When I opened it, the internet browser and a word processing document were open. The internet browser was open to my email, and it quickly refreshed with new unopened messages, mostly from the local online message board with notices of things for sale or events coming up in town, along with the barrage of daily monitoring alerts for particular search terms related to the towns the paper covered, and press releases from elected officials and the county government and nonprofits, and there was one email from my father about whether I wanted that medication to slow my nerve function. There were a few emails from my editor, who wanted to know how I was doing and talk to me about the potential sale, if I saw another path, anything she could do besides sell, if she should hold steady and hope the town takeover plans would be thwarted. She even asked if I wanted to come back, to cover what was happening, because even though I was compromised by my boyfriend, the other reporter had given notice and she needed someone. I felt a pang of longing for a minute: for the paper or for her or for the person I thought I'd be. I could go back! I thought. There was another path, theoretically. But really I couldn't, really that part of me or version of me was half-crumbled inside me. No no, I told myself, you don't really want that anyway, no no no!

I didn't respond.

I sat there for a few minutes, blankly.

Then I looked up on the paper's website my few articles about smoke and fire, before those things were taken from me. The articles were okay, I thought. Not groundbreaking, and the one about smoke was so short and barely covered even the surface of things. I could have gone deeper but I'd had so few words to cover it and hadn't pushed for more and just tried to cram into it what I could, to warn people to be careful. But it was bland, could it really have made anyone fearful of smoke? Oh well, I thought, oh well oh well oh well . . .

I was about to minimize the internet browser when I thought: was there anything I wanted to know, before I started dictating, which could take hours and hours and hours?

Not that it would change what was in the notebook, not that I'd edit it as I dictated, since I wanted a perfect replica.

But yes, there was something I wanted to know.

I wanted to know where the Axon had come from.

I wanted to know what it was I had submitted myself to.

Of course I should have known it would all come back to this little world I was living in, and I wondered after my googling whether the other reporter knew and hadn't told me, whether my boyfriend knew.

Anyway.

I said *Mirror on!* and I looked up the Axon and there was a mix of vague information and social media discussions on the first few pages, each of which I clicked with my mouse, with the gentlest click that still was excruciating, but I kept going and going between pauses of pain until I saw some interview in some specialty magazine about pseudoscientific metaphysical biotech with the founders of the company selling the Axon and of course those founders were Lee's landlords. They had tried but failed—well, they didn't say *failed* but sometimes you have to read between the lines—tried but failed to create a machine that could truly and quickly read minds, and by read minds I mean replicate a person's thoughts instantaneously in text or image, that was still a ways away. But in the meantime they claimed that their technology could actually do something much more important, something more than replication; it could access and interpret your mind, but not just your mind, you body too, the things going wrong in it, and—well, I knew all the claims made about the Axon, everything they said was what Lee had laid out for me.

I sat there for a few minutes, staring at the screen.

This seemed very important.

But still I didn't completely connect the dots until a few minutes later.

I guess I need things to be really obvious.

In the moment I just thought: They really seem to believe in it.

In the moment I thought: If only you two had consented to an interview, way back when, maybe I could have been Lee, could have been the one pseudo-treating people, offering convoluted placebo effects, I could have been the one listening in on people.

Although I couldn't have had this thought right then, because I only understood I'd been monitored after I minimized the internet browser, which revealed the last word processing document open on my computer, which had words. A big block of words, words Mirror must have picked up that last day the computer was open. But the words weren't all mine.

When I realized that, I closed my eyes and covered them with my palms.

Covering your eyes with your fingers is no good because fingers always leave gaps.

The truth is that I don't really ever want access to the inner workings of the minds of people I love. I try to figure out what they are thinking, but in the face of actual evidence all I want to do is look away.

At the same time, whenever words are in front of me, I struggle not to read them, no matter what they are. So my hands fell and I began to read the block of text, which was difficult because it lacked commas and periods. But it was clearly one side of a conversation my boyfriend must have been having on the phone. Some of it was about him. He was worried again that he was morally compromised, so it was easy to guess what he'd been talking about. But he was clearly also discussing me and the Axon and Mirror. He said, It all makes me uncomfortable. He said, Well because it's extremely invasive. So—yes, I understand people are giving away information about themselves all the time. He said, And this is for a much more important. . . . He said, I feel creepy reading the worksheets but if they. . . . He said, The disorder—no I still don't know the why of that, except that it really is her own body's way of telling her to change her life. He said, No, I didn't, I really didn't! Well I did—like herbs to make the—so it's likely it would—come out. He said Well she did quit. Today. So yes, I'm happy. She's been so miserable. She'll be much happier. He said, Everything I did was to make her feel better. Just to think differently. He said I honestly don't—I don't know if it made any difference. Maybe she never would have . . .

※

I read the words again and again and again and again and again.

※

And again and again and again and again.

※

And I zeroed in on *I still don't know the why of that, except that it really is her own body's way of telling her to change her life*, I zeroed in on *No, I didn't, I really didn't!*

※

Of course if he lied to me he could lie to anyone, he could lie to her, he could lie to himself, and that would be an answer, an ultimate cause, wouldn't it? But I don't think so, I don't think so, I think it happened and he saw it as a sign, a sign of what was bad in the world, or a sign I was meant to come along on his weird journey. . . . And so what, I thought, so what if someone else had tried, tried and succeeded I guess, in changing me in certain ways? Didn't they have my best interests at heart, or my interests mixed with their own in their heart? Didn't I always want Mona to change herself via chemical interventions and hadn't I tried that on my mother and weren't those out of love, and maybe it was the same, or not exactly the same, but—but—

I pulled out my notebook and took a big suffocating sigh because how frustrating and demoralizing and awful would it be to dictate the long contents of my notebook and worksheets to my computer, because I loved my computer but I hated Mirror because I hated my voice and Mirror never understood me. But when I began to speak, something strange and wonderful or at least helpful had happened. I no longer had to say each word and sentence two or three or four times. Instead each word appeared perfectly rendered. My computer finally understood me perfectly.

And

I've been speaking for so long now. At first it was exhilarating, for the words in the notebook to be so perfectly rendered by Mirror. Why did it work now, really? It must be that she's stopped somehow errorizing my words from afar but I like to think that perhaps my time of rest, if it could be called rest, really did do something, it smoothed my voice. Or I don't know. Anyway I spoke and spoke and spoke this notebook, only taking breaks when the disorder started burning, even though my hands were just hanging there they burned badly at times, and I'd close my eyes and cry until it ended, and then again I spoke and spoke and spoke, so enraptured by the words appearing magically before me that I ignored the alarm for the practice evacuation. It went on and on although it didn't sound like how they said the practice alarm would sound. Maybe it was a real fire. Maybe it is a real fire. Maybe it's not actually for practice. Maybe the practice fire became a real fire. Maybe all practice is real. I see my phone buzzing beside me, my boyfriend calls and calls and even Lee calls, now she wants to talk to me but I don't need her anymore, and anyway the story is almost done and I don't have time to incorporate any more comments. I am worried, a little worried, but once I started the document I couldn't stop, and anyway the government said they would stop more fires, and although it is very dry here, scientifically speaking drier than anyone has ever recorded before, it's not as dry and hot and dangerous as other places, and I can't believe it would all go up in smoke, although there it is, there are plumes of smoke, but it could be the prescribed fire. I take a break from dictating this to go outside and breathe in the smoky air, pleasant like a campfire, and remembering how I learned and reported on how smoke is bad for pregnancy, I breathed in more and more, the burning smoke, *please evacuate*, I think to the potential baby, *please evacuate*, and now I'm back, and I should leave but I can't, I need to finish, I'm close to the finish, maybe once I finish I'll grab this computer and bolt. But will I? Or will I do what I decided to do as I talked and talked and the excitement of Mirror understanding me ebbed, and my voice got so very tired, and my words started to seem false, not literally false but maybe at least cracks start to appear in the truth or meaning of what I was trying to say. Even though I've been reading from the notebook, the notebook was kind of like my mind, both places where I have some platonic ideal of what I want to say or mean or convey, but once the thought is said, each word is one more heavy step on a thin sheet of ice. Crack! Crack! Crack!

Anyway. I need to touch those keys.

So here we are and there isn't anything left to tell and soon I'll be done speaking, which is good because my voice is almost ground to dust, and I'm eyeing hungrily the keyboard of this laptop. I don't know. I could keep trying, I could beg Lee for another treatment, I could force myself to finish the last worksheet, I could find some new healer, if I just keep looking maybe I could find the right person for me, I see now on the screen of my phone that I keep getting calls and calls, or I could respond to my father and procure the nerve-slowing medication, just to see, just to see, I'm sure there are more pharmaceuticals I could try, more alternative treatments, really I barely scratched the surface of all the things I could try, and maybe if I had a stronger will I would. In the worksheet I never finished I hear my mother scream: Failure! But I don't care. It's over. I'm done.

Done except for this!

Because when I'm done talking, I'm going to lift my hands and lay my hands on these keys and type no matter what, I will to try to fix the connective tissue between my computer and me that somehow got all distorted, or maybe it was never distorted, maybe the pain is the pain that comes just before two things merge even more intimately together. I don't know what will happen when I lay my fingers on the keys and type without stopping. But I imagine that I begin to type a whole new document (and I know how I'll start: *My name is Kim Smith, I am from Huntington, West Virginia, I am 29 years old . . .*) and the disorder stings first my fingertips but I don't stop, I keep going, the pain shoots into my forearms, it burns like white-hot iron, but still I don't stop, and the pain keeps going, further, like it always wanted to, I will be filled with pins and needles and stabbing and throbbing and burning, the pain will move through me and search inside me for every place it has never visited, metastasizing, it will push against everything, it will rise without argument up to my biceps and squeeze my arms there, it will dig into my shoulders and curl around my neck and scream up into my cheeks, my mouth, my wet pink tongue, then it will fall, fall like it always dreamed of falling, this is what I always wanted! it will say, I didn't ever want you to stop typing, I wanted you to keep typing because that's the only way for me to grow and grow! It will fall like my shoulders were ledges it always wanted to jump off, the pain will tumble into my lungs, crawl into my belly, clench my heart, trace each rib, it will seed itself in my gut, it will push into my liver, unfilterable, it will descend into my cunt, it will pour into my thighs, my calves, it will fill my feet and dart insistently into each toe, it will finally be complete, the pain will be a symmetry of body, it will fully inhabit me, I will cry and weep and scream and writhe, I will be held by the pain from the inside, I will be cradled and bright on the inside, and the pain will wonder inside me: Can I break through her, can I break through her, can I shatter her like glass, and I will realize that I thought the disorder was born so long ago but really it wasn't born, just conceived, and now this is its birth, or is it an abortion, and I will tell it: You don't understand, there is nowhere for you and me to go, there is not any distinction between us anymore, you are no longer those disappearing evanescent flashes, and maybe that was the worst part of it: you kept disappearing, here and not here, here and not here, here and not here, but now the disappearing is over.

Acknowledgments

There are so many people I want to thank, and books, too, but for the sake of brevity: thanks to the book *Introduction to Fire in California* by David Carle, which informed a few sentences on a poster in the section "The Practice Emergency Evacuation Meeting." Thank you to Valerie Laken, who read many of these pages with such care and offered crucial guidance; thanks to my other teachers and peers at Pacific University for your thoughtfulness and support. Thank you, Tess Elliot, for our years together at the Point Reyes Light; I treasure them. Thank you, Stephen Sparks, for making it possible for me to spend my working hours surrounded by books. Thank you, Mariah Stovall, who helped me wrangle this manuscript into a novel, and to the University of Iowa Press, for bringing it into the world. Thank you, Dad, Sylvia, Anna; I love you all so much. Mom, wherever you are: I miss you, I love you. Thank you to my dearest, the light of my life, Michael Kuntz, for always believing that this book would make its way into the world, even when I didn't.